MW01137439

Praise for Wolf

"The passion between these two will burn you up. So be ready for one hot steamy ride... One you definitely won't be putting down until the end and even then it will leave you wanting it to never end!! Two thumbs up!! A must read book and series!!"—*Joey, GoodReads*

"This book was a suck you in book...You will not be disappointed. I love every one of the boys from the MC Sons of Sangue; its so hard to choose." — *LaWanna, GoodReads*

"As always, this author has hit it out of the park. Grigore "Wolf" Lupei is yet another Son of Sangue to fall in love with. The romance between him and Caitlyn is one to set the readers heart on fire."—*Sue, Goodreads*

"This is a great story with glimpses from all your favorite Sons of Sangue and their Mates, tons of action, emotion and steam!" — *Melody, Goodreads*

"This is a series that I find very entertaining. It has a bit of everything - the feeling of family, a strong paranormal romance, the vampire angle, the biker camaraderie and brotherhood, some violence, some conflict and some jealousy & amid the seriousness there is always a bit of humour — *Deb. GoodReads*

Other Books by Patricia A. Rasey:

Viper: Sons of Sangue (#1)
Hawk: Sons of Sangue (#2)
Gypsy: Sons of Sangue (#3)
Rogue: Sons of Sangue (#4)
Draven: Sons of Sangue (#4.5)
Preacher: Sons of Sangue (special edition)
Xander: Sons of Sangue (#5)
Ryder: Sons of Sangue (#6)
Love You to Pieces
Deadly Obsession
The Hour Before Dawn
Kiss of Deceit
Eyes of Betrayal
Façade

Novellas:
Spirit Me Away
Heat Wave
Fear the Dark
Sanitarium

Wolf

Sons of Sangue

Patricia A. Rasey

Copyright © 2019 by Patricia A. Rasey.

All rights reserved. No part of this publication may be reproduced, distributed or transmitted in any form or by any means, including photocopying, recording, or other electronic or mechanical methods, without the prior written permission of the publisher, except in the case of brief quotations embodied in critical reviews and certain other noncommercial uses permitted by copyright law. For permission requests, write to the publisher, addressed "Attention: Permissions Coordinator," at the address below.

Patricia A. Rasey
patricia@patriciarasey.com
www.PatriciaRasey.com

Publisher's Note: This is a work of fiction. Names, characters, places, and incidents are a product of the author's imagination. Locales and public names are sometimes used for atmospheric purposes. Any resemblance to actual people, living or dead, or to businesses, companies, events, institutions, or locales is completely coincidental.

Book Layout ©2013 BookDesignTemplates.com

Ordering Information:
Quantity sales. Special discounts are available on quantity purchases by corporations, associations, and others. For details, contact the email address above.

Wolf: Sons of Sangue / Patricia A. Rasey – 1st ed.
ISBN-13: 978-1-7977193-3-7

Dedication

To those of you waiting for WOLF—
This one's for you!

To my bestie, Lara—
here's to 20+ more years of friendship!

To Barb, for years of friendship—
thank you for not only reading my chapters
as I finish them, but offering great advice when I'm
stuck.

To my husband, my boys and their wives—
and especially my grand babies!
You guys are the loves of my life!

Acknowledgements

Thank you to my cover artist, Frauke Spanuth, from Croco Designs for creating the Sons of Sangue. Wolf is a wonderful addition!

And a HUGE special thank you to my editor— you make me a better writer!

CHAPTER ONE

"WHO THE HELL ARE YOU?"

"The better question might be 'How the hell did you get in here?'" Grigore squared his shoulders. "Because, if I bothered with a question, that's the one I'd want an answer for. And every dumb fuck who let me slip by would get his ass handed to him or be given his walking papers."

Grigore "Wolf" Lupei stood backstage at Detroit's Progressive Arena. Sure in the hell not by choice, otherwise he'd still be in Oregon with his MC, the Sons of Sangue. The fact he was actually positioned within striking distance of the beautiful pop star currently on stage made him madder than a hornet. He shouldn't have gotten anywhere near her without proper credentials.

The six-foot-three, 240-plus-pounds of all muscle roadie asking the question might've been a scary presence to a normal person. But to a blood-sucking vampire? He wasn't even a blip on Grigore's radar.

The man's brows drew together. "What are you? A dumbass?"

Since Grigore stood about three inches shorter than the jerk, he supposed it gave the man bravado. The fool.

"No, I'm the man about to hand you your ass."

1

The big guy took a roundhouse swing. Grigore blocked it, then punched him in the face, snapping his head back. Blood splattered, and the man cried out, his hand covering his broken nose.

"Shit!" he griped.

Grigore might've told him who he was at that moment and saved him a serious beatdown, had the bonehead's cronies not come to his rescue. Suddenly, Grigore was surrounded by a legion of men hired for the singer's protection. He didn't bother counting how many circled him. After all, this would be over in a matter of minutes, then he'd look up Caitlyn Summers's manger, Ryan Baxter, who had hired him.

While the man with the broken nose wisely took a step back, the other men came forward. Grigore easily blocked the biggest share of the punches and kicks, sending each roadie sailing through the air one-by-one. Most stayed down after being knocked silly, their cranium hitting cement walls or the floor, while those not-so-smart came at him for another round. Within moments, all of the men were groaning, wisely staying put. Grigore, on the other hand, remained standing, barely feeling what the men had doled out.

The first man glared at him. "What the fuck do you want, asshole?"

"Careful, I might think you want a little more pain. Show some respect or I'll toss you out myself."

Ryan Baxter, dressed in slacks and a collared shirt, took that moment to show his face. His eyes rounded as his gaze swept the sea of men before landing on Grigore. "I guess Caitlyn's mom had the right man for the job."

"It's a good thing I accepted if this is all you got."

Ryan nodded toward the first man. "Go get cleaned up, Josh. Take these guys with you. I have some business to discuss with Wolf."

"You know this jerk?"

"I hired him, so you best get used to taking orders from him. Now get out of here before I decide to fire the lot of you." He turned to Grigore and shook his hand. "Glad to see you decided to join the tour."

"I said I'd be here. I keep my word."

Caitlyn's angelic voice carried to his ears as she sang on-stage, oblivious to what was going on behind the scenes. Her focus was where it needed to be, on her fans. Following tonight's performance would be soon enough for her to find out her ex-boyfriend was about to become her personal bodyguard.

Christ, his dick half-hardened at the thought of following Cait around twenty-four-seven. She may hate him, and rightfully so, for walking out on her fifteen years ago without so much as a goodbye. Grigore, though, still held a special spot for her in his heart, and he supposed he always would.

But he'd be damned before he ever told her.

The last thing he needed was for her to think they go could go back to what they had before. She had her life in the spotlight, while he had his reasons for needing to stay out of it. He was here because he had a job to do—keep her alive. His cock might have another pursuit in mind, but that wasn't going to happen.

Damn good thing he had a will made of iron.

"You didn't check in to get your passes and clearance."

Grigore smiled, but there was no humor in him. As a matter of fact, he was damn pissed. "No, I didn't. And yet I managed to get all the way back here without having done so. Had I been the man wanting to hurt Cait, no one would've stopped me. Your security is lacking, Ryan. You need to fix that."

"That's why I hired you." His smug smile said he had all the answers. "Security issue fixed."

"Wrong. I'm here to protect Cait, and you can bet your ass I'll do my job." He growled, letting Ryan know exactly how unhappy he was about the current situation. "You fix the hole that allowed me to get back here in the first place. Caitlyn's mother trusted me enough to give you my name and I aim to see that trust isn't misplaced. You found me and called me, asked for my help. Well, I'm here now and I take this job very serious. We both do our jobs and Cait won't have a worry in the world. We find the fuck who threatened to kill her and I'll personally take him out. Once the threat is removed, I can get back to my life in Oregon."

"You sound pretty confident you can make that happen."

"I just took out a good deal of your men."

"Point taken."

"This asswipe will pray for Hell before I get done with him." Grigore wrung his hands together, wanting to wrap them around the throat of the person daring to threaten Cait's life. "You do your job, Ryan. Run the show, fix your security. Let me do what you hired me for. From here on out, Caitlyn Summers isn't going to be out of my sight for a second. She may hate me for it, but since she already does, not much is going to change."

Ryan half-smiled. "Still glad you're here, man," he said and walked away.

Grigore watched his retreating back until he turned the corner at the end of the hall. Regardless of the flaw in Ryan's security, the man was likable enough. He seemed to have Cait's best interests at heart, which alone accounted for a lot in Grigore's book.

He took the seven metal stairs to side-stage where he could watch Cait in action. The vampire part of his nature rose swiftly as soon as he saw her. Grigore tamped it back, nearly growling his frustration. He was in a shit-ton of trouble. Caitlyn Summers wasn't just beautiful. No, on a Richter scale she was a nine, causing near or total destruction of anyone's heart should they be unlucky enough to fall for her. With her long golden-blond hair and azure blue eyes, she was a fucking knockout, if not more so than the day he walked out of her life fifteen years ago. It would've been for good, too, had it not been for her manager's phone call, insisting he join the tour because some shit-for-brains had sent several untraceable letters threatening her life.

Cait wore a silver mesh dress, ending at her upper thigh. Large round pearls studded the gorgeous ensemble. Four straps of beads and pearls lay across her upper arms and shoulders in place of sleeves. Thankfully, the dress was high around the neck, showing nothing of the generous swell of her breasts. As it was, the five-inch silver heels were enough to shake his libido awake.

He had already seen her naked and could still vividly recall every inch of her flawless creamy-white flesh. What the hell she had been doing with the likes of him, he'd never know. Walking out of her life had done her one hell of a favor. She may not have recognized it when she awoke and found him gone, but look at her now. Her screaming fans and sold-out shows around the world proved as much. He knew for a fact she filled stadiums wherever she went.

Tonight's show kicked off the American tour, and Grigore planned to be there every step of the way—no matter what the pop star had to say about it. If someone was out to kill Caitlyn Summers, he'd have to do so over Grigore's dead body. And since he was immortal, this faceless coward had his work cut out for him.

CAITLYN STOOD CENTER STAGE, silver heels planted shoulder-width apart, as she belted out the last note from her encore. The roar of the crowd was deafening, putting a large smile on her face. She'd never get used to the rush her fans gave her when she performed live.

Nothing like it in the world.

Opening night had been a complete success. Her fans had sung along with some of her more popular songs and also seemed to enjoy the ones off her newly released chart-topping eighth album.

Life couldn't get better. Well, other than the annoying death threat she had received a little over a week ago. Part of Caitlyn didn't take seriously the couple of letters that had arrived, telling her that she needed to die and this faceless person was going to make sure that happened. The world was full of crackpots. The other part of her was terrified he might try to make good on his threat.

Her mother had demanded she cancel the tour, something Caitlyn could never imagine doing. Her fans had secured concert tickets months ago just to see her perform. No way in hell was she disappointing them.

Ryan assured her he had taken care of security and had somehow convinced her mother that her precious daughter would be in very capable hands. Whatever he had done to ensure that, Caitlyn couldn't be happier. She didn't need the specifics; the results were more than sufficient. A few nights prior, her mother had finally stopped insisting she cancel the tour. And seeing her fans' reaction to her high-energy show tonight, Caitlyn couldn't be more pleased to have won that battle.

Her gaze swept the sold-out arena, stopping to the left of the darkened building. Lights illuminated the exits, which were all empty but one. Her focus fixed on the large man filling the open space. She couldn't see much from where she stood, not with the stage lights blinding her. But as they dimmed, signaling her cue to leave the stage, she couldn't help but notice the longish hair and tattoos covering his massive arms. Something about the way the man stood there, arms out on each side of him, hands braced on the cement walls, evoked a memory. Someone she hadn't seen in fifteen years, and yet, he never seemed far from her recollections.

It couldn't be.

Not a phone call, a text … or anything. It was as if he had vanished, fallen off the face of the Earth. But even so, she'd recognize that cocky stance anywhere. The man dropped his hands from the half walls, turned and headed into the corridor, disappearing from sight. Surely, it was nothing more than her overactive imagination. No way in hell would Grigore Lupei turn up here, of all places.

Hanging the microphone on the stand, she formed a heart with her hands over her chest and said, "Goodnight! And thank you for coming to my show!"

The noise from the fans rose in volume as she was escorted from the stage by three roadies, followed by her hired musicians. Having done an encore, it was time to head for her dressing room and a large bottle of water, not to mention to kick off her ridiculously high heels. Though she wore them often in her line of work, she preferred a pair of flats or flip-flops.

Ryan met her backstage, handing her a bottle of water, and followed her entourage to the door where the venue had pasted a star with her name. "Great job out there tonight, Caitlyn. What a way to open the tour. I'm sure you'll be all over social media tomorrow."

She opened the door and Ryan followed her through, shutting out the rest of the crew. Fresh fruit and cold bottles of water decorated one end of a long table along the far wall. The other end had a pot of hot brewed tea and a small jar of organic honey, one of Caitlyn's go-tos following a performance.

Uncapping the water, she lifted the bottle to her lips and took a long drag. "I certainly hope so. It makes my day to surf the Internet after a show and see all the videos and pictures posted by fans. It tells me they really enjoyed themselves."

"Judging by what I saw out there, they got their money's worth."

Caitlyn closed the distance to her manager and gave him her back. "A little help?"

Ryan slid the zipper down her dress, while she crossed her arms over her front to hold it in place. Walking behind the dressing screen, she shimmied out of the garment, and stepped out of her heels, before pulling on a pair of dark-washed slim-fitting jeans and a vintage concert tee. She slipped on her OluKai leather flip-flops, then stepped around the divider.

Ryan leaned one hip against the table bearing the fruit basket and bit into a large red apple. "There is something you need to know."

"What's that? Please don't tell me anything that might kill my buzz. Tonight was an awesome show and I'm feeling pretty damn good about it."

He fidgeted with his apple, having trouble keeping eye contact. Whatever it was, Caitlyn was pretty sure she wasn't going to like it. What the heck had her mother done now?

"We hired a new man to oversee your personal security. He'll pretty much shadow you twenty-four-seven."

She arched a brow as a feeling of unease settled over her. "Who?"

The dressing room door swung inward.

"Me."

All of the oxygen seemed to suck from the room in an instant. She'd recognize that deep timbre anywhere, even if she hadn't been staring directly at her past. Her heart nosedived to the pit of her stomach.

Grigore Lupei.

Caitlyn hardly survived him the first time. She'd never survive him a second.

He stood just as big and menacing as she remembered, maybe even more so. His presence filled the room now, making it nearly impossible to draw her breath. Dear, Lord, she didn't need hot tea. She needed a large glass of Irish whiskey.

"I guess it's no surprise you aren't happy to see me."

Happy to see him? No. Way. In. Hell! He could take his sorry ass and walk right back out the door. Ryan may have hired him, but she was the boss. She certainly could send his ass packing.

And that's exactly what she intended to do, right after she found out how it was even possible for this man to be standing in front of her.

"Maybe I should leave the two of you alone," Ryan said.

"No."

"Yes," Grigore said at the same time. Not giving her answer consideration, he turned to Ryan. "Give us a minute. This is about to get real ugly."

Caitlyn ran a hand through her hair, pushing the long strands from her face. Her stage makeup had yet to be washed off, no doubt making her look clown-like considering her newly donned attire. And right now, she needed Grigore to take her seriously.

"What in the living hell are you doing here?"

"Making sure that death threat of yours doesn't go beyond just that … a threat."

It frustrated Caitlyn that Grigore stood here, privy to the fact some whack job had threatened her life, and she hadn't even asked for his help. Not only that, she was shocked he'd even care.

"How did you know?"

Grigore chuckled, the deep sound pleasing to her ears. Oh, hell no! She was not about to go back down that road. "Your mother told me."

"My mother?" Her tone raised on the last syllable. "I should've known. No wonder she'd suddenly gone silent about canceling my tour. That little sneak!"

"She's looking out for you, Cait, and for good reason."

"That's my business, not yours. And not hers, either. Why on earth would she turn to you? I'm sure there are hundreds of guys capable of doing the job."

His face sobered. "Not in my eyes. Nor, apparently, in your mother's. The deal is done. You can't get rid of me."

"The hell I can't," she squawked, her palm slapping a very solid and muscular chest. Caitlyn couldn't help thinking how things had changed. She was in her mid-thirties and a few pounds heavier. Grigore, on the other hand, had filled out nicely. He wasn't quite so fit or alarming fifteen years ago. Still the same arrogant bastard, evidently. "You're fired."

"You can't fire me."

"Why?"

"Because I'm not getting paid."

"What?"

"I don't need your money, Cait. But you do need me. Sorry, Sunshine, I'm not going anywhere until this threat is dealt with."

Caitlyn wanted to stomp her feet, throw a hissy fit, and turn juvenile. Problem was, though, she was a grown ass woman, and a very tired one at that. She needed to get in her limousine, head for the hotel, and get some sleep for the night. Tomorrow, she had a full day of press with television and radio stations, not to mention another show in Detroit to prepare for—one her mother planned to attend. Lord, she was going to give her a piece of her mind, right after she managed to get rid of the big guy now crowding her space.

How she intended to manage that, she wasn't quite sure. Right now, though, she needed a bed and a pillow. *And* to get as far away from Grigore "Seriously Hot" Lupei as she possibly could. His presence was calling to that grown ass woman side of her.

And *that* was not a good thing.

CHAPTER TWO

CAITLYN SUMMERS SAT BEHIND A THICK GLASS WINDOW AND beamed a thousand-watt smile at the man interviewing her. Grigore didn't know how she had the energy after spending the last four hours being carted from one television program to the next, finally ending with the radio station he now stood in. While neither he nor Cait got much sleep the night before, she hardly looked the worse for wear.

He supposed having him lying on the hotel bed next to hers had something to do with neither of them getting much shut eye. But Grigore wasn't about to let her out of his sight. Not even for a New York minute. He had meant what he said. No one was getting to her unless they went through him. Keeping her in his eyeshot at all times ensured no fuck-ups.

The DJ, grinning from ear to ear, seemed enamored with the pop star. But what man wouldn't be? From where Grigore stood, there wasn't a more stunning woman on the planet. He had spent the last fifteen years trying to convince himself otherwise to little or no avail.

Her soft laughter came over the speaker above him, if for nothing more than to annoy him. Not that there was anything wrong with the sound. Hell, no. It washed over him, making him wish they didn't have so much water under that bridge already. The vampire side of him wouldn't mind acting on their chemistry still simmering beneath the surface. Being a vampire, he not only had enhanced strength and night vision, his sense of smell was off the charts. And her scent was definitely kicking up his desire.

Now? He hoped to hell they were done with the press, where Caitlyn would be safe and secure and out of the public.

Caitlyn stood, took off the headphones, and shook the DJ's hand, which caused a rosy hue on the man's cheeks. Moments later, she exited the booth and bounced off Grigore's chest where he waited right outside the door. He wanted to laugh at how fast her smile turned into a frown.

Tightening her jaw, Caitlyn batted at his biceps and glared at him. "Must you?"

His brows pinched. "Must I what?"

"Go around scaring the dickens out of me."

He chuckled. "Sunshine, I'm not trying to frighten you. I'm trying to keep you safe."

"Well, then, stop hovering. I never know when I'm going to turn a corner and run right into all that muscle."

"You find it sexy?"

She blinked. "What? No! I mean... Oh, hell! Let's just drop this conversation and pretend it didn't happen."

"Whatever you say, boss."

"Funny that. If I were your boss, that would mean I could fire you."

"Which you can't." Grigore slapped her lightly on the ass, earning him a squeal and a dirty look. "Let's get moving, boss. Your limo awaits."

"Fine." She hid her delectable mouth behind her hand and yawned. "I'm exhausted and I have a show to perform tonight. All I want right now is a nap."

Without another word, she headed down the hall, not bothering to look back and see if he followed. Of course, he would. She wasn't going anywhere without her shadow. Besides, the view from behind was stellar.

Downstairs and through the glass doors, the driver held open one sleek black door of the limo. Caitlyn ducked her head and crawled into the cool interior. Grigore followed suit, but when he meant to sit next to her, her pointed finger indicated he take the adjacent seat. He shrugged his shoulders. No matter to him, it was still close quarters no matter how she wanted to look at it. And judging by the rise in the scent of her desire, she must have thought so too.

He settled back against the cool leather, a smile creeping over his face. He couldn't help it. As much as Caitlyn wanted to deny the fact, he affected her, and just not in the ability to piss her off.

"What in the world do you find amusing, Grigore?"

"The fact I get under your skin so easily."

She harrumphed. "You do. So please, don't let that stop you from heading back to wherever you've been the last fifteen years."

He no longer tried to hide his grin. "So you have thought about me."

She jerked her gaze back to his. "Seriously? *You* walked out on me, as I recall. In the middle of the freaking night …

while I was asleep, I might add. It was kind of hard not to wonder what happened or what I did to warrant you leaving me. For a year, I kept thinking you might come back. That was before I gave up hope."

"Why the hell did it take you a year? You were better off without my sorry ass." His hand swept the interior of the limo. "Case in point. When I hit the road, you were driving a piece-of-shit rat-trap that had seen better days. Now look at you."

Her forehead furrowed. "What in the world does any of this have to do with you leaving me?"

Grigore took a deep breath, letting it out slowly. "Because I saw you had serious talent. I was only going to hold you back."

"That's a line of bullshit and you know it. My having talent had nothing to do with you … us."

"The hell it didn't."

He gritted his teeth, causing an ache in his jaw. The woman was exasperating. Why couldn't she see he had been holding her back? Had it not been for her talent and being meant for something much bigger than he had to offer, he would've never left.

"I refuse to get into this conversation with you, Cait."

"It's Caitlyn."

Grigore rolled his eyes. "Fine, Cait*lyn*," he spat the last part of her name, "then you can stop calling me Grigore. Only my mother called me that."

She glanced out the window, her hands absently toying with the hem of her beaded tank. "You never used to mind it."

"And you never used to mind me shortening your name."

She glared at him. "Well, since we're about to spend a lot of time together, what is it I'm supposed to call you if not your given name?"

"Wolf."

"You still go by that moniker?"

"My grandfather gave it to me." He shrugged. "Besides, I think it's fitting."

"You're telling me."

His gaze narrowed. "And just what the hell is that supposed to mean?"

"You could clean up a bit and stop trying so hard to look like one."

Grigore titled his head back and bellowed a laugh. "Hallelujah. Now you get why you shouldn't be seen with the likes of me … other than as your temporary bodyguard. This is who I am, Cait*lyn*. Take a good look because I'm not about to change for you or anyone, and I'm sure in the hell not one of your pretty boys you've been carting around on your arm like candy in front of the tabloid photographers the last decade."

Her delectable mouth rounded, though, not uttering a single word. Good, he had finally rendered her speechless. She turned her head and looked back out the window, the muscles in her jaw gone to stone. If she was busy being pissed at him, then maybe he wouldn't be thinking about jumping her bones. That wasn't the job he was here to do. Sleeping with her would only complicate matters and not change the end result.

When his job was done here, he was leaving.

Grigore looked past Caitlyn and out the window as the city of Detroit breezed by. This had been his stomping grounds growing up. So much had changed in the past fifteen years. Oregon had become his home, the Sons of Sangue his brothers. He wasn't about to change who he was for anyone, not even for Cait.

Had it not been for his accidental meeting with the Sons of Sangue at a bar along the coast, them following his drunk ass afterward along the windy road, that motorcycle crash would've ended him years ago. His injuries had been severe. Grigore had missed the steep curve, flipped over the guard rail, and gone head-first over the side cliffs, hitting every damn tree on the way down. He had been going too fast to make the turn. Leaving Caitlyn had left him raw and reckless. Had it not been for the Sons giving him their vampire DNA and turning him, he wouldn't be sitting here today, and Caitlyn's life would still be in grave danger.

He wasn't about to let anything happen to her. Whoever the fuck was threatening her, Grigore planned on sending him straight to Hell.

CAIT LOOKED AT HERSELF IN the mirror after the night's show, having removed all of the stage paint from her face and eyes. What she saw was an ordinary woman in her late-thirties staring back at her, not the pop star everyone adored. At her age, she could hardly be considered young anymore.

How long before the next youthful star took her place on the charts? Lucky for her, she didn't look anywhere close to her actual age, thanks to her mother's genes. Grace didn't look a day over fifty, when in actuality she had hit sixty this past year. Her father had passed away from cancer some years ago, shortly after seeing his only child achieve her first number one hit single.

There wasn't a day she didn't miss her daddy.

Her mind drifted to the man occupying the room's second bed, just on the other side of the bathroom's closed door. He had yet to see her without makeup since his arrival. The night before she had slept without removing it, leaving her pillowcase an absolute mess by morning. Sure, years ago, when she was a young girl of twenty-three, Grigore had seen her plenty of times free of cosmetics, but that was before age had lined her face and the rigors of her career left her with unsightly dark circles under her eyes.

Why the hell do I want his approval?

Because he didn't look a day older than when he had walked out of her life fifteen years ago. Caitlyn had always been attracted to older men, and Grigore was no exception. In fact, he had been downright hot and still was. He had been nearly her current age when they first met, which meant he had to be nearing fifty now. She loved the soft gray streaks threaded through his hair and the white in his beard centered on his chin. The small scar on his forehead, jagging into his eyebrow, only added character to his already rugged handsomeness. Other than a spattering of more tattoos, it was as if he hadn't changed at all.

Cait splashed cold water on her face, resigned to the fact that sooner or later, she was going to have to leave the bathroom. No way could she add a bit of foundation and blush without making herself look silly. Instead of going natural, though, Cait opted for a bit of concealer and powder to hide her tiredness the best she could.

Taking a deep breath, she turned off the light and left the bathroom. A bedside table lamp barely illuminated the area, leaving most of the room thankfully in shadows.

Grigore rested his head on his hands crossed behind, while his long, thickly muscled body stretched out on the mattress. Her gaze couldn't help traveling the hair of his chest as it sprinkled nicely over his deliciously well-formed pecs, down his abdomen, and arrowing straight to the top of his unbuttoned jeans.

A shiver passed through her as she recalled with clarity the size of the body part concealed behind the zipper. The man she wanted to despise right now had given her a great deal of pleasure too many times to count. Nothing she had found since came close and certainly not with any of the pretty boys he had referred to earlier. Truth be told, most of the men she wore on her arm were for the sake of the media. Once the lights went out and the cameras were gone, Caitlyn mostly went home alone.

"Like what you see?" The deep timbre of his voice startled her from her musings.

Great. Could things possibly get any more embarrassing?

Heat rose up her neck and pooled in her cheeks. She skirted the bed he lay on and trotted over to hers. Quickly slipping beneath the covers, she pulled them up to her chin. Maybe she could blame the churning air-conditioner for her pebbled nipples. Because surely, he had nothing to do with that or the dampness between her thighs. Cait needed to get a handle on things before she did something stupid, like cross over to his bed and take what was calling to her baser needs.

Lord, she hadn't had sex in nearly two years.

Ending that dry spell had never been so tempting… "I don't know what you're talking about. Shouldn't you be asleep?"

"I wouldn't be doing my job then would I? I meant it when I said no one will get by me, Cait. I'll protect you with my last breath."

She turned and looked into his dark eyes. "And then what? You're leaving?"

He nodded. "When my job is done here, I'll be going back. I don't belong here."

"With me? Or here in Detroit?"

"Both."

Flipping to her side, she pillowed her head with her hands and watched him, curious about the man he had become. "Where does Wolf belong?"

He shrugged. "My home is in Oregon."

Cait couldn't help but wonder if he had a woman waiting for his return. She had noted on the first night he wore no ring. "Do you have a … you know…"

His beard moved with the curve of his lips. "No, Cait, I don't. Do I have a what?"

She pulled on her lower lip with her teeth, trying to convince herself that she didn't care. "Have a woman to go back to?"

"As in a significant other?"

Cait nodded.

"Do you?"

A smile slipped up her lips. *Touché.* "I asked you first."

"There isn't any one person in my life, Cait. I like my solitude. Or at least I did before I had to get on my motorcycle and ride east because some shit-for-brains threatened your life."

"You shouldn't have had to interrupt your life because some idiot decided I'm not worthy of breathing air."

"What was in the letters?"

"Apparently, I must not have given him the attention he thought he deserved at some chance meeting."

"The world is full of people who feel entitled. I'm glad Ryan called, Cait. There is no one better equipped to keep you safe. I'll go back to my life soon enough."

"Are you happy? With your life, I mean."

He turned his head and stared back at the ceiling. Finally, he said, "Reasonably. What about you?"

"Happy? Or do I have a boyfriend?"

"Both."

The air between them was charged, thick enough she could've sliced it with a knife. There was no way she was making it through this entire tour without getting her heart broken for the second time. She'd need to insist he get his own room at the next stop. Cait couldn't sleep next to him and not want him. And she wasn't ready now, if ever, to go down that road again.

"Happy yes, boyfriend no."

He looked at her again. Emotion swam in his stormy eyes, making her wish she could get inside his head. "A woman as beautiful as you and yet no boyfriend?"

Her heart swelled at his admission. She shouldn't be ecstatic that he still found her attractive, and yet she was. "I could say the same thing about you."

Grigore chuckled, returning his stare overhead. "Not that I haven't had my share of women, but I don't think there's anyone out there wanting to lay claim to this ugly mug."

"I wouldn't say that. Since your arrival, I've seen the way women look at you when you pass by, Grigore."

"Yeah," he grumbled. "Well, I'm probably old enough to be their dad."

"Not old enough to be mine."

He chuckled. "I still have several years on you."

"You didn't seem to mind before."

Grigore sat up and leaned forward, clasping his hands between his knees. "I did, but I was selfish enough back then not to care. What's this really about, Cait?"

"Reminiscing." She dropped her gaze. "I was just trying to catch up."

"All this talk about significant others? Look, Sunshine, as much as I'd like to take up where we left off, it isn't going to happen."

Her heart anguished at the reminder. But there was no way in hell she was going to let him know how much she still cared. Or how much that fact pissed her off.

"Thinking pretty highly of yourself, Grigore. I never said I wanted you back."

"You didn't have to, Sunshine, your nipples said it for you."

Her mouth dropped open. *So he had noticed.*

Grigore winked at her, which only further infuriated her. "Now get some sleep. We head out for Cleveland bright and early."

With that, Grigore lay back, crossed his arms behind his head again and said not another word. Now, instead of desiring him, she felt more like pummeling him, the arrogant bastard. With a final huff, she flipped over to her other side and gave him her back. Yep, first thing come morning, she'd have a talk with Ryan. He better make damn sure he got them separate rooms in Cleveland or she'd cancel the damn tour herself.

CHAPTER THREE

GRIGORE WALKED INTO THE KITCHEN OF GRACE SUMMERS'S home, the scent of baked goods and bacon wafting to his nose. Damn, he missed home cooking. Not that human food did anything for him anymore, resulting in him eating very little. The only nutrition he needed for survival was human blood. He couldn't help but wonder what Caitlyn might think of his new feeding habits.

A smile lifted his beard. He bet she wouldn't be offering up her artery anytime soon.

"Well, look what the cat dragged in." Grace framed his face with her palms, lifted onto her tiptoes and placed a kiss on his whiskered cheek.

Grigore could see where Cait received her youthful looks. "Looking beautiful as always, Mrs. Summers. Thank you for inviting me over."

She stepped back to the stove and tended to the frying bacon. "You know you have an open invitation."

Caitlyn grumbled as she entered the room. She kissed her mother's cheek, then stole a mini muffin from the cooling rack and plopped it into her mouth.

Grace waved her tongs at her daughter. "You be nice to this man, young lady. He's the reason I didn't make you cancel your shows."

Rolling her eyes, she stole another muffin. "Not like I would've listened, Momma. Last time I checked, I was a grown woman capable of making up my own mind."

"Even if you're wrong." Ryan walked through the archway into the kitchen and bussed Grace's cheek, before nabbing a piece of bacon from the plate where some were left to cool. "I love it when we're home. Grace, no one cooks like you."

She wagged her tongs at him. "You're just saying that because you rarely get home-cooked food while you're on the road with my daughter."

"True." Ryan took another bite of the bacon. Grigore found it odd that Caitlyn's manager found himself so at home in Grace's kitchen, making him wonder about him and Cait's relationship. "But regardless, your cooking rocks."

Grace turned to Grigore. "You aren't eating?"

"I'm not really hungry but thank you."

"Nonsense." Grace grabbed a plate and loaded it with eggs, bacon, and toast, setting the plate next to her daughter's at the breakfast bar. "Eat. You're a growing boy."

Grigore chuckled. "I'm hardly a boy, Mrs. Summers."

She plopped a mini muffin onto his already full plate. "Quit already with the missus. You call me Grace."

"Thank you, Grace."

Grigore groaned at the thought of eating even a portion of the food placed in front of him. No way could he eat the entire meal and not pay for it later. He could eat the food, but it would take longer than normal to process. Some of his brothers had no problem eating regular food, but he wasn't as lucky. This amount of food would earn him a massive stomach ache later in the day.

He sat beside Caitlyn hoping her mother would take his confession of not being hungry over his lack of good manners for not consuming what was placed in front of him.

Caitlyn picked up a small glass of orange juice and took a sip. "You used to love Momma's cooking."

Grigore forked a large bite of egg and placed it in his mouth, chewing slowly, then washed it down with water. He opted for a white lie. "I do. Grace is a fantastic cook. You never mentioned we were coming here. I ordered room service. You were sleeping so I didn't want to wake you."

Taking him at his word, Cait said, "I didn't hear a thing."

"You were snoring loud enough to wake the dead."

Cait's cheeks reddened. "I don't snore."

Ryan laughed and said, "You do when you're over-tired," then bit into a piece of Texas toast, slathered in butter.

She shook her head and returned her gaze to her mother. "What did you think of last night's show?"

"It was very nice, dear."

"Nice," she repeated with a chuckle.

Grace's brow pinched. "I highly doubt this far into your career you need my glowing review. What do you want me to say?"

Cait laughed. "Nothing, Momma. I'm glad you enjoyed yourself."

"You were the prettiest girl up there."

Grigore couldn't agree more with her mother. Although it was Caitlyn's show, she had three female background singers who couldn't hold a candle to her. At least not in his eyes.

"Where you off to next?"

"Cleveland, Momma. Thankfully, it's just a short bus ride."

Grace looked at Grigore. "You're riding with her?"

"I think she needs a break from me." He chuckled. "I'll be following the bus on my motorcycle. I prefer to ride that way. Besides, I can keep a better lookout from the outside and not be surrounded by that cage."

"Speaking of?" Ryan finished the remainder of his plate. "We need to get on the road. We have a three-and-a-half-hour ride ahead of us and a soundcheck before tonight's show."

Caitlyn quickly finished her plate of goodies, then wiped her mouth with a napkin. "Then we best hit the road. Momma, can you fix the driver a plate? He stayed on the bus for security reasons."

"Of course, dear."

Ryan pushed back his plate and waited to escort Caitlyn back to the large decorated vehicle waiting along the curb. Grigore's motorcycle was parked just behind. He spoke the truth about his need to follow. He couldn't keep an eye on things outside of the bus by being trapped inside.

He thanked Grace for her hospitality, even if he hadn't eaten much from his plate, then he left the house before the other two so he could do a quick sweep of the bus. Even though the doors had been locked and the driver had remained onboard, he wanted to make sure no one had gotten past the man while they were inside her mother's quaint home.

At Grigore's approach, the driver opened the doors with a swish. He stepped onto the first step and made his way into the cabin.

"You see anything unusual?"

The driver shook his head. "All's quiet."

"That's what I like to hear."

Grigore walked across the tiled floor, past the kitchen and living area, and through the small hallway. He peeked inside the bathroom, then into the curtain-lined bunks, finding them both empty. Continuing on, he passed into Cait's on-the-road-bedroom and master bath, finding everything secure.

Satisfied, he headed back for the front of the vehicle when his cell rang in his pocket. He nodded at the bus driver, then stepped off the bus and pulled out his phone. One of his Sons of Sangue brothers' name, Ryder, appeared on the screen. He tapped the answer button and placed it to his ear.

"Bro, how's it going?"

"I was about to ask you the same thing," Ryder said. "Viper wanted me to check with you, see if you could use some help out there."

Grigore chuckled. "I would think with his great-grandfather's brother, Mircea, on the loose, he'd need all the help he could get on his end, not worry about me. How's Gabby? You speak with her yet?"

"Believe it or not, moving to Oregon. We're looking for a house. She decided to forgive my sorry ass for my part in her uncle's death. Not that Raúl didn't get what he had coming. As kingpin to the LaPaz cartel, he had been responsible for a lot of murders."

"Glad she saw the light. So you're not moving her into the clubhouse?"

Ryder chuckled. "Hell, no. Not with you living there."

"I'm not there now, bro."

"Which is exactly why she's staying with me until she finds a home along the coast she likes. Then you'll have to find a replacement for my room. I'll be moving in with her."

The clubhouse was going to be damn lonely without him, but Grigore would adjust easily enough. It never seemed long without visitors anyhow. "That's great. Glad you made it work. She doing okay?"

"Losing Raúl was tough on her, no doubt about it, but she understands the why. Gabby is resilient. Plus, having her old friend Brea Gotti here is helping. The two are wasting no time catching up. Adriana, her best friend from Mexico? She's clearing things up down there for Gabby, and then she's moving up here as well. Adriana left her fiancé because he thinks he can take over the reins of the La Paz cartel and she wasn't having any of it."

"Good for her. And of course, Gabby as well."

"Back to the reason I called. If you need my help, bro, just let me know."

"I think you have your hands full with Gabby right now." Grigore wasn't about to be the reason Ryder left town again so soon. "I'll be fine."

"Well, if you change your mind, Preacher, Rogue, and Gypsy have offered their help as well. Their old ladies said they'd also be on board to help a brother. Don't think you're in this alone, Wolf. We're family."

Emotion clogged his throat. Grigore wasn't used to needing anyone. It was nice knowing his brothers had his back. "Thanks, bro. I'll call you if things get hairy."

"Be careful, bro. The Sons of Sangue have lost enough men lately. We don't need you adding to the numbers."

Grigore laughed. "That ain't happening, Ryder. One lone asswipe isn't a match for the likes of me."

"Catch you later."

"Take care of Gabby."

"No worries there." Grigore could hear the smile in his MC brother's tone. "You keep Caitlyn alive."

"Whoever this fuck is, he has to go through me, bro."

Grigore tapped END on the phone, then pocketed it as Caitlyn walked down the sidewalk with a plate laden with food, heading for the tour bus. Thankfully the vehicle had not been printed with her name and looked no different than a glorified RV, with their fancy decorative paint jobs.

"Ready?" Grigore asked.

Caitlyn nodded as she passed him, earning a chuckle from Ryan. "Dude, you really are on her bad side."

"Don't I know it."

"YOU NEED TO GET HIM HIS own room, Ryan. This isn't negotiable."

Caitlyn sat cross-legged on the beige Italian leather sofa and looked out the tour bus window, watching the mostly flat landscape pass by on the Ohio Turnpike. They had about an hour to go before arriving in Cleveland at their hotel along the lakefront. She couldn't bear another sleepless night, lying in such close proximity to the man she despised, or at least had despised until the moment he walked back into her life.

Which infuriated her even more.

He left me in the middle of the night without so much as a goodbye.

She'd do well to remember how he had broken her heart. Fifteen years and he had yet to give her an explanation worth a damn. The one he had offered earlier was no doubt orchestrated to make him feel better about leaving because it sure in the hell didn't make up for how she had felt the morning she awoke to an empty bed. No note ... nothing. His phone number no longer working. She had no way of contacting him and no idea where he had gone.

And yet, somehow, after all of these years, Ryan had managed to track him down.

He sighed next to her. "What if the hotel is over-booked? I'm sure a lot of the rooms are taken due to *you* coming to town. Can't you make an exception, Caitlyn? Grigore will be pissed if I change any of his demands. At least let me talk to him first."

She turned her glare on Ryan. "*I* employ you, Ryan. Grigore doesn't. I don't give two shits if he's pissed. What about me being upset? Does that not matter?"

"Of course, it does. But, Caitlyn, we're trying to keep you safe."

"My complaint has to do with not getting sleep. My focus needs to be on my career and giving the best performances I can."

Not on the hot as sin man lying in the bed next to mine, night after night.

The fact that he still cares was unsettling to her, because like it or not, she was still attracted to him.

"I don't care what you have to do, I want this fixed ... tonight. I won't spend another night without having my privacy. Call the hotel, Ryan."

He sighed, pulled his cell from his pocket, looked up the number, then dialed. She could hear the ring on the other end as he stood and headed for the back of the bus. Caitlyn didn't care what Grigore had to say over the change, nor did she care if he slept in the damn hallway as long as it was outside of her room. Enough was enough. This was her tour, her career. She couldn't spend the entire tour with him slam-dunking every damn battle. This win was going to her.

"Done," Ryan said, returning to the living area. "You will be the one to tell him. I'm not getting in the middle of your pissing matches. That is one scary dude and I'm not about to make him mad."

"Is he on the same floor as us?"

Lord, she didn't want to be the one to tell him he was not only out of her room but floors away. He'd never go for it and likely wind up in her room anyway, sleeping on the floor if he had to.

"You have adjoining rooms."

Her gaze widened. "Seriously? You couldn't—"

"Caitlyn." Ryan's tone raised. "You got what you wanted. He's not in the same room. There's a door connecting you, which should satisfy him."

"What about a suite? Penthouse? Something with two rooms farther apart?"

"All taken. Apparently, you aren't the only thing going on in the city."

"He better not want to keep the doors open between the rooms. Otherwise, we might as well be staying in the same one."

Her manager rolled his eyes, clearly exasperated. "Tell him you will leave the adjoining doors unlocked. Look, that's the best I could do on short notice."

Caitlyn took a deep breath, returning her gaze to the window. A very tired expression looked back at her. "That man is hard-headed, to say the least. Let's hope he's okay with the new arrangement. Start calling ahead for the rest of the tour dates. Make sure Grigore has his own room from here on out."

She couldn't help but think back fifteen years to the middle of the night when he'd gone, leaving an irreplaceable hole in her heart. Caitlyn had been clueless as to what had made him take flight. They had been best friends who had shared everything, at least it had been that way for her.

Before going to bed, they'd had a disagreement about her career and her reluctance to do anything more than play in small, local clubs. Her life with him had been happy. Leaving him to follow a bigger dream wasn't an option, never would have been. If it came down to choosing her career or him, she would've chosen him. After the argument, they had gone to bed and had fantastic makeup sex, but then she'd woken up to find him missing in the morning.

The years following, she set out to make a name for herself, make him regret his actions. For years, she'd hoped he would contact her to no such luck. Of course, she would've told him to take a flying leap off a very tall building. Then, two days ago, without warning, he came waltzing back into her life, reopening all of those old wounds and making her wish things could be different. Getting rid of him this time wasn't about to happen. Grigore had made it his mission to keep her safe, which meant he'd be sticking to her like glue.

"You ready for tonight?" Ryan asked. "We have two more sold-out shows coming up in Cleveland at the coliseum."

"Absolutely. I love giving my fans a great show. They're my entire reason for not canceling because of this stupid threat. At least I don't have to worry about whoever wants me dead. I'm sure Grigore won't let anyone within striking range of me." She looked back at Ryan. "How did you find him anyway?"

"It wasn't easy. Your mother, as you know, was the one to suggest him. Said if anyone could keep you safe, her money was on Grigore. My Internet search found a couple of men with the same name, though neither lived in the States. It was pretty obvious Grigore Lupei didn't want to be found. No social media accounts, no known addresses, nothing. I have a friend in law enforcement who did me a favor."

Ryan smiled lopsidedly. "Of course, that's on the down low. He could get in trouble for his help. He found a couple of small-time arrests for Grigore in Oregon, ones that basically amounted to squat. It looked as if the law may have had a hard-on for him but couldn't make anything stick. Anyway, he's a known member of a motorcycle club called the Sons of Sangue. My friend found a last known number for him, and the rest is history."

"How did you ever convince him to join the tour? Not only that, but not accept payment?"

"It wasn't hard, Caitlyn." Ryan raised a brow. "Contrary to what you believe, that man cares. As soon as I told him there was a death threat on you, there was no need to convince him. Even though he refused compensation, Grigore hopped on his bike and headed East."

CHAPTER FOUR

Finished securing his bike, Grigore walked the perimeter of the lakefront hotel, noting nothing out of the ordinary. They had arrived a few minutes prior, parking near the rear of the building. No one had followed the bus, of that he was sure. The Ohio Turnpike was an open three- and sometimes four-lane highway, making it easy enough for him to keep an eye on neighboring vehicles.

Ryan had ushered Caitlyn inside upon arrival, using a security entrance set up for high-profile guests, with the promise to stay by her side until Grigore scouted the premises.

His leather chaps slapped against his thighs. The cool winds coming off the bay and overcast sky carried a threat of oncoming rain. Thankfully, they had beat the storm. No matter, he would've weathered it out rather than ride inside the bus, which would've hampered his view and ability to keep an eye out for tailers.

Reasonably satisfied and seeing nothing to raise the hairs at his nape, Grigore continued into the lobby to the front desk, giving them his name. He procured a key, then turned and inquired which room Caitlyn Summers was staying in.

The stoic face of the reservationist gave nothing away. "I'm sorry, sir, but I'm not allowed to give out any information regarding possible guests."

"Good." Grigore headed for the bank of steel elevators. "Let's keep it that way."

Visitors mingled in the lobby, most giving him a wide berth as he passed, many looking down their straight-patrician noses. He supposed his motorcycle cut, with its Sons of Sangue rockers, gave them pause and labeled him as an outlaw, someone who normally didn't stopover at expensive joints. He certainly didn't give a flying fuck what deep-pocket socialites thought of him.

Grigore punched the UP button on the panel between a couple of elevators and waited for the car to arrive, his vampire hearing picking up most of the conversations happening nearby. There was mention of the night's concert featuring Caitlyn, but nothing regarding the threat. There seemed to be a bit of speculation that the superstar might be staying at the hotel, though it stemmed more from excitement in possibly seeing the woman cross through the lobby. There was also someone referring to letting just *anyone* stay here, likely aimed at him.

Grigore smiled, stepped into the elevator and turned. His gaze zeroed in on a woman dressed to the nines, who had probably been the one offended by his presence. He winked at her just as the car's doors slid closed, then pushed the button for the eighth floor and the car started its ascent.

Seconds later, the doors slid open. Looking at the numbers posted on the wall, he took a right and walked to the end of the hallway, the carpet muting his booted footfalls. Grigore slid his key card into the slot on the handle then opened the door and entered the room.

His backpack lay on the king-size bed … one bed, as in singular. What the fuck? His gaze traveled the lavish room before landing on an adjoining door. Grigore quickly crossed the carpeted floor, turned the bolt and swung open the door, only to be greeted by another closed one … one without a handle.

Heads are going to roll.

Grigore struck the metal with his fist. "Caitlyn, open this damn door."

Seconds later, the door swung inward and a very red-faced Ryan Baxter stood on the other side. "Sorry, Grigore. Caitlyn insisted."

Grigore ignored Ryan altogether as he pushed past the man, bumping shoulders, before coming face-to-face with the object of his current fury. She may pay Ryan's bills, thus obligating him to abide by Caitlyn's demands over Grigore's, but Caitlyn, by God, was going to listen to him if he had to hogtie her to his damn bed.

"What the hell, Cait?"

She turned an innocent look on him. *As if she had no clue.* Which infuriated Grigore even further. He wasn't an idiot to be toyed with, and the sooner she realized that the better off they'd both be. He was here to protect her damn life, for crying out loud.

Grigore barely reined in his temper. "I'm sure you're the reasoning behind the change of plans."

"If you're referring to the sleeping arrangements, then yes."

He turned to Ryan. "Give us a minute."

"My pleasure." Ryan all but chuckled. "You two iron this out. I have work to do and a soundcheck to prepare for."

The door closed quietly behind him. Before the lock even clicked into place, Caitlyn's gaze turned stormy.

"Let's get something straight here, Grigore." At his raised brow, she corrected, "Wolf. I make the final decisions on this tour. And this one? Is non-negotiable. I can't sleep with you in the same room. I need my space."

He spread his arms wide. "You used to sleep beside me every night, if I recall, and you slept just fine."

"I used to fuck you, too. And *that's* not happening either." Hell, even angry she was gorgeous. Just the mention of fucking her and his cock took notice. "I need my own room, Grigore."

He took a deep breath and paced across the floor to the window, looking out across the lake. Waves slapped against the concrete barrier below, the skies stormy, much like the one brewing inside him. Hell, he warred with himself over picking her up and taking her back to Oregon, her fans and crew be damned, because there was no doubt Cait was going to fight him every step of the tour.

The non-sensible side of him wanted to toss her on the king-size bed and fuck her to exhaustion as his vampire DNA demanded. He wasn't used to abstaining and being this close to the one woman he had never managed to exorcize from his heart was making it hard. Hell, he was fucking hard. Every inch of him.

He turned and faced her again, her gaze dropping to his lap. Grigore hadn't had the chance to strip out of his chaps, but he'd be damned if he apologized for the erection cupped by his jeans between the leather.

"Like what you see?"

Her gaze snapped up a bit too late. He caught the gesture and the rising scent of her desire. If he were a fool, he'd carry through with tossing her onto the bed. Trouble was, he was no fool. Fucking her would be one hell of a colossal mistake. They both knew it. He had a job to do and slipping between those delectable thighs peeking beneath her short floral skirt was not it.

Christ, could that skirt be any shorter?

"Do you have no manners?"

"You're the one staring at my crotch."

Caitlyn shook her head and turned her back. As if she could dismiss him so easily.

"We aren't finished here."

She whirled around on her bare heel and stalked toward him. Using her palms, she shoved him toward the adjoining doors. "We are done, Wolf. I have a soundcheck to prepare for. I suggest you get ready as well. Take a cold shower, do what you need. We leave in an hour."

"Fine," he conceded. "But this conversation isn't finished by a long shot. If you insist on your own room, then these doors stay open."

"No."

"Yes," he said, then did the most natural thing in the world to him. Grigore gripped the hair at her nape, leaned down and took possession of her full, bow-shaped lips.

VLAD TEPES ROLLED OVER IN bed. The sound of his phone chirping awakened him from his slumber. He picked up the cell and looked at the numbers illuminating the blackish room. It was the middle of the afternoon, but Vlad preferred the dark, the light-blocking shades making it easier on his sensitive, vampire eyes.

He sat up, disentangling himself from the two blondes sharing his California king and slid from the bed. Punching the answer button, he took the phone to his ear and padded silently to the bathroom.

Vlad glanced briefly in the mirror at the black, tangled mess of hair and brushed it from his eyes. The morning's tumble had been quite enjoyable, making him not yet ready to kick the twins from his bed. The more tight-lipped of the two knew how to please a vampire with a voracious sexual appetite. He wouldn't mind a little more time with that one. Watch out for the quiet ones, he had always heard, and this one certainly lived up to the saying. Damn, but she must have been an acrobat in her past life.

"Hello," he answered, his voice hoarse from sleep.

"Dear brother, it seems that I have awakened you."

Dragging his hand through his longish hair again, though this time due to extreme agitation, Vlad bit back every curse name for Mircea that came to mind. His earlier good mood dissolved instantly. "And where the fuck, may I ask, have you gone? Taking my servant Nina with you, no less. Very bad manners, Mircea. She doesn't belong to you."

"That's where you're wrong, brother. I've taken quite a liking to Nina and have made her my mate."

"Without my permission?"

Mircea chuckled, the sound getting on his last nerve. "I'm a primordial, Vlad. I don't need your damn permission."

Vlad growled into the receiver. "Have you phoned to brag, or is there another purpose to this call?"

"If I were calling to brag, it would be to inform you that your beloved twin grandsons were already dead. But since they're not, then it seems there really is nothing for me to brag about."

If his fool of a brother even thought to hurt Kane and Kaleb, he better bring an army. After all, they now carried some of Vlad's primordial blood. "Threatening me, Mircea?"

"It's not a threat, you old fool. It's a promise. I suggest you keep a close eye on them in the near future. I'd hate to see something untoward happen to either of them."

Mircea's chuckle lit his ire like a skyrocket. It was time to flip the tables and give Mircea a surprise of his own. "I should warn you, Mircea, my blood relatives are stronger than you give them credit for."

"They were born of your bloodline but they don't carry your actual blood, Vlad." He heard Mircea's yawn. Had he been standing within arm's reach, Vlad would have taken great pleasure in shoving Mircea's teeth straight down his arrogant throat. "There's a big difference when it comes to primordial strength."

Vlad smiled, satisfaction alleviating his annoyance. "It's a damn good thing I gave them my blood then isn't it?"

"What?" Mircea growled. "Nevertheless, you old fool, it won't matter what you've given them, you son of a bitch. They can't stop what they don't see coming. Once I've finished with them, I coming for you."

The gall! Vlad laughed, humor lacing his fury. "Be careful, brother. Next time we meet, I won't be so merciful."

Vlad ended the call, not bothering to save the number. His brother had likely used a burner phone. Kane and Kaleb needed to know about the threat. Vlad's blood may have given them his primordial strength, but Mircea would not fight fair. Whatever his brother had planned for their future, they needed to be prepared.

And he'd call them, right after he took care of the prettier twins lying in his bed. They'd go a long way in helping to take the edge off his fresh temper. Vlad wasn't about to allow his brother the upper hand, nor allow Mircea to get under his skin. He needed to keep his head about him.

Walking out of the bathroom, he paced to the bed and tossed back the sheets, finding his two playthings the way he had left them, pleasingly naked. His cock instantly hardened as he knelt on the mattress, the edge of it dipping beneath his weight. Once he finished would be soon enough to alert his grandsons to his brother's recent threats.

Vlad lay between two of the leggy blondes. He crossed his arms behind his head, his fangs filling his mouth. "Who wants first dibs?"

The close-lipped one smiled lazily, not bothering with an answer. Instead, she climbed astride him, fisted his erection, then slowly slid down, impaling herself on his length.

Fu—uck!

He hissed, his fangs aching with an entirely different kind of hunger, which he'd most certainly partake of once his sexual appetite was spent.

Life is good.

Why the hell his brother couldn't enjoy the finer things life had to offer and not waste time on this idiotic vendetta of his, he'd never know. Soon, Vlad would put an end to the annoyance that was his brother. At the moment, though, Mircea had no business in his bed.

KANE FOLLOWED KALEB'S CHOPPER around the bend in the road before pulling back on the throttle on the straightaway and getting the jump on his brother. Rubber ate up tarmac. Trees and brush blurred as he passed them at 120 miles per hour. Adrenaline coursed through him, the Twin Cam Screaming Eagle 110 roaring powerfully beneath him.

This time of year, Oregon's lush landscape was breathtaking with its brilliant oranges and vibrant reds. The cooler temperatures made for perfect riding weather. It was times like these Kane craved the open road and time spent with his vampire twin. They may not always see eye-to-eye, but there was no one he loved or trusted more than Kaleb. The two shared a special bond that could only be broken by death.

Cara Brahnam, Kane's mate, was an entirely different kind of love. She consumed him and their bonded love was for all of eternity. He was already anxious to return home, knowing she'd be there to warm his bed. No one could be a more perfect half to his whole. Finding out she carried his child? Damn, Kane had nearly shed tears of joy, actually feeling his heart expand. To think he had ever been selfish enough to think he could never love another child. Not since the birth of his first born son, Ion, had he felt such elation, only to have that joy stripped from him years later with his only child's death.

It was all he could do to keep from telling Cara she had to quit her job as a detective with the Sheriff's Office. He'd known exactly what kind of a leap she'd tell him to take. Cara was a feisty one, he thought with a smile, and damn if he didn't love that side of her. She had promised Kane she'd be careful and mindful of the special cargo she now carried. Nothing was more important to her, she had assured him. And even though Kane wasn't a fan of her partner, Joe Hernandez, the human male had her back. Having kids of his own, Joe wasn't about to allow Cara to take chances on the job.

Kane and Cara had recently discussed the idea of starting a family, only to find out that she had already conceived. Kane couldn't be more ecstatic and was anxious to tell Kaleb. His brother would be the first to know outside of the two of them, though he had a strong feeling Suzi would be among the circle who knew as well after today. No way would Cara keep that kind of news from her best friend. The two had taken a day to bond over pedicures and shopping, which was something Kane would never quite understand.

Exactly how many pairs of shoes could one female own?

Seeing Riley's Gas Station and Dairy Mart ahead, Kane turned on his signal and headed for the adjacent picnic area. The shelter house tables were devoid of customers, being mid-afternoon. They'd have the place to themselves for the time being.

Kane parked his bike, cut the engine and stepped over the seat. Unsnapping the skullcap, he dangled it from the rubber handgrip of his motorcycle and headed for one of the tables. Kane sat on the top of one, his booted feet on the bench. His brother mimicked Kane's seating, nearly taking up the second half of the table.

Kaleb leaned forward, clasping his hands between his knees. "What's up, bro? Afraid I might've won?"

"Not even on a good day." Kane laughed, patting Kaleb on the shoulder. "There's something I want to tell you."

Kaleb put his hand over the newly added Vice President patch on his leather cut, colorful tattoos covering every inch of that arm. "Fuck. Tell me you aren't rescinding the presidency already?"

Kane smiled, looking at the reinstated patch now sewn onto the left side of his own vest. "Not a chance, Hawk. I'm feeling pretty good about being back at the helm."

"Good, because I'm looking forward to handing you all of the drama of the club and spending more time with Suzi and Stefan."

"Family's important. I know that to be true in my case as well. Cara's pregnant."

His gaze widened. "You're serious? That's fucking great news, Viper! Damn, you move fast. You two just decided—"

Kane chuckled. "Turns out she was already pregnant and I was worried about broaching the subject with her for nothing. Not sure if a condom broke, nor do I care. I couldn't be happier to be getting another son."

"I'm sure Suzi will be thrilled Stefan will finally have a cousin. I can't wait to tell her."

"Cara will no doubt beat you to the punch. She called me about an hour ago, while I was at the clubhouse waiting for you. Said they were going shopping and that I should let you know."

"Those two share everything." Kaleb rolled his eyes. "Probably more than we'd want to know."

Kane's phone vibrated in his pocket, cutting short his good humor when he saw the name on the screen. He showed the screen to his brother before hitting the answer button, then placing it on speakerphone.

"What's up, Vlad? You don't usually call unless there's a reason," Kane said. "Hawk's here. I have you on speaker."

"Good. I needed to talk to the both of you anyway."

"You in the States?" Kaleb asked.

"I'm still at my home. Just crawled out of bed actually."

"It's mid-afternoon."

"When you have a pair of gorgeous ladies lying in your bed, Kane, there is no good time to get out of it."

Kane guffawed. "I don't suppose."

"Something neither of you would know much about since you both ball-and-chained yourselves to just one female. Only a couple of fools would deny themselves the pleasure of many."

"I'll be sure to let Cara know you called her an old ball-and-chain."

"Don't you go ruffling her feathers. You know I love her like my own." Vlad cleared his throat. "Speaking of family, let's stop beating around the bush and get to the reason I called. Mircea has surfaced."

"Where?" Kaleb asked. "I'd love to get my hands on the son of a bitch."

"Not before me, little bro," Kane said, referring to him being just minutes older. "You've seen him? Where is he?"

"The yellow bastard wouldn't have the nerve to show his face to me. Mircea has to know I'd take his head forthright."

"And rightly so." Kaleb grinned at Kane. "Let us at him. He won't know what hit him. Did he give any clues to where he might be? Or were you able to at least trace his call?"

"Neither, Kaleb. Mircea is too smart for that. He most likely called me on a throwaway phone. It seems he only called to issue more threats. It's what he's good at. I informed him that the two of you have been given my primordial blood, so he'll be careful when he finally shows his face."

"Of course, he will," Kane said. "No matter, he's no match for the two of us."

"He won't come alone." Vlad sighed. "It appears I was right in my assumption that he's taken my servant Nina as his mate. So when he does surface, we'll be dealing with two primordials. I called to tell you that you should travel together. Don't give him the chance to ambush the two of you."

"Duly noted, Grandpa." At Kaleb's endearment, Vlad grumbled. "We'll be on the lookout and let the rest of the Sons know to be as well."

"Make sure your boys travel in packs. I have a feeling Mircea won't stop until all the Sons are extinguished. Don't take him lightly, boys."

"I do hope he comes gunning for me first," Kaleb said. "I'd love to be the one to separate that big head of his from his shoulders."

"What do you want us to do with Nina should they turn up in Oregon?" Kane asked.

"The same as you would Mircea. She made her bed."

"You coming to Oregon?"

"If I find out Mircea's there, Kaleb, I'll be there before you can blink. I have some things to settle here first, starting with the women still in my bed. Once I'm done buttoning things up, you can expect me."

"We'll be looking forward to it." Kane smiled. "Besides, that ball-and-chain of mine has some news for you when you get here."

Vlad laughed. "You give those lovely girls hugs for me. I don't need them aiming for my balls."

"We'll do that," Kane said, then ended the call. "You ready for some action, Hawk?"

"Absolutely. Let's just hope he comes looking for us first and not anyone else in the MC. We've lost enough brothers over the past couple of years."

"Agreed." Kane's lips thinned. "Things would be a lot less complicated had Vlad let me take the son of a bitch's head when I had the chance."

CHAPTER FIVE

CAITLYN FROZE AS GRIGORE'S LIPS SLANTED OVER HERS, seizing her heart. Her breath caught. But instead of pushing him away as warning bells flashed in her muddled brain, she melted beneath the feel of his soft, full lips against hers. His beard abraded her skin all too familiarly, recalling memories best left in the past. Her knees nearly gave out and might've buckled had he not ended the soul-searing kiss.

Get a grip, for crying out loud. She mentally slapped herself.

Nothing's changed.

Ending the kiss was exactly what needed to be done. Thankfully, Grigore showed some semblance of willpower, proving she had none when it came to denying this man. Never had, hence the need for separate hotel rooms. And since it had been at least two years since she last had sex, her libido was off the charts. Grigore was the one man she'd never been able to fully purge from her system.

She hated him, hated herself for not being able to resist a simple kiss. Worse yet, clinging to him as if her very life depended on touching him. She'd been happy on her own. At least that's what she had told herself until he came marching back into her life a couple of days ago. She should be telling him to go to hell, to hit the road and not look back. Not kissing him. Damn it! He had been the one to leave her, and she'd do well to remember that.

She groaned, stepping back and putting much needed distance between them. Grigore oozed sex, as if the very word had his picture beside it in the dictionary. Allowing him back into her life was idiotic at best. But thanks to her meddling mother and manager, he now stood two feet from her looking ready to pounce. He certainly earned the nickname Wolf. Grigore was more predator than man. And damn if that didn't further tickle her libido.

He's here to protect you. Nothing more.

She should stamp off limits across his forehead. Something to remind her not to go within touching, or in this case, kissing radius.

Was it possible to extremely dislike a person and yet want to jump his bones at the same time? Apparently, in Grigore's case, it was not only possible but probable. Fine! She'd keep her distance and her damn libido to herself, not to mention her traitorous heart. Because out of all the people on the planet, he was the least deserving of it.

"Don't do that again." Cait clenched her teeth so hard her molars hurt. "If you do—"

He raised a hand to stop her tirade, no doubt sensing it was forthcoming. He knew her all too well. "I apologize. I was out of line."

"You? Apologize?"

He nodded, casting down his troubled expression. "I shouldn't have kissed you. It won't happen again."

"You bet your sweet patootie it won't. Or I won't stop with separate rooms next time. I'll insist they get someone else altogether for my protection."

His nearly black gaze lifted, searing her where she stood. "I made a promise, Cait, and I don't make a habit of breaking them. You will not get another protector. And another thing, you will sleep with these damn adjoining doors open."

"No."

She actually stomped her foot. What grown woman did that? She wasn't in the habit of acting like a toddler who wasn't getting her way.

"Why do you think I found it necessary to want my own room? I need my privacy and I need a break from all of this." Her hand did a sweep of his body, causing him to chuckle.

His amusement twinkled in his dark gaze. "Glad you find all of this hard to resist."

"I didn't say—"

"You did." He winked at her.

"I—"

"Cait, I need to be able to get to you at all times. This door"—his hand indicated the backside of the metal panel—"doesn't have a handle. If you scream, I'll be forced to break down the fucking door, costing your tour, and more specifically you, a lot of money."

"It's steel, Wolf." She rolled her eyes. "No one is breaking through that door."

His gaze challenged. Surely—

"Look, Sunshine, I think you have a soundcheck you're expected to attend. After all, you're the star." Sarcasm dripped from the last word. "We can beat this dead horse, but the result is that it's still dead. These doors are staying open if you want your own room. Your non-negotiable term is having separate rooms … duly noted. My non-negotiable term is that the doors remain open."

His cell phone buzzed in his pocket. Grigore pulled it out and read the message telling him the limo had arrived.

"Get your cute little ass around," he told her. "Your limo is downstairs waiting. Ryan apparently thinks the media and fans seeing you pass through the lobby might be good for business. I disagree, but it's too late to change that now. You have a show tonight and I'm in charge of getting you there unharmed. I don't take that lightly."

Cait let out a loud puff of air. The man was exasperating. "Fine. You're the boss."

His smile returned. "If that were the case, I'd be in that bed fucking you right now, your show be damned."

Her mouth dropped open, but he had left her speechless.

"Since I'm not throwing you over my shoulder caveman-style, I guess that means you're the boss. Let's get your pretty little self in gear and head out before Ryan sends a search party."

Cait's heart hammered, blood roaring through her ears, and damn if the juncture of her thighs didn't ache at his suggestion. Nibbling on her bottom lip, she glanced from her dress bag containing tonight's outfit to the bed. She shook her head, stomped across the room, and grabbed her things before heading for the door.

She needed to get a grip on her raging hormones. No one had a right to look that freaking hot. Every delectable muscled inch. Cait may not like him very much, but damn her hide for hungering over his lewd suggestion. This was going to be a very long tour, which she'd be lucky to survive. Not because of the crack-case that threatened her life, but from wanting Grigore. Her heart would be left in tatters. She'd do well to remember that next time he leaned in for a kiss.

Grigore's chaps slapped against his muscular thighs as he followed her from the room. Caitlyn stopped and looked back at him. Her gaze took in his disheveled appearance. The chaps, the motorcycle vest, the damn snug-fitting black T-shirt. And she wasn't even going to think what the front of his jeans looked like cupping his … oh, dear Lord. She did not just look at his junk again.

His lips turned up. "See something you want, Sunshine?"

She ignored his question. There was plenty she wanted, none of it good for her. "Are you seriously going to wear that?"

"You didn't give me time to change."

"Fine. I'll wait here while you get changed." One of his brows rose, challenging her directive. "Okay, not in the hallway. I'll wait in your room while you use the bathroom."

"Do you have a preference?"

Caitlyn clamped down the need to suggest anything baggy, or to announce that form-fitting T-shirts and jeans were banned from the rest of the tour.

"Removing the chaps would be fine. The vest can stay."

At least the vest would go a long way in hiding the mouth-watering muscles beneath his tight shirt. Heck, even his biceps were sexy, stretching the shirt sleeves. God surely must be displeased with something she did to bring Grigore crashing back into her life like an out-of-control locomotive.

Cait followed him into his room where he unbuckled the front of his chaps, not bothering to use the privacy of the other room. She supposed it wasn't as if he was completely disrobing, but her gaze couldn't help following the actions of his capable hands. Chaps gone, and rooms secured, they headed back for the elevator. Grigore grabbed the garment bag from her, while Caitlyn punched the button and they waited patiently for the elevator to arrive.

Grigore remained blessedly quiet on the way down to the first floor, and through the lobby to the waiting limo. Although Caitlyn heard some of her fans' screeches as she crossed the marble tiled flooring, thankfully none of the people approached. Grigore following her most likely had been the reason. Usually, fans would hope to snag selfies and autographs, which she normally didn't mind. Today she was relieved the menacing-looking man kept everyone at bay. Even though he was a gentle giant when it came to her, Caitlyn would bet with the wrong person there would be nothing softhearted about him.

The sliding glass doors whooshed open. The limo driver quickly skirted the vehicle and opened the back door. This time, Grigore sat across from her without having to be directed. His long muscular legs stretched out in front of him, bumping against her bare ones peeking out beneath her short skirt. The air-conditioning had no hope of controlling the heat rising from the mere contact.

Cait was in trouble. Should Grigore make good on his threat to carry her caveman-like to either one of their waiting beds, she wasn't sure she'd have the power to resist. From where she was sitting, he was definitely her biggest weakness, not to mention all kinds of wrong for her. Grigore knew his way around a bed, and to say he was an expert at pleasing a woman wasn't doing him justice. As if to add to her torment, his tongue darted out now, wetting his lips. Oh, what that thing had done to her in the past...

Crossing her legs, she squirmed against the leather seat, as if that might give her a bit more breathing room in the vehicle's interior. The knowing, sexy smile on his face told her he had somehow detected her exact thoughts.

Damn the man.

"All you have to do is ask, Sunshine. I'll have the driver raise the partition."

Cait clamped her teeth and looked out the window. No sense pretending she didn't want him; he'd know the lie the minute it left her lips. But that didn't mean she intended to act on her attraction to him.

A cold day in Hell came to mind.

It was a good thing she had packed her vibrator because she was going to need it when she got back to the hotel. Let

Grigore hear the damn buzzing. He wasn't a stupid man; he'd know exactly what she was up to. It would serve him right for insisting they leave the adjoining doors open. Caitlyn snuggled into the leather upholstery and smiled.

IF GRIGORE HAD HIS WAY, he would've put a kibosh on this whole "meet-and-greet" thing. With someone threatening Caitlyn's life, bringing fans into a ten-to-one type of setting could turn into a potentially bad situation. He had no way of vetting people beforehand. Sticking to her side like glue was his only option for keeping her safe.

When he had brought up the idea of canceling the little reception on their limo ride to the venue, Caitlyn had picked up one of her stage heels and nearly impaled him. Another of her non-negotiable terms, Grigore thought with a flattening of his lips.

According to Caitlyn, these fans had coughed up a good deal of money to be one of the special few who got to meet the pop star in person before the night's show. They were promised an autograph, the opportunity to take a photo with her, and to receive a VIP bag filled with swag.

Grigore stood at Caitlyn's back as she spoke to each person individually, far enough not to interfere, but within spitting distance should things turn ugly. She treated each person with kindness and humility, thanking them for coming to see her. She'd always had the makings to become a huge star, something Grigore saw early on.

Leaving her had been the right decision then and it would be again when his job here was done. Once the tour was completed and this asswipe dealt with, he'd be riding his motorcycle solo back to Oregon. It had nearly shredded him to do the right thing the first time. He hoped the second time didn't completely destroy him.

The door opened to the backstage room and another man walked through, escorted by the crew manager, Josh. "Sorry to interrupt, Caitlyn. We have a late VIP ticket holder. I escorted him personally so he didn't get lost along the way."

Grigore nodded at Josh, knowing exactly what he meant. He wasn't allowing this person free rein behind the stage. In this current group of ten, nine fans being women, this late arrival was the only man among the bunch.

Cait's gaze widened as she took in the newcomer, then thanked Josh before he backed out of the doorway. Her reaction told Grigore that she knew the man. And by the way he looked at her, Grigore would bet his motorcycle cut it was on an intimate level.

He couldn't be sure, but maybe this was one of her arm candy playthings he happened to spot on one of the tabloid television shows or magazine covers. Caitlyn dropped the man's gaze and continued through the line of women who had arrived earlier and on time. Grigore was certainly glad to see she didn't give this douche more attention than the women.

When the tall, thin model-like man reached the front of the line, he grinned. "Caitlyn."

"Tyler." She acknowledged, proving his theory that they were acquainted. She lowered her voice and nearly hissed, "What are you doing here?"

"I came to see you." His tongue darted out, wetting his lips. "Can we talk?"

"I'm not sure there's anything to be said."

Tyler gave Grigore a cursory once-over, easily dismissing him. The man apparently didn't see Grigore as a threat. Moron. "Please, Caitlyn. A few minutes is all I ask ... alone."

"Absolutely not." Grigore's jaw tightened with tension. "Sorry, bud. Whatever you have to say to Caitlyn will be done in front of me."

She gently laid a hand on Tyler's forearm. "Give me a minute."

After thanking the rest of the fans and completing their VIP experience, she opened the door and asked Josh, who had waited outside the reception room, to usher them to their seats. Caitlyn closed the door and returned her attention to Tyler.

"What about him?" he asked, with a nod of his head in Grigore's direction.

"He stays." Caitlyn kept her gaze on Tyler, who didn't look all too happy with her announcement. "What do you want?"

"A second chance."

She laughed, but Grigore felt the tension rolling off her. Something about the man bothered her on a deeper level. "Not going to happen. Look, Tyler, it's nice to see you, and you're welcome to the VIP bag and to stay for the show, but that's it."

"I don't give a damn about the show."

"That's right." Cait's smile could have frozen over Hell. "You never did. You only cared about being seen in the limelight. What's the matter? Are the acting jobs drying up?"

Tyler glanced at Grigore, anger rolling off him in waves. Likely giving up on the idea of trying to remove Grigore from their conversation, he glared back at Caitlyn.

"I don't need you to get jobs."

"No, Tyler, you don't. You need talent for that."

"Who's the muscle?" Tyler used his thumb to indicate Grigore. "Taking to fucking goons these days?"

When Grigore meant to step forward, Caitlyn held her hand out to stop him. "My bodyguard is none of your concern, Tyler. Neither is who I choose to sleep with. I'll have Josh return your money for your VIP ticket and escort you from the building. You're obviously not here to see the show."

"I paid for the damn ticket and I'll be damned if I don't stay for the show."

"Fine." She raised a brow. "Do what you want, Tyler, but this conversation is over."

With one last look at Grigore, the man stormed from the room. Grigore wasn't about to chase after him and leave Caitlyn alone in the room. And with Josh escorting the rest of the fans to their seats, he had no choice but to let Tyler go it alone. He'd make sure the crew kept an eye out for him, but not until after he talked to Caitlyn. She had a show to do and the last thing she needed was to worry about some loser from her past.

Although, said loser could be the one issuing threats. That deduction he'd keep to himself for the time being.

"You okay?"

Caitlyn's breath shuddered. "I've been better."

"What the hell did that fuck do to you that has you so worked up?"

She shook her head and briefly glanced away. At first, he didn't think she'd answer, but then Cait looked back and squared her shoulders. "We dated until I found out his only reason for being with me was the notoriety he received from the media."

"He tell you that?"

She harrumphed, shaking her head. "Of course not. I had to find out from one of his girlfriends who he had also been fucking. Then? He tried to make a joke out of it, with me being the butt-end. I stopped dating, tried to keep out of the public eye. It's no wonder my tour has brought him back out of the woodwork. Tyler's all about making the headlines and since he can't do it on his own, he figures he's got a second shot with me. He's past news, Wolf."

"You slept with him?"

Her downcast eyes answered him. For that alone, he wanted to follow the fuck and beat some sense into him. "We all make mistakes, Cait."

When she brought back her moisture-filled gaze, it was like a kick to his gut. Somehow he knew they were no longer talking about Tyler. "Did you?"

"Sleep with other women? I'm no saint."

"No." She stepped closer, placing her pale hands on his tanned, tattooed forearms. "Did you make a mistake when you left me?"

"We're standing here, aren't we?"

"What do you mean?"

"Had I not left you, we'd still be in that shitty little apartment back in Detroit with me getting ready to sign up for AARP." He stepped back from her and gestured toward the door. "It's time for you to hit the stage, Caitlyn. Your fans await."

She took a deep breath and headed for the door. When she opened it, she turned back, Grigore damn near running into her. "So you stand by your decision to leave me fifteen years ago?"

He squared his shoulders. "Not only do I stand by it, Sunshine, I'd do it again."

CHAPTER SIX

G RIGORE'S SIXTH SENSE NEEDLED HIM, RAISING THE HAIR ON his tattooed forearms. His gut rarely steered him wrong in the past and he wasn't about to start ignoring it now. Caitlyn stood in the spotlight, damn near glowing like an angel sent from Heaven in her gold sequined dress, microphone raised as she hit a ridiculously high note.

Using his walkie, he alerted Josh. "Keep your eyes and ears open. Let the rest of the crew know something doesn't feel right."

"Because…" Josh let his response hang, apparently not about to take Grigore's word for it. *Stupid boy*.

"Because I fucking said so, d-bag. Make sure no one gets beyond any of the checkpoints without proper ID double-checked. That means crew and media as well. I'm not about to take chances with Caitlyn's wellbeing at stake. And since she's paying your damn paycheck, I suggest you don't either. And no matter what, make sure that last guy you brought to the VIP room is in someone's sight at all time. If he so much as leaves his fucking seat, he's followed. Got it?"

"Affirmative."

The walkie-talkie went silent. Grigore's point of contact was the crew manager, Josh, whose job it was to communicate with the rest of the men. Wolf didn't want the hassle of micromanaging the team; that's not what he came here to do. He had one job, and that was to make sure some shit-for-brains never got his hands on Caitlyn.

Two hours had passed without incident since the meet-and-greet. Grigore rubbed the hair on his forearms. But now? Something was amiss, he could feel it. Tilting his nose in the air, he scented nothing out of the ordinary. He heard Ryan Baxter's gait as he approached, alerted to the man long before Grigore turned and greeted him.

"Josh says there might be a problem?"

"Good. The fuck actually took me seriously."

Ryan smiled. "Probably more so out of the fear of receiving another beatdown from you."

"Wise decision." Grigore stroked his beard as he looked back to the stage. "I can't tell you what it is, but something just doesn't feel right. I wanted everyone on high alert."

"Then it's nothing you saw?"

Without giving Caitlyn his back, he looked at her manager. "Call it a sixth sense, Baxter. It's never steered me wrong before."

"Don't take this the wrong way"—he glanced at the stage—"but I sure the hell hope it's wrong this time, Wolf."

"You and me both." Grigore returned his attention to Caitlyn. "Make sure Josh is doing his job. If he doesn't take me seriously, then you find someone who will."

Ryan placed a hand on Grigore's shoulder. "I'm on it. You keep Caitlyn out of the crosshairs of this psycho."

"Don't worry. I promised to keep her here on God's green earth and I aim to do just that. The person who needs to worry is the one who threatened her in the first place, because I make no such promise to him."

Grigore heard Ryan's answering chuckle as his dress shoes struck the concrete in his retreat, leaving him once again alone to watch Caitlyn. He took the steel steps to the stage, careful to stay out of the eye of the public. She swayed seductively to one of her slower tunes. Damn, her ass looked fine hugged by all those shiny sequins. He could easily imagine peeling her out of the no doubt costly garment. Of course, he wouldn't, but that didn't mean she couldn't play a major role in his wicked fantasies.

Later, after the show, he'd need to get Ryan to keep an eye on Caitlyn for a bit when they arrived back at the hotel so he could look up a little sustenance. He hated leaving her side for even a moment, but sinking his fangs into some young lady's carotid wouldn't earn him any points with the pop star. She'd likely freak the fuck out, and rightly so.

Maybe he'd even find a hot little number to help work off some of his sexual frustrations while he was at it. If he didn't do something soon, even the adjoining rooms wouldn't be enough to keep him away from Cait.

His willpower was seriously beginning to mock him.

Caitlyn may hate him but there was no doubt in his mind she still wanted him. That much was apparent from the scent of her desire when things heated up between them. Grigore was sure tonight would be no different, regardless of her non-negotiable term of sleeping in separate rooms. To make sure he was the stronger of the two, he'd need to slake that hunger elsewhere.

Grigore peered around one of the props and into the audience, particularly the first few rows where the VIP section was located. A quick scan of the rows didn't produce Tyler.

Where the fuck?

He stepped back and pushed the button on his walkie. "Josh, tell me you have the latecomer in your sight."

Silence greeted him. Son of a mother…

His gaze landed back on Caitlyn who did a little dance number to one of her more upbeat songs. She certainly knew how to move, probably giving half the young men in the audience woodies. Grigore wished he could stand back here all night and enjoy the show, but he needed to find Tyler like fucking yesterday. Scanning the crowd again turned up nothing.

Placing his walkie by his lips, he growled, "Josh? Where the fuck are you?"

Nothing.

"Motherfucker, I'll beat you to within an inch of your life if you don't answer me."

Grigore took the steel steps by twos down to the back corridor, finding it completely empty. Where the hell were all the roadies? He knew he couldn't leave his post without someone to watch over her. Caitlyn was his number one priority. Fury radiated through him, threatening to bring out the vampire. Grigore returned to side stage and took several deep breaths. He needed to calm down. Acting on anger resulted in making stupid mistakes. And that he couldn't afford.

He tried one more time, holding the walkie to his mouth. "Josh," he hissed, still receiving dead air.

Caitlyn walked to the front of the stage, singing part of the chorus before holding out her microphone for the audience to join in. The noise grew to a deafening volume. No wonder the crew wore earplugs. With his sensitive vampire hearing, it was overloud, not that it would hamper him from hearing any other oddities.

Looking back out over the audience, he still didn't spot the moron from earlier. Crew members lined the front of the stage, making sure the attendees stayed behind the wooden barrier. He sure in the hell hoped Josh was doing his damn job and that was the reason he wasn't answering his call.

Grigore's gaze traveled the stadium, seeing in the dark fairly well, thanks to his vampire DNA. Nothing seemed out of the ordinary. A few more crew members were spotted walking the floor, but still no Josh. Or Tyler for that matter. Fans screamed, sang, danced, jumped up and down—

Back the fuck up!

His gaze returned to one of the dark, unused press boxes near the rear of the stadium. A lone man leaned against the steel and Plexiglas railing. What appeared to be a long-range rifle rested at his shoulder and aimed at the stage, more specifically Caitlyn. Wolf's gaze flew back to her, where a red glowing dot now centered on her forehead.

Motherfucker!

He took off with speed unmatched by a human, reaching her about the time he heard the ping of the rifle being fired. Pushing Cait to the side, Grigore took the bullet to his left pec. His body jerked and he stumbled backward several steps. His eyes heated and his gums ached with the threat of the emerging vampire. He gritted his teeth to keep that from happening.

"Son of a motherfucking bitch," he growled, his hand covering the bleeding wound. He didn't think it hit anything vital to stop his heart, but it stung like a bitch nonetheless.

Lots of blood flowed from between his fingers. Fuck, the bullet must have grazed an artery. He'd survive the wound, but not without considerable blood loss. His need for sustenance increased tenfold.

Caitlyn screamed. Hysteria blossomed in her rounded gaze as she fixated on the blood seeping between his fingers. "You've been shot."

Grigore covered her mic with his free hand to silence their conversation. "Focus, Sunshine. I'll live. I need to get you out of here."

Picking her up, he cradled her against his uninjured side and ran for the back of the stage, her band members quickly following suit. Luckily, he hadn't heard any more shots fired from the rifle.

Ryan Baxter skidded to a halt just inches from them. "Is Caitlyn—"

"She's fine." He handed the cordless mic to Ryan. "Calm this crowd down before pandemonium hits. Kids could get trampled out there. I need to find this motherfucker, but first I need to secure Caitlyn."

Ryan quickly mounted the stairs to the stage, trying his best, along with the crew, to calm the crowd and get them out of the venue without incident. *Fuck!* This was sure to bring the authorities and make major headlines.

Moments later, Grigore had Cait contained backstage in her locked dressing room, waiting for Ryan to watch over her. With any luck, the piece of shit who tried to shoot her was having trouble leaving the building due to the fans charging the exits.

A knock sounded on the door. Grigore turned the lock and cracked it open, finding Ryan on the other side. He further opened it and allowed her manager into the room.

"Lock the door behind me. No one gets in but me. Got it? Don't open this motherfucking door unless you hear my voice."

Grigore heard the lock click into place before he took off through the stadium, heading for the stairs. His wound had already begun healing, but he could tell the lack of blood had made him weak. His head swam, leaving him slightly dizzy as he took the steps, heading for the box office seats. Reaching the top landing, he leaned over, sucked in air and passed the fuck out.

CAIT PACED THE DRESSING ROOM, moments after Grigore having been carried in and laid upon a wooden bench. She gulped in oxygen, trying desperately to calm her jangled nerves and not wind up having a full-blown anxiety attack. Someone had tried to kill her. Of course, the threat looming over her was no surprise, hence the need for Grigore. But to have a gun actually pointed at her? Had it not been for Grigore, right now she'd be zipped up in a black body bag on her way to the morgue.

Looking down at him, she couldn't help but note his pallor. Grigore was pale, so much so, his skin appeared nearly translucent. Dr. Wensink reported the nicked artery had somehow miraculously healed itself, but not before considerable blood loss. She had said the body was capable of things modern science couldn't explain. This certainly was one of them.

Dr. Wensink had left moments ago to see about transporting Grigore to the nearest hospital due to his obvious blood loss. Thankfully, she had been in the audience to see the show. Upon witnessing the shooting, she had immediately come backstage to offer her help.

Caitlyn's hand trembled as she lay it gently on the opposite side of Grigore's bare chest, taking in the meager piece of taped white gauze covering his wound. It was the best they could do from the first aid kits found backstage. Blood congealed in the hair on his chest. She sucked in a sob, knowing this was her fault.

The good news?

Grigore was going to be okay and he'd saved her life by taking the bullet meant for her.

The bad news?

Someone had gotten close enough to take aim and if it wasn't for Grigore, she'd be dead.

His lids fluttered open, his dark gaze landing on hers. He tried to sit, but Caitlyn applied a bit of pressure to his chest, keeping him on his back.

She brushed his long hair out of his face. "You need to stay still. Doctor's orders."

His brow creased. "Doctor?"

"There was one in the audience who came to help after she witnessed you getting shot. Good news, she says the artery healed itself. But you need blood." Caitlyn smiled, trying to hold the tears at bay. Grigore didn't need a blubbering female on his hands. "She's arranging transport to a hospital."

Grigore brushed off Caitlyn's touch and sat up. "Like hell. I don't need a fucking hospital. Like the doctor said, the artery healed itself."

Stubborn man.

"She also said you needed blood, and that you should be checked over."

"I'm fucking fine," Grigore growled as the doctor reentered the room. His gaze landed on the woman. "Sorry, doc, but thank you for your help. No further assistance is needed."

The doctor blinked in befuddlement, obviously shocked by his quick recovery. So was Caitlyn. Grigore should still be flat on his back, not acting as if the bullet to his chest was nothing more than a flesh wound.

"I'd still feel better if you were checked over and given some blood," the doctor said. "You lost a lot. I'm surprised you're even sitting, to be honest."

He looked at Caitlyn, then to Ryan, who stood near the rear of the room on his phone. "Can you guys give me and the doc a minute? This won't take long. Then we can get back to the hotel where we'll discuss what the hell happened and how a fucking rifle got into the building. We'll need to beef up security for tomorrow night's show."

"You won't be doing anything." Cait wagged a finger at him. "You're going to the hospital. No arguments."

Ryan shoved off the wall, patted Grigore's good shoulder and said, "Excellent job tonight, man. We'll give you some time with the doctor."

Ryan ushered her from the room, to wait with him in the hall. The arena seemed eerily quiet now. Caitlyn wasn't used to hanging around venues after the show. Usually, she was one of the first to leave. It didn't help her nerves to know the gunman hadn't been located.

"I'm worried about Grigore, Ryan."

"As you should be. That man just saved your life. But thankfully, the doctor said he'll be okay."

Caitlyn bit her lip to still the trembling. She was a hair-breadth away from becoming a sobbing mess. "She also said he needed blood, and he's refusing. Did you see how pale he was?"

"I'm sure the doctor knows what she's doing. She'll no doubt talk him into a quick trip to the ER. You and I will go back to the hotel so you can get some rest. I've arranged for a police escort. I've also hired some of Cleveland's finest to patrol the venue for tomorrow's show. No one will get past."

Her face heated. "Exactly how did that happen the first time? For Heaven's sake, Ryan. The man walked in with a loaded rifle."

"I know. I'll be speaking with the crew. There's no excuse for a breach. It won't happen again or heads will roll."

"Let's just hope one of those heads isn't mine."

"A couple of detectives will meet us back at the hotel. They want to question you."

"But I don't know anything." She sighed heavily. "If I did, I wouldn't be in this predicament and Grigore would be on his way back to Oregon. Not sitting in there with a hole in his chest."

The door opened and Dr. Wensink walked out, looking a bit paler than before. What had Grigore said? "Doctor?"

She stopped and smiled, her gaze seeming a bit unfocused. "He'll be fine. No need for him to go to the hospital. I'm going to cancel the call for an ambulance. You both have a great night."

The doctor gave them her back and walked down the corridor. *Odd.* Caitlyn turned and entered the room, finding Grigore pulling his bloodied shirt over his head.

"Exactly why aren't you going to the hospital?" Caitlyn noted his cheeks were no longer pale, but rosy with color. She narrowed her gaze. "Don't you look one-hundred-percent better. What the hell happened in here?"

He shrugged, shoving his arms into his vest and pulling it on over his shoulders. "Turns out I didn't need a hospital after all. You heard the doctor. Just like the artery, I miraculously healed."

GRIGORE PACED HIS HOTEL ROOM like a caged animal. He had managed to sip a little sustenance from the good doctor's carotid back at the venue before hypnotizing her to call off the ambulance and forget the fact he sank his fangs deep into her neck. With the oddity of his plasma and his vampire DNA, he couldn't risk a trip to the hospital. The donation of her blood fixed one of his problems, but not the other.

He still wanted to get inside Caitlyn's tight little sleep shorts she wore in the next room. Now that his one hunger had been fulfilled, the other raged out of control. Cleveland's finest had shown up earlier with their questions, but in truth no one knew anything. Ryan and Cait had followed that meeting with one of their own over the next night's show and their plans to step up security. Grigore had listened in ... barely. Hell, he couldn't get his mind focused on anything other than his need to be near Caitlyn, to hold her in his arms and bury himself deep inside her. He had come too damn close to losing her.

Fuck, she had him by the balls.

Always had.

Now that she was alone in her room, preparing to get some shuteye, Grigore was thinking about his insisting on leaving the adjoining doors open. He couldn't get away from her scent, and that had his dick hard enough to ram through steel. He needed to get his mind off slipping between her thighs and focus on something more productive, like not relying on Josh and his motley crew to protect Cait.

Fucking her wasn't going to get that done.

Grigore grabbed his cell from the nightstand, found Ryder's number in his contacts and hit send. It was late here, but Oregon was three hours behind them, making it eleven o'clock their time. The phone rang several times before Ryder answered.

"What's up, bro? Everything okay?"

"Everything went to shit tonight," Grigore grumbled. "We had a near disaster on our hands and shit-for-brains Josh couldn't be found."

Ryder chuckled. "And Josh is?"

"Crew manager and head of fucking security."

"You want to start from the beginning? Tell me what happened."

Grigore reiterated the night's events, ending with his sipping from the doctor's artery. "When I get a hold of Josh's motherfucking neck, he's going to wish he'd answered my call. He better have a damn good explanation."

"I'll talk to Viper. I'm sure he'll want a few of us to head out and help you with security."

Grigore scratched his beard. "I'm not going to argue with you this time, Ryder. I can't be everywhere at once and this crew isn't good enough for my liking. I can't take a chance with Cait's life by letting my ego get in the way. But make sure

Viper and Hawk have their backs covered with Mircea as well."

"We have plenty of primordial blood around here to take him out. That son of a bitch won't know what's waiting for him."

Grigore laughed. "Good to hear."

"Where you off to next, Wolf?"

"Pittsburgh, day after tomorrow. There won't be a show that night as we have a couple of days' rest in between, so you have plenty of time to get here." Grigore briefly peered through the adjoining doors, seeing Cait propped against her pillow, knees drawn up, reading a novel. "Although, you might want to stay back at the clubhouse, Ryder. You take care of Gabby. Besides, Viper and Hawk may need your help. The more primordial blood the better, should Vlad's brother make an appearance."

"You're probably right. I'll check with Preacher, Rogue, and Gypsy, since they offered their help. I'll let you know who's on their way. You know if I'm needed, I'll be there."

"Thanks, Ryder." Grigore walked over to his bed and sat down. "I appreciate it. Not that I don't think I can handle this crackpot, but I can't trust the crew manager to be my eyes and ears."

"You got it, Wolf. It's what brothers do. We help one another. I'll be in touch."

"Sounds good, man."

Grigore ended the call and set the cell back on the nightstand. He'd feel better with a few more of the Sons on watch. Cait's life was too big a risk to think he could've done this on his own.

The light in the adjoining room extinguished and he heard the rustling of covers as Cait no doubt settled in for the night. He sighed. At least one of them would be getting sleep. Grigore still had another kind of hunger simmering beneath his skin and damn if he didn't want to cross between the doors, and crawl under the sheets with her.

Instead, he stood and headed for the bathroom.

One cold shower coming up.

CHAPTER SEVEN

K ANE GLANCED AROUND THE SONS' MEETING ROOM FILLED with members and newly appointed club prospects. Normally, the prospects waited outside and weren't invited in while a session was in order. But since the subject of this gathering would include a few of them, Kane had asked that they all stay for the time being. A few hang-arounds stood outside the closed door, having yet to prove themselves.

He dropped the gavel against the strike plate. Conversation died down around the room. "I call this church meeting to order. Some of you already know why you were summoned here today. Wolf needs some help on a job in Cleveland, so we're stepping in. Ryder? You want to give the lowdown?"

Ryder Kelley filled the members in on what had taken place at last night's concert in Ohio. There would be another show tonight, but since Caitlyn's manager had already secured a number of local police to patrol the arena and surrounding area, Grigore's MC brothers weren't needed until the crew arrived in Pittsburgh, giving them a couple days to ride out.

"So who's in?" Ryder asked.

"Hell, I'm all over that." Bobby Bourassa stroked his long beard, a smile curving the whiskers surrounding his lips. "I'll be glad to take Tena along. She can be a tough nut. I'm sure she'll want to offer her help as well."

"Count Kimber and me in." Anton Balan tapped the table with his index finger. "I'd be more than happy to help Wolf out."

"Thanks, Preacher and Rogue." Viper looked around the room. "Anyone else?"

"I offered," Ryder said, "but my hands are a bit full at the moment and Wolf said he'd rather I stay here and take care of my shit."

"I agree with Wolf. I'd also rather those with pregnant mates and babies stay here as well. No sense putting your family at risk."

"Fuck that." Grayson Gabor smiled. "Tamera and I are in. I could use a little action."

"What about Lucian, Gypsy?"

"Suzi and I can keep him, Viper." Kaleb shrugged. "Stefan would love having him around."

"I'm not sure that's a great idea, bro. We have our hands full with Vlad's brother on the loose."

"I agree." Grayson nodded. "Tamera and I will follow in her Range Rover. We'll take a prospect along to help watch Lucian. He'll never see the danger. Besides, this might take a while and I'm not comfortable leaving him for a long period of time. Tamera would never go for that either."

"Then we're agreed." Kane glanced about the room. "The rest of you will stay here to keep an eye out for Mircea. Should Vlad's brother show his face, don't be a hero. You call either Kaleb or me. That primordial's a loose cannon, and since he's bringing another with him, it's going to take our own primordial strength to take on the two nut jobs. That means me, Hawk, Ryder, or even Draven and Brea are to handle Mircea and his mate. No one else. Am I clear?"

Heads nodded in agreement around the room. Kane continued, looking at the prospects standing along the back wall. "Tamera will choose one of you to make the trip east to help take care of Lucian. The rest of you are commissioned to keep a watch for Vlad's brother. You're mortal, so don't make the mistake of crossing him. You see him, you call one of us immediately."

He turned back to the table of Sons. "Any other business at hand?"

The doors abruptly swung open, catching the men's attention. Vlad strode in on a growl, "Let's take care of my brother once and for all, shall we? Can there be any business more important than impaling that son of a bitch?"

VLAD SAT ON THE SOFA OPPOSITE his two great-grandsons and plopped his booted feet onto the center table of the clubhouse. The rest of the motorcycle club had taken their leave, except for Ryder and his plaything. He supposed she was more than that to the man, as he heard the word mate tossed around by a few of the members. Sooner, rather than later, they'd most likely be bringing another vampire into the mix.

Not that it was a bad thing. Hell, no. Strength came in numbers and his grandsons were building a nice family among their crew. But for him? Vlad laughed in the face of romance. Why would he ever want to tie himself for eternity to one mate? Not when there were so many females willing to feed his vigorous hungers. Nope. He'd leave the mating to his kin and their friends.

Vlad planned to stay happily unmated for his eternity.

He took the proffered glass from Kane's hand. Fine whiskey, which he quickly downed. Spending so much time in his brother's company of late, he had taken to drinking his share of wine. Hell, he nearly forgot the pleasant burn of a good rye until it slid down his esophagus and warmed him from the inside.

Balancing the now empty glass on the arm of the sofa, he glanced at his grandsons. Ryder and his lady friend had already excused themselves to their quarters. "Where do we start?"

"If you're referring to looking for your wayward brother, your guess is as good as mine, Vlad." Kane took a sip from his own whiskey. "Mircea could be anywhere, but something tells me he's near. Maybe not in the same town, but I'm betting he has a flat somewhere in Oregon and is laying low. He won't strike until the timing is right. Mircea isn't stupid by any means and won't chance losing his opportunity again."

"My brother is nothing if not cunning." Vlad rubbed his free hand down his jaw. "He's going to want to stake out the clubhouse and your homes. The coward would no doubt rather strike when you're alone, but he wants you both. Should he take out either of you first, it would eliminate the element of surprise, opening him to an all-out war before he could slink away like the snake he is."

"You think he's stupid enough to try to take us both on at the same time?" Kaleb asked.

"I do." Vlad raised a brow. "He's vain enough to think he can accomplish it if you don't see him coming. Don't be foolish to think of him as anything less than a formidable opponent."

"Are you here to offer your help, then?"

Vlad laughed. "I'm here to take the son of a bitch out myself, Kane. I'd much rather have the honors. But if he somehow gets past me, I need you boys on the lookout. Don't let your guard down for even a second. And for fuck's sake, don't leave your families exposed. Maybe you should move them into the clubhouse."

"But you just said he'll want to strike while we're together." Kaleb's lips thinned. "Wouldn't that put us at further risk?"

"With Ryder here, that makes three primordials against two, not to mention the addition of your mates. He won't strike with the odds against him. So if you leave the clubhouse, do it in numbers. Don't go out alone."

"And where will you stay?" Kane asked.

"I don't want Mircea knowing I'm near. It's better that no one knows my whereabouts."

Kaleb chuckled. "The way you mask your scent, do we ever?"

"Be assured I'm a phone call away. But I'll be close, son … very close."

———

THE SECOND GIG IN CLEVELAND had gone off without a hitch. Thankfully, nothing had happened to warrant Grigore's attention. Caitlyn had been phenomenal and the show high energy. No one likely went away disappointed from the two-hour set. Her vocals were flawless. Grigore would listen to anything she sang, any damn day of the week, regardless if it was chick music. She was *that* good. His normal choice of music, though, was country. Not the new-fangled pop stuff they played on today's radio stations. He liked the good old boys, such as Hank Williams, Merle Haggard, and Johnny Cash.

His brothers gave him shit whenever he ran his music through the speakers at the clubhouse. Most of them favored heavy metal or industrial. He could listen to it, but preferred the stuff he grew up on. His old man had been a huge fan of Waylon Jennings until the day he died. At the funeral, Grigore had the director play "Farewell Party" sung by Waylon. His father would have loved it, and surely he had been looking down with a smile.

Grigore finished his sweep of the grounds at the fancy hotel in Pittsburgh that Ryan Baxter had secured for them. A few nights in the penthouse of this place must have cost a small fortune. No adjoining rooms needed here. Hell, Grigore didn't think he had ever stayed in a penthouse, or a hotel this elaborate. Chandeliers hung from the two-story ceiling of the lobby, with cascading, diamond-like lights twinkling about the room. An atrium with potted greenery where one could sit and enjoy reading or a cup of coffee was positioned to the right of the bank of chrome and glass elevators. A low din of conversation came from inside.

The penthouse had its own elevator car. Only the top floor keycard would operate it, which was great from a security standpoint. No one would be able to get to Caitlyn once she was secured in her suite.

The heels of Grigore's boots thudded off the marble tiles as he headed for the elevators. More than a few heads turned in his direction, sending him the similar scorn he had experienced in Cleveland. To the ones looking upon him in disdain, he saluted as he passed. He'd give them a reason to turn up their snooty noses, he thought with a grumble. Next stop? New York City. Those fancy-smancy hotel guests would surely have coronaries when he strode through the lobby of one of their fine establishments.

Grigore didn't care one iota what people thought of him, but he needed to remember it was Cait's reputation at stake. He may have thick skin, but she didn't need the negative attention he'd bring. His exact motive for staying on point and the hell out of her pants. When this gig was over, he was leaving. He'd not subject her to the kind of disapproving publicity that would no doubt follow being seen with someone like him. Oh, Grigore had made jokes about the arm candy she frequently wore when she was in the eye of the press. But in truth, any of those men were much better for her career. He'd do well to remember that.

Sliding his keycard through the slot, he waited for the elevator doors to swoosh open, then stepped inside. He resisted the urge to flip the bird to those guests who continued to stare, especially since he had just entered the elevator reserved for guests with money. Real money, not the kind in his bank account. He wasn't poor by any means, having accumulated a small nest egg over the years, but it was nowhere near the amount of wealth Caitlyn had become accustomed to.

Once the car reached the top floor and the doors slid open, Grigore walked into the main sitting area, the penthouse having no actual door. The place was decked to the nines, making Grigore feel completely out of place. He'd never fit into Caitlyn's lifestyle, all the more reason to pack up his shit and hit the road once he eliminated the threat to her safety.

Ryan stood and met him halfway to the elevator. "Now that you're here, I'm going to head downstairs. We don't need Caitlyn for a soundcheck until the day after tomorrow, but we do have a couple of television spots and one radio interview in the morning you'll need to make sure she gets to. Otherwise, she's all yours. If you need me in the meantime, call my cell."

The elevator doors closed on Ryan just as Cait walked into the sitting area from what Grigore assumed was one of the two bedroom suites. She wore a coral, chiffon floral sundress that breezed around her ankles as she padded barefoot across the tiled floors. Sitting on one of the Italian leather sofas, she tucked her legs beneath her, setting her phone on the armrest and looked at him.

"You want to fill me in on what's going on?"

Grigore shrugged. "We lay low here for a couple of days. You don't go anywhere without me. The show is in two days. By that time, some of my MC brothers will be here to help with security."

"I pay my own security team, Grigore."

He chuckled and patted his chest where the bullet had entered. "You see where that got me."

"Back to my point. I already knew what the coming days' schedule was, I was referring to you being shot." She narrowed her gaze. "I saw the wound, the amount of blood you lost. Damn it, Grigore, you were so pale I didn't think you were going to make it. Then what? A half hour later the doctor walks out of the room looking stoned, and you've miraculously recovered. How the hell does that happen?"

"It's in my DNA, Cait. Let's not worry about something that didn't happen. I'm here and I'm healthy."

"Amazing. It's as if you were never shot at all." She stood and walked toward him. "Take off your shirt, Grigore."

"What the hell for?"

"I'm concerned. I need to make sure the wound didn't get infected."

"I'm fine." Grigore knew he'd have a lot of explaining to do if she saw his non-existent wound. Only a tiny red mark remained and that would be gone in another day. "Why don't we talk about this security of yours."

She stopped inches from him, locking gazes. Damn, but she had the prettiest eyes he'd ever had the pleasure of looking into. "How much are your guys going to cost me? I have a budget—"

"Don't worry, Sunshine, you can afford free."

"I already took charity—"

"You call this charity?" He gripped her shoulders, resisting the urge to shake the hell out of her. "What we are doing for you is not charity. You can keep your damn money. I'm fucking doing this because I care what happens to you. I always have. And my brothers help protect what's mine."

Fuck, he did not just say that out loud. And he sure in the hell hoped it went right over Caitlyn's head with the little fit she was throwing.

"You may be doing it for me out of old times' sake, but your friends—"

He damn near shut her up with a kiss, one he so desperately wanted. "This isn't open for discussion, Sunshine."

"Good, then neither is this." She shoved his T-shirt over his chest so quickly he hadn't had time to react.

Touché. Well played, Sunshine.

Cait gently ran her fingers through the hair on his chest, his dick taking notice. One look down and she wouldn't miss his reaction to her fingers' exploration.

Grigore tried to yank the shirt from her hands, but Cait was relentless. She drew her lower lip between her teeth, making him want to nibble on it as well. The scent of her rising desire didn't escape his notice, making what was semi-hard now rock hard. Christ, it had been too long since he fucked a woman, making this a precarious situation. He wanted her bad. Touching her, though, was a Very. Bad. Idea.

"Cait," he hissed through clenched teeth.

Her innocent gaze came back to his. "Where were you shot, Grigore?"

He should've thought to dress the non-existent wound with gauze even though it hadn't been necessary. "Cait, listen—"

"Grigore, no one heals that quickly. Two days ago, a bullet passed through here." She poked her forefinger on target. "I saw the wound and the blood. It looks as if the bullet simply bounced off. Why? What are you? No human can heal that quickly. You should be lying in a hospital bed, hooked to IVs. And yet, here you stand, good as new."

Fuck! He hadn't been careful enough. Kane would have his ass and rightly so. No one could know what he truly was now. But what choice did he really have? There was no way he could hypnotize Caitlyn into forgetting he had been shot. Should someone bring it up, she'd have no memory of the event.

He gripped her shoulders again and backed her to the leather sofa, gently urging her into it. "You aren't going to like what I'm about to tell you."

Her hazel eyes widened.

"I'm not trying to scare you, Sunshine, but there's something you need to know about me." At least now, she wouldn't want anything to do with him, making leaving her much easier in the end. "What I'm about to tell you, you cannot repeat. This isn't up for negotiation. My people could get hurt if this got out. I … could get hurt. You must promise. If you break that promise, I'll erase your memory of me. You won't even know I exist, which hell, is probably the wisest choice at this point."

But damn him for not wanting her to forget him.

"You have my word, Grigore. You must know I would never want harm to come to you. What is it?"

"There is no easy way to explain, so I'll show you."

He turned his back to spare her from watching the changes. His gaze heated. The bones in his face popped, changing shape. His fangs elongated, scraping past his lower lip. Grigore allowed the monster to come forth before slowly turning. His black gaze landed on her widened one.

"Vampire?" Cait gasped, her trembling hand going to her lips. "They're not real."

Grigore smiled tentatively, knowing she couldn't possibly miss his razor-sharp fangs. He expected her to run scream-ing for the spare room, slam and lock the door, call her man-ager. Which, of course, would force him to do exactly as he had threatened, erase her memory and head for the hills, leaving her to fight this unknown bastard on her own. He had fucked up.

Instead, she stood her ground, her trembling fingers now outlining the contours of his rugged, misshapen face. "How did I not know?"

"When we were together, I was human. This happened after I left. I was in a bad motorcycle accident that should've taken my life. My brothers saved me."

"They made you a vampire?"

He nodded.

"You're dead then?"

Grigore chuckled. "Sunshine, you saw me bleeding just days ago. I assure you, I'm very much alive. You're thinking of fictional vampires. While we have some of the traits you see in movies and books, most of them are just that … fictional. My DNA is different than yours, which means I heal very quickly, as you saw firsthand."

Her pink tongue darted out and wet her lips. "You drink blood? That's the reason you didn't eat my mom's cooking. For that matter, I don't think I've seen you eat much this entire trip. You always had excuses."

"That part is true, Sunshine. We survive on blood. It's our sustenance, our fountain of youth. If I continue to drink it, I stay alive."

"For how long?"

He shrugged. "Forever, I suppose. Or unless someone cuts off my head or stops my heart from beating."

Her hand reflexively covered her carotid.

"Don't worry, Sunshine, I won't drink yours … not unless given permission, of course."

CHAPTER EIGHT

CAITLYN WAS FLIPPING OUT, FULL-ON PANIC MODE. AND YET she was trying her damnedest not to freak out in front of Grigore. Vampire? What the hell? She couldn't help but rub her neck, drawing his black, marble-like gaze back to her throat.

Stop it! Stop rubbing your damn neck and drawing attention to it.

Vampires aren't real.

Of course, they weren't. Had she just entered into an episode of the *Twilight Zone*? What. The. Hell? Cait had seen the rapid healing of Grigore's body after a near mortal bullet wound. When he should've been heading for the ER, he instead walked out of the arena as if it were a mere scratch. He sported fangs, his face had transformed into a vampire, proving what her rational mind tried to dispute. But her heart? Only saw the man she had fallen in love with.

"Can you go back to being you now, Grigore.? You're kind of weirding me out." Cait dropped her hand, watching as his features slowly returned to the man she had fallen hopelessly in love with years ago. No wonder he hadn't aged and looked just as hot today as he did then. "The fact the bullet hit to the side of your heart, that's the reason you were able to recover so quickly? An inch to the right—"

"I'd be dead. There's no coming back from that, Sunshine. Even as a vampire."

He reached out to her and she took a step back, slapping his hand away. "Then why the hell don't you wear a bullet-proof vest?"

Grigore stepped forward and backed her against the wall, not allowing her room to retreat farther. "Why, Cait, I wasn't aware you cared."

Caitlyn smacked his chest and hard, but she'd bet he barely felt it. He didn't even bat an eye. "I may hate you for leaving, dipshit. But I'll always care, even if you are … are this."

"Duly noted." His face hardened. "I suppose I deserve your hatred. And this? It's called vampire."

Her breath quickened, her mind not yet ready to accept what she had seen with her own eyes. A vampire, for crying out loud. She placed her hand at the side of her throat again, regardless if he had no intentions of eating her.

"You left me in tatters, Grigore. It took me a long time to move forward with my life."

"And look at you now."

She dropped her hand hiding her carotid and fisted them at her sides. "I loved you, you ass, and you threw me away. Why?"

"Christ, Cait. I was going to hold you back. Look at me." He gripped her by the shoulders. "Really look at me, damn it. I haven't changed a fucking thing. I have long hair. I ride motorcycles and sport tattoos like they're clothes. Hell, I look like

I'm at least twenty years your senior with this damn pre-mature gray. If people didn't immediately mistake me for your father, they'd turn up their fucking noses at your choice of companions. There wasn't a record company or PR person that would've taken you seriously with me at your side. And you weren't about to ditch me, Sunshine, even if it was for your own damn good."

A tear slipped from her lashes. Grigore released her and used the pad of his thumb to wipe away the moisture. "Can't you see, I did it for you. Had I left you a way to get a hold of me, you wouldn't have taken the path you did, leading you here … to all of this."

"You should've given me the choice."

"And what would that have been?"

"You."

HER ADMISSION SHOULDN'T HAVE cut him to the heart. But it did. Ripped a fucking hole right in the middle. Grigore had been acting on her behalf when he left, even though she hadn't seen it that way. He had made the right choice then and he would do so again, no matter what she had to say on the matter. A biker, let alone a vampire, would not be good for her or her career, not to mention exposing him as such would be putting his club's secret in danger. It was simple. Grigore, nor the Sons of Sangue, could be put in the spotlight. They had managed to steer clear of the media thus far and would continue to do so.

Grigore framed her face with his palms. Lord, she wasn't just beautiful, she was fucking gorgeous. But there would be no hope of ever claiming her. They simply were who they were. No fate or meant-to-be bullshit. Life had handed them a raw deal. Caitlyn would move on, find herself a nice man to settle down with and have babies, though the thought of that ever happening was like a punch to the gut. He hoped to hell he never met the man who was lucky enough to live out his life lying beside Caitlyn nightly because he wouldn't trust himself not to drain the lucky bastard.

For him? There would be no other. Grigore would continue on, live life as usual. There would be no mate because no one could ever take Cait's place. The love of his life stood inches away. Too fucking bad she wasn't his to claim.

He ground his teeth. Damn himself for wanting nothing more than to carry her to the bed just beyond the walls of the room where they stood. "If that's true, Cait, then I made the right fucking decision."

Cait jerked from his touch and backed away. "You're a fool, Grigore."

"I won't argue with that."

Her arm swept the room. "You could've had all of this … with me."

"Is that what you think I want?" He laughed, not feeling any of the humor. "I've only ever wanted *you*, Cait. This shit doesn't mean crap to me."

"Then why didn't you choose me? Why did you run away?"

"I fucking chose a better life for you." He jammed a hand through his hair and paced from her to keep from reaching out again. He no longer trusted himself to do the right thing. "I chose a better life for you. I'm a fucking vampire, Sunshine. I can't be seen with you. The media hounds you day and night, looking for a story. Should someone discover my secret, it would be devastating for me and my brothers. Don't you get it? We'd be hunted down like animals. We'd be slaughtered until my kind ceased to exist."

"Maybe if we—"

He cut her off. There was no way in hell he'd allow her to try and *find a way*. Christ, if he thought there was one, he'd have found it long ago.

"No, Cait. We"—he used his fingers to indicate the two of them—"aren't happening. *Ever.* This conversation is over. My brothers will arrive in two days and they can't find out that you know our secret. You want protection? There is no one stronger or more cunning to do that. We're hunters, predators. It's what we do."

He watched the shiver pass over her shoulders. She worried her lower lip. "You aren't an animal."

"No?" He raised an eyebrow as his gaze zeroed in on the rapid pulse beating at the base of her neck. "Let me near your neck and I'll prove you wrong."

Her trembling hand flattened over the hollow. "You would drain me? You're not capable of it."

"I may not drain you." His nostrils flared as he scented the sweet essence of her life's fluid. "I don't need to take all of your blood to sate my hunger. But don't think I'm not capable of slaking my need on that artery you keep trying to hide from me. Show me this piece of shit threatening you, though, and I'll gladly drain the fucker of every last drop. *That's* an animal, Sunshine."

She turned her back on him and paced soundlessly across the marble to the floor-to-ceiling windows and looked out across the sprawling city beyond. Her shoulders drooped as she palmed the window and leaned her forehead against the cool glass, her breath leaving a circle of mist.

He was doing the right thing.

Then why the hell did he feel like such a shit? When he had left years ago, Grigore was one hundred percent sure he was doing what needed to be done. After all, as the old saying went, if you love something…

He had been a fool.

Fifteen years had passed and he still pined over the loss. When he took this job, he didn't expect to find Caitlyn just as broken as he was. He figured she would've moved on, no longer shedding tears for the past, her heart filled with hate. And yet, beneath all the anger she harbored toward him, she still cared. Who knew, maybe had he stayed he'd be clean-shaven, his hair shorn, wearing Dockers instead of biker chaps and trying to fit into her world. He shook his head. It wasn't him and he didn't have it in him to change, then or now.

Approaching the window, he stopped beside her and looked across the darkening sky. "Will you ever forgive me?"

She turned her haunted gaze on him. "For leaving?"

"For being such a fool."

Cait faced him, standing within reach, tears free-falling down her face. "I'm not sure I can. You have no idea the pain you caused or the depression I slipped into. Only my music carried me through. Goodnight, Grigore."

With that, she headed for the suite she had exited earlier and softly closed the door. The turn of the lock echoed through his head. Christ, he never thought doing the right thing could hurt so damn much.

Grigore headed for the other suite, the living area dividing them. Tomorrow would be a better day. They'd forget this whole damn conversation and go back to being Cait and her protector. Except, now she knew his secret, one that was sure to forever damn him in her eyes.

It would be the final nail in the coffin that was his heart, sealing his lonely fate forever.

SHIVERS WRACKED HER BODY, the heater blowing warm air into the room doing little to chase away the chill. Cait tucked the covers beneath her chin, but she doubted that her goose-flesh had anything to do with the temperature of the room. Winter was two months away and she was trembling as if icicles were hanging from the eave spouts.

Her thoughts returned to the man lying in the other suite. The term vampire flashed behind her closed lids like a bright neon light. Did vampires even sleep? Grigore was very much alive, that much being apparent from the loss of blood he suffered from the gunshot wound to his chest. He was warm, even hot, to the touch, not cold as stone or seemingly fresh from the grave. But what about all the other fictional traits? Aversion to garlic, holy water, crosses? Sunlight hadn't seemed to faze him. And turning into a bat wasn't likely.

Although, he did go by the moniker Wolf.

Oh hell, that was shifters. Her imagination was getting a little carried away.

But if one existed, who's to say the other didn't?

Caitlyn flipped onto her back and stared at the ceiling. *Batshit crazy*. Completely off her rocker. Grigore had sworn her to secrecy, but who would she tell? No one was likely to believe her anyway. Vampires were a product of folklore and people's imagination … that was until about fifteen minutes ago. One very large and menacing looking vampire stood but inches away from her. Had she not seen his transformation with her own eyes, she'd never have believed it possible.

Every time she closed her eyes, Grigore was in full monster mode, black eyes, fangs and all. He was a nightmare come to life. And yet, he was still Grigore, the man she had fallen hopelessly in love with over fifteen years ago. The man she still loved, if she were being completely honest with herself. Having him by her side day in and day out had proven as much. Oh, she still hated him for leaving her; nothing he had said excused that away. He couldn't begin to know the pain he had caused, the depression that had set in.

Her heart panged.

He would leave her again.

Grigore was a man of his word, and if he said he was leaving once his job was done, Caitlyn didn't doubt it for a minute. A tear leaked from the corner of her eye, making a trek to her ear. She wiped it away, refusing to shed another over the bastard. If Grigore meant to leave, then she'd not allow him to see her despair.

Besides, Grigore did have a point. Caitlyn lived her life in the public eye. The media could be ruthless in their pursuit of a juicy tidbit. The risk of exposure for him would be too great. Cait wasn't quite sure how or when he fed, but if a reporter caught that on film, it would be all over the news. She didn't want to think about the ramifications.

Rolling back to her side, she punched the pillow, bunching it beneath her head. A vision of Grigore, the man, not the vampire, floated through her mind. In all of the years following his departure, she had hated him for leaving, despised the fact she compared every man she dated to him. Hell, he had likely ruined any chances of her ever falling in love again.

Grigore had been *it* for her.

Now, facing the possibility of him disappearing from her life again, Caitlyn wasn't sure her heart would survive it. But Grigore couldn't stay hidden forever, nor did she want him to have to live that kind of anonymity. If he wanted to have any kind of a life, he'd need to return to his home … to Oregon.

Her gaze went to the window. She hadn't drawn the drapes. This far up, no one would be able to see in anyway.

The nearly full moon cast a glow across the carpet, leaving the rest of the room cast in darkness.

Was Grigore awake? Did he lie in bed thinking of her?

Part of her wanted to get up, pad across the distance between them and crawl into his bed. Cait didn't necessarily want or need to have sex with him, although the idea had merit. She simply wanted to be held. If for just a night, she wanted to feel safe and coveted by the one man who had the power to turn her life upside down.

So why was she still lying here?

Caitlyn sat, scooting to the side of the bed. They were adults, and no one was there to judge. If she only had Grigore a few more days to a couple of months, she didn't want to be left with regrets. Having him so close and yet not touching him was killing her.

She had become accustomed to getting what she wanted. And right now, that was Grigore. Nerves fluttered through her stomach. What if he turned her away? Cait drew her lower lip between her teeth and stood to retrieve the silky matching robe to her white, nearly sheer nightgown. Mind made up, she slipped her arms into the sleeves and tied the sash around her waist.

If she wasn't so damn nervous, she'd have giggled with excitement. Cait planned to slip into his bed, whether she found him awake or not, and cuddle up to his heated, deliciously hard body.

At least her shivers would cease.

Making the trek in silence, she stopped outside his closed door, not yet having the courage to knock or test the knob to see if it was locked. Vampire or not, he was still Grigore, *her* Grigore. And he lay just feet beyond the door.

His deep voice startled her. "Caitlyn Summers, if you know what the fuck is good for you, you'll take your sexy little ass back to your bed … *now*."

She sucked in a deep breath, the need to be with him sliding up the charts faster than a new record release. "Grigore…"

"I'm warning you, Sunshine. I'm at the end of my rope."

Cait turned the knob and opened the door, seeing him lying on his bed bathed in moonlight.

"You have to the count of three."

His voice was husky with desire. Cait knew if she didn't do as she was told, they would be fucking like rabbits. Her stomach clenched. It had been too damn long.

"One."

She took a tentative step forward.

"Two."

Another couple of steps.

"Three."

She closed the distance and stood next to the bed, looking down at the only man she had ever given her heart. Grigore ran a hand down his beard and sighed heavily.

"You should've listened to me."

Reaching for her, Grigore gripped her forearm and pulled her down to the mattress, flipping her onto her back. His heavy thigh lay across her leg, trapping her to the bed. Gripping her wrists, he pinned them over her head and stared down at her, his eyes no longer human, but black and marble-like. Cait saw her reflection in them, seeing her need for the man now holding her to the bed.

The changes in his features, the fangs, they should've scared her, sent her running for the covers she had abandoned. But Grigore was still the same man on the inside, the one she had invited into her bed years ago. She'd be damned if she denied him now.

"Time's up, Sunshine."

CHAPTER NINE

GRIGORE WRESTLED WITH THE DEMONS IN HIS HEAD. LORD, he wanted to fuck her in the worst way. His cock lay stiff against her thigh, proof of his need. Never had he wanted another woman the way he did Caitlyn Summers. Never would he again. Damn, he might as well sign up for a monastery, once he left the tour behind as no woman could ever take her place. No one had come close in fifteen years.

If he were smart, he'd release her, carry her back to her room and lock her inside. Sleeping with her would only complicate matters and make it tougher on both of them in the end. Somewhere along the way, though, his propriety seemed to have taken its leave. Because there was no way the vampire side of him wasn't taking the gift she offered. Christ Almighty, he didn't deserve her.

Where the hell was Preacher when he was needed?

Grigore could certainly benefit from a few Hail Marys.

Cait's chest rose and fell in exertion, whether it was from fear, nerves, or need, he wasn't sure. Oh, she wanted him, vampire or not, that much he could detect from her scent.

"Lord help me, Cait. What the hell do you want?"

She drew her lower lip between her perfect row of white teeth, apprehension in her gaze. "You."

"Then why do I sense your fear? This is who I am, Sunshine. What I am. I can't hide my ugly side when my emotions get caught up. This is what you'll be fucking if we go any further. Not Grigore the man, but Wolf the predator."

Telling her about vampires had been a mistake. Showing her had been an even bigger one, but he would be damned if he'd regret it, not when it showed her what she was getting into bed with ... literally.

Cait tugged and he released his grip on her wrists. She brought her hands to his face, tracing the contours. "This is not ugly, Grigore. Different, but not ugly, not to me."

A slight smile lifted one side of his lips. "Glad you don't think so, Sunshine, because these fangs, this mug, it's part of the whole package. You can't have one without the other."

"Will you bite me?"

Grigore chuckled. Bracing his forearms on each side of her head, he leaned in and placed a soft kiss on the tip of her nose, then whispered, "Only if you want me to."

She sucked in air, a slight inhalation, but he had detected it. "I'm not sure—"

"Relax, Sunshine. We have donors, a secret society of women who feed us. It's against the rules to feed from a human if a donor is available. Telling you that I'm a vampire? Well, that technically broke the rules too."

Her forehead crinkled. He wanted to trace the soft lines with his finger, ease the worry. "Whose rules?"

"The Sons of Sangue."

"The MC vest you wear. Your brothers who are on the way here to help."

"Yes. You'll meet them soon, Sunshine. And whatever happens here, they can't know I told you about us."

Her pink tongue darted out and wet her lips. "What would happen if they found out?"

"I would be punished, and deservedly so. I knew the rules coming into this." He sighed heavily. "But as for you, they would erase your memory of me having ever been here."

Cait's gaze widened. "How?"

"We're experts in hypnotism." Grigore shrugged. "It's how we can survive in anonymity. We normally feed from a donor society who offer themselves to us. They know what we are but are sworn to silence. But when they aren't available, like now, I can feed from anyone but I must then erase the person's memory of it."

"That's why the doctor looked stoned when she left the room after tending to you?"

He nodded. "I needed blood to heal. It was a grave wound. The bullet nicked a large artery."

Caitlyn said nothing, just stared into his eyes. He could see her indecision. As much as he wanted this, she wasn't ready. If he asked her, however, she'd say yes. No doubt about it. Hell, she had walked across the living area with the sole purpose of crawling into his bed, knowing full well what would happen.

Grigore needed to be the bigger person, be the one who said no. Until Caitlyn was one-hundred-percent onboard, he wasn't about to take what she offered. For fuck's sake, the last thing he wanted come morning was to see regret in her beautiful hazel eyes.

"About this…"

"Yes?"

"It's not going to happen, Sunshine. You aren't ready for all of this." He chuckled. "Hell, you probably still hate me for leaving you."

Cait looked down for a moment, long enough that Grigore knew he hit the truth.

"It's okay, Cait. I deserve it. I may have had the best intentions, and still do, but I also know how much I hurt you." He ran a knuckle down her cheek, bringing her gaze back to his. "I'm not sure I'll ever be the man you need me to be, or the one you no longer despise, but until then this isn't going to happen. I won't do something, whether it's mutual desire or not, unless we are both on the same page. I'm still leaving when this is over. Not because I despise you, but because our lives are worlds apart. Hating you isn't in my DNA. Lord, I worship everything about you. I can't, and won't, ever take a pity fuck from you."

"This isn't pity." Her gaze heated. "I came in here because I wanted you."

His smile turned sad. He flipped her on the mattress so that they spooned, wrapping her in his embrace. "I know, Sunshine. But desiring someone and liking them are two different things. Besides, you need time to come to terms with this whole vampire thing. You may say it doesn't bother you, but I can sense your fear. I don't want you scared of me when we get busy. I want you all in. You go to sleep and I'll hold you right here if you'd like. You have a big day tomorrow."

"You'd let me sleep here and not want anything?"

"I *want*, Sunshine, more than you know. But I'm okay with just holding you for now." He placed a feather-light kiss on her temple. "You have interviews tomorrow. Get some sleep."

Grigore gathered Caitlyn more tightly against him, their heads resting on the same pillow, much the way they used to sleep. Holding her felt right, like he had come home, even if he knew it wasn't to be. He guessed if he was going to be here awhile, then he'd at least have this tenuous truce. He'd gladly hold her every night while they slept, blue balls be damned. He supposed he'd better get used to servicing himself in the shower because he sure in the hell wasn't going to take any other woman while the one he truly wanted slept in his arms nightly.

Caitlyn may not know it yet, but now that she was sharing his bed, he wasn't about to allow her out of it. Being next to her was the best way to keep her safe. At least that's the excuse he intended to give her.

If he couldn't fuck her, he'd at least be able to hold her.

Tightening his arms, he kissed the slender slope where her neck met her shoulder, then closed his eyes and listened to her breath grow shallow as she fell to sleep.

CAITLYN HAD FINISHED HER interviews for the day and awaited his return in the penthouse. They had one more day of rest before her next show. Grigore had left her alone for a few minutes, thinking it wouldn't hurt since the only way up to the suite was through the elevator just outside the atrium where he now sat. No one was going up without his notice. He figured they could both use the reprieve.

Being with each other twenty-four-seven played havoc on their emotions. Grigore was beginning to feel as if all good intentions were about to fly out the window, especially after having spent the night holding her in his embrace. Sleep had eluded him most of the night, not that he needed it. Being next to her was certainly not conducive to getting rest. Not when all he could think about was what he had turned down hours earlier.

Intended or not, Caitlyn's state of dress today seemed a bit more provocative. Her silky halter tank cut well past her cleavage, leaving his gaze frequently landing on her very nice set of tits. Lord, his tongue itched for a taste. Add that to a pair Daisy Dukes with just the right amount of ass cheeks showing and he was fucking hard from head to toe.

Whatever made him think he could handle this?

Grayson had sent a text fifteen minutes ago saying they were about twenty minutes out and should be arriving soon. Thank God. Having his brothers and their mates underfoot would go a long way in helping to keep his libido in check and his hands to himself.

Ryan had secured separate rooms for them one floor down. Each of the brothers would receive a keycard gaining them access to the fire escape door leading into the penthouse. Should something go wrong, they wouldn't have to take the elevators to the lobby in order to access the one for the penthouse.

He was anxious to see his brothers, not realizing how much he had missed them. Grigore hadn't flown solo in years, and although he liked his quietude most days, he loved the camaraderie he shared with his MC.

Glancing around the lobby, he saw nothing out of the ordinary. A mother sat three tables down breastfeeding her infant, which of course brought back to mind a lovely pair he left upstairs, further agitating him. His brothers wouldn't get here soon enough. Taking a sip of the coffee he had in front of him, he tried his best to blend in. Better to keep an eye on those around him.

Guests came and went, the lobby a constant flurry of activity. Most paid him little mind as he sat in his corner, flanked by a large indoor plant. From his vantage point, he had a clear view of the entrance and the elevator doors. No one was getting by without his notice.

His gaze flitted back to the lobby doors just as they swooshed open, Anton and Bobby walked in, all chaps and leather vests, making some of the more elite patrons gasp. Grigore suppressed his chuckle as he stood and headed toward the entrance to greet them.

Grayson and the mates followed behind, with little Lucian's arms wrapped around his daddy's neck. A smile crossed Grigore's face as he took in the gang. Damn, he was glad to have his brothers onboard. Their presence would go a long way in making him feel more secure about keeping Cait safe.

He reached out and shook hands with Anton, then Bobby, shoulder bumping them in a half hug, before moving onto Grayson. Grigore then tousled the dark-reddish hair on top of Lucian's head. The women chatted about the grand lobby before heading for the reception desk to secure their rooms and get their keycards.

The last to walk in was a friend of Kimber and Tena, Anton and Bobby's mates, a guy he recalled was named Chad, and Lefty, one of the Sons' prospects. No doubt the last two had babysitting duty for Lucian since neither were vampires and were of little use to him.

"Damn. Nice fucking place," Anton commented as his gaze swept the lobby interior, no doubt also looking for anything out of the ordinary.

Anton had gone undercover in a covert operation to bring down a Mexican drug cartel and the Devils MC who had been working with them. His intelligence would no doubt be beneficial here.

Tamara, Grayson's mate, walked up behind Anton, tapping him behind the head. "Language, big guy. Little ears."

Anton's cheeks reddened. "Like he hasn't heard it all before."

"Sure, he has, Rogue, but once he starts repeating you Cro-Magnon men, I'll be doing more than slapping you behind the head."

Grayson chuckled, scratching a spot just beneath his ear. "I'd take heart, Rogue. Tamara's adamant in trying to shield Lucian from the worst of us."

"I don't blame her a bit," Kimber, Anton's mate, spoke up. "Once Rogue and I have a baby, I'll feel much the same way."

"Jesus—," Grigore stopped from saying more, his own face heating from the glare Tamara aimed his way. "Whatever. Let's stop acting like a bunch of women and head upstairs where I'll introduce you to the pop star we'll be protecting."

Tena shuffled in her stance. "I can't wait to meet her. I've been a huge fan of Caitlyn's for a while."

"Calm down, doll face, I'm betting she shits like the rest of us." Bobby ducked and missed Tamara's swat, leaving him chuckling as he tucked Tena beneath his arm. "Let's go meet this woman who has Wolf all tied up in knots."

"Fu—," Grigore stopped himself and rolled his eyes. Good thing he wouldn't be in baby Lucian's presence often or he'd wind up with a knot on his noggin. "Screw you, Preacher. Ain't no woman who has me tied up in knots or otherwise. We were an item back in the day. Past tense."

"Whatever you say, bro." Bobby blew a raspberry. "Lead on."

Moments later, the elevator car arrived on the top floor and the Sons of Sangue members and their mates spilled into the living area. Caitlyn's eyes widened at the lot of them, no doubt seeing them as the motley crew they were. At least the men, anyway. Grigore would never say that about the mates. One thing his MC brothers had was good taste when it came to the ladies.

"Caitlyn." Grigore closed the distance, stopping within touching distance, choosing to keep his big paws to himself. "I'd like you to meet my family from the West."

Introductions made, the women gathered around Cait while she cooed over the baby. She lifted Lucian from Tamara's arms, cuddled him in her embrace and played with him as if it were the most natural thing in the world. Grigore couldn't help imagining her with a baby of her own. Truth of it was, he didn't want to think about the possibility of it because it wouldn't be with him. Another reason once this gig was up he was heading west. Watching Cait move on with another man would damn near unman him.

"So what's the plan, Wolf?" Anton asked. "These venues are large and it won't be easy to keep eyes everywhere. We need to go in on the same page."

"We'll meet with Ryan Baxter, that's Cait's manager, tomorrow during the soundcheck. After that, I'll introduce you to Josh, the crew manager, and we'll get a feel for the venue. We'll solidify a plan once we get a layout of the place."

"Any idea who might want her dead?" Grayson asked.

"Not a clue, Gypsy." Grigore rubbed his nape. He had an inkling the truth might be closer than he originally believed. No way a rifle would've just walked through those gates. He lowered his voice. "We need to keep an eye on everyone, including the present crew."

Bobby's gaze widened. "Anyone in particular?"

"The crew manager, Josh, was MIA when the bullet hit my chest, Preacher. Something about that doesn't sit well with me. I had tried to reach him via our walkie before it all went down. All I got was silence from him on my end."

"You think that's possible? Maybe a motive?"

"None that I know of, Rogue. But most definitely we need to look into him and his background."

"What about this Baxter?"

Grigore shrugged, taking in a deep breath. "Anything's possible, Gypsy. But he was quick on the scene when it all went down. No way he would've been able to take that shot and then been backstage so quickly."

"Anyone else we need to be aware of?" Bobby asked.

"Some dude named Tyler. Should be easy enough to find the deets on him. He's an actor, likely a B-Lister as Caitlyn referenced him only wanting her back because he needed acting jobs. The two have to be plastered all over the net, especially news about their breakup."

The man crawled under Grigore's skin from the moment he saw him. Tyler was slimy that way, not afraid to use someone else for his gain. "He was at one of her VIP meet-and-greets at the last show. Caused a stink then never showed up in his seat that I was aware of."

"I'll see what I can dig up before tomorrow's event."

"Thanks, Rogue." Grigore slapped him on the shoulder, his gaze briefly drifting back to Cait.

"She's a beauty, no doubt about it." Grayson whistled low. "Why the hell aren't you tapping that?"

Grigore creased his brow, anger thinning his lips. Grayson was only putting voice to Grigore's thoughts, so why it angered him to hear it he refused to examine.

"Because it's against club rules, bonehead."

Grayson laughed, not the least bit offended. "Not if you alter her memory of the event. If she doesn't remember you become a freak of nature when you get all hot and heavy, then the club doesn't care. Just ask Rogue. It was awhile before Kimber knew the truth about him."

"You really are an ass, Gypsy." Anton shook his head and laughed. "Coming from the man who wouldn't even fuck the woman he was mated to."

Grayson shared in the amusement. "What can I say? I can be pretty pig-headed at times."

"At least you admit it." Tamara walked over and planted a soft kiss on her mate's lips. "But you wouldn't be you otherwise. I love you, warts and all."

Grayson slapped her ass, then pulled her in to his side. "Damn good thing you didn't give up on me."

There was a knock on the fire escape door. Grigore's muscles went taut. Everyone who had a key for that entrance was already present.

"Relax," Tamara said. "I texted Chad and told him to come to that door, so they could get Lucian without having to go to the lobby first. Lucian's tired from the trip and ready for a nap."

Grigore crossed the tiled floor. A quick peek through the eyehole confirmed Tamara's statement. He opened the door and stepped back. Chad lifted his hand in a high-five, but Grigore only raised a brow.

"Or maybe not." Chad laughed off Grigore's diss, unoffended. He waltzed over to Cait as if they had already been introduced. "You must be the famous Caitlyn. Ooooh … I am thrilled to meet you. My name is Chad, by the way, personal nanny to Lucian."

Cait's smile widened, lighting her face. "Nice to meet you, Chad. And who is your friend here?"

Chad turned and smiled at the prospect, whose cheeks grew rosy as he shifted his stance. Grigore knew Chad batted for the other team. As for the other guy? Another look at the prospect and Grigore couldn't help but wonder if he wasn't more interested in Chad than Cait.

"This is Lefty. He belongs to the Sons."

"As if he's a possession?" Caitlyn's judgmental gaze landed on Grigore. What the fuck? Chad's words, not his. "I'm not sure I understand."

Chad rolled his eyes, waved a hand in the air, and chuckled. "Honey, he's a prospect for the motorcycle club. Until he earns their respect, they might as well own him."

The prospect didn't deny the accusation, and wouldn't, not with four Sons standing in the room to pass judgment. Frank "Lefty" Miller knew his place. He was there to do the Sons of Sangues' bidding, no matter what they needed from him. Cait may not agree with the way his club did things, but it wasn't her place to question their actions either. The Sons

of Sangue wouldn't get up in her business or concern themselves with how she ran her show, and she had no place
challenging theirs.

Cait handed off Lucian to Chad and approached the four
men. Grigore stifled a groan. Just once, he wished she'd
keep her opinions to herself. Grigore was ready to run the
happy reunion off before she embarrassed him in front of his
MC. Cait looked mad as a hornet and this time he hadn't done
a damn thing.

CHAPTER TEN

THE ELEVATOR DOORS CLOSED ON HER GUESTS BEFORE Caitlyn padded across the marble floor to the sofa. Exhausted, she sat heavily in the pillowed corner, tucking one of her bare legs beneath her. She hadn't gotten much sleep wrapped in Grigore's arms the night before. She had felt warm and protected with him, drifting into an easy doze at first. But once his movement behind her had nudged her awake, erotic visions of the man who held her made it difficult to return to dreamland.

Waking up needy hadn't helped the matter either.

Try as she might, Caitlyn couldn't hate Grigore. She had done her best to hang on to her anger of years' past. Spending a considerable amount of time in his company these past few days had begun to chip away at the carefully constructed walls she'd built around her heart. Her opposition was weakening.

Heat settled between her thighs as she looked at him now. She was a woman with needs, and the man she desired above all others was certainly obtainable. Though he had turned her down last night, she bet his own resistance was wearing just as thin as hers. Her gaze followed Grigore as he poured a tumbler full of whiskey and carried it to a seat opposite her, thankfully putting much-needed space between them. Cait didn't think she could trust her self-denial had he sat next to her on the soft Italian leather.

His smile was knowingly confident, as though he understood exactly what she had in mind. "You really need to stop looking at me that way, Sunshine."

One of her brows rose. "In what way?"

"Like I'm on your menu."

Her face heated, surely blotching her pale skin. "I'm not—"

His chuckle stopped the white lie from falling easily from her lips. "Not that I ain't flattered. There is nothing more I'd like to do than oblige."

"Wow. There really is no limit to your ego, Wolf. I spent one night in your bed because of my need for comfort. That doesn't mean I'm ready to jump in the sack with you today."

It was his turn to raise a brow. Grigore didn't look as if he believed her lie for a second. Damn it, she sucked at fibbing. He adjusted the front of his jeans, likely making room for the considerable bulge she now spotted. Cait glanced back up, locking eyes with him, mortified for having been caught looking.

Her face further heated. She didn't think she'd ever been so embarrassed. "Look, we can't…"

He shrugged. "I like the word *could* better. Can't is such a strong word."

"So is hate, as in I still hate you."

Grigore shook his head, his amusement reaching his eyes. "I don't believe that for a minute, Sunshine. You should hate me, no doubt. But after last night, I think you're warming up. It's more of a dislike."

"Nothing happened."

"We might not have fucked, but I could smell your desire. It left me hard most of the night. I'm sure you could feel—"

"Have you no manners? Of course, I could. But there's no reason to bring up the fact I spooned your erection. It's embarrassing."

His humor continued. "For who? Surely, not for me. I fully admit I want to fuck you. You on the other hand—"

"You're right, I don't," she finished for him.

"That's not what I was going to say, Sunshine, and you know it. Even had I not felt your squirming the night away, your scent was a dead giveaway."

"That's twice you referenced a smell to... I don't think smelling someone's sexual desire is possible."

"It is for a vampire. We have a terrific sense of smell. So today, when you looked at me, and even now..."

"You can detect when I desire you?"

He nodded, and she groaned.

"Your vampire friends too?"

The twinkle in his eye said it all. Caitlyn was no longer embarrassed; she was beyond mortified. How could he keep that little tidbit to himself? She hung her head and placed her palms over her face.

"Cait?"

She groaned into her hands, her face nearly on fire from humiliation. How could she look them in the eye again? Had

Cait not needed their help, she'd send them all packing without so much as a goodbye, starting with the maddening man
who was a witness to her shame.

"Sunshine?"

Caitlyn lifted her gaze, glaring at him. "You jerk."

"What did I do?" He held his hands out, palms up. "Clearly,
you want me. What the hell is wrong with that?"

She stood, fists balled at her sides, then marched across
the space dividing them, stopping just shy of touching him.
"You could've warned me."

"And said what exactly? Mind your desire? Stop the infat-
uation? Quit crossing and uncrossing your damn legs?"

"You could have told me everyone in the room was aware
of what I felt for you."

"Only to further add to your humiliation."

"At least then I wouldn't have been thinking about fucking
you."

In his answering silence, they could have heard the sound
of a pin dropping. His whiskers curved upward, drawing her
gaze down to his kissable lips. Cait blinked, took in a deep
breath and swallowed. Hell, she was doing it again and since
he could scent it, he already knew what she had in mind.

"You know I can scratch that itch. All you have to do is
ask."

He caught her hand in mid-strike and yanked her to his
lap. She gasped. Easily palming one of her thighs, he ma-

neuvered her so that she straddled his muscular legs, bring-ing her center against his hardness. There was no doubt what he wanted, what they both did.

"I'm a hairbreadth away from taking what you're asking for, Sunshine. I only have so much control."

Gripping the unbound hair that framed his face, she low-ered her head, sealing her lips over his. He groaned. Caitlyn was tired of fighting the urge that taunted her. She should've sent him packing the moment he walked back into her life, regardless of his commitment to safeguard her. Instead, in the span of a few days, he had broken down every one of her defenses, leaving a powerful craving she could no longer deny.

Stubbornly controlled lips met her wild kiss. In fact, Grigore's every muscle was strung taut now. No way would she allow him to deny her, not this time. Cait shimmied her hips along the rough material of his jeans, earning her an-other groan. Taking the briefly won opportunity, Cait pushed her tongue past his lips and into his mouth. What was hard became pliant now, as Grigore yielded.

His thick forearms wrapped her back, holding her tight as he kissed her in return. Teeth clashed, tongues sparred. Her achy breasts flattened against his muscular chest. Pebbled nipples begged for his touch.

Tonight, she'd be damned if she'd allow Grigore to deny her. No spooning, no wishful thinking.

Cait released his hair, running one of her hands down the soft cotton of his tee to his hip where they were damn near joined. She tilted back, sliding her hand to the front of his jeans and slipped the button free of the hole. Cait skimmed her hand beneath the material to encompass him in her grasp. His erection was primed, thick enough that her small hand couldn't completely encircle him.

Grigore tore his mouth free on a curse, tilting his head to the ceiling. Razor sharp fangs gleamed in the lamp light. Had she not known Grigore, knew the man he was, then the vampire in him would have scared the daylights out of her, sent her running for her room. If she were smart, she'd do so anyway. But there was the part of her heart, the part that never gave up, which had her seeking more.

She slid her hand from root to tip over the silk-like steel, smoothing a drop of pre-come over the crown, watching with fascination as his face turned vampiric. Grigore was positively frightening, looking more lethal than any Hollywood vampire.

Her panties grew wet as she witnessed his change. But instead of alarming her, as it should, she found him sexy as hell. Her libido shot up the chart. This new side of Grigore only added to his allure. She tightened her fist on his cock and he growled.

He brought his gaze back to her, eyes black and shiny as marbles. "You need to stop, Cait, before I lose control."

She wet her lips with her tongue as she released her hold, stood, and wiggled out of her jean shorts and silky underwear. Her gaze dropped to the front of his denim. Cait leaned down, reached for his zipper and slid it slowly over the rest of the impressive bulge. Grigore's knuckles whitened from his tight grip on the arms of the chair.

"Cait…," he warned.

She ignored his word to the wise and freed his erection. But instead of leaning down for a taste as she desired, she had a more urgent need. Straddling his lap again, Cait fisted his cock, positioning him at her center and slid onto him. Grigore hissed as she fully seated herself, tilting her head and exposing her neck to the vampire. Hell, she didn't care if he sank his fangs into her arteries and took his fill. Just the thought had her racing toward an orgasm.

Grigore's fingers splintered the wood beneath his grip. His breath sawed out of him, his Adam's apple bobbed in his throat, and yet he remained deathly still.

It occurred to her that she hadn't bothered with a condom. "I'm on the pill. I'm clean—"

"Christ, it doesn't matter," he said through clenched teeth. "I'm a fucking vampire. Even if you weren't clean, you couldn't infect me."

He growled when she shifted her hips ever so slightly.

"And I can't get you pregnant."

"What about Tamara?"

He grunted, gripping her hips and holding her stationary. "You'd have to be a vampire…"

His words trailed off as Grigore thrust upward, silencing them both. It had been far too long since she last had sex with anyone other than her vibrator, and even then, she had often used the man filling her now as fodder for her fantasies.

Having him here was better, more seductive than she could ever recall. Everything about him was bigger, more danger-ous, and far sexier.

Grigore yanked down the front of her low-cut tank, the thin material easily ripping down the center. He brushed aside the rent fabric and found her braless. Leaning forward, he drew one of her nipples into his mouth, nicking the sensitive flesh with his teeth. The sharp sting was quickly soothed by the pad of his tongue.

When he leaned back, Cait caught sight of the small bead of her blood on his lips before he licked them clean. His look of pure animalism was her undoing. She began to convulse around him, white lights stealing her breath as she rode him hard. His name tumbled from her lips just before she hunched her back and laid her forehead against his shoulder with a final shudder.

Grigore wrapped a forearm tightly around her back, stood and backed her against the nearest wall, thrusting arduously into her. Her back slid up the drywall with each drive until his grunts signified his own orgasm. His ass muscles tightened beneath her heels and he murmured her name.

They stood stationary for what seemed forever but was no doubt more than a couple of minutes as they both gath-ered their breath. Cait brushed the hair from her eyes and looked at Grigore, his features slowly returning to the man she knew.

Grigore pulled out and released his hold, allowing her to slide to her feet. "I'm sorry."

What? He wouldn't dare apologize for giving her the single best orgasm of her life. She slapped him square on the sternum. While she stood nearly naked before him, he still wore most of his clothes, his jeans now circling his ankles. Grigore backed up and pulled them over his hips before looking at her again and boy, was she pissed.

Cait hoped it showed on her face. "Grigore Lupei, don't you dare excuse away what just happened. I don't regret a minute of it. As a matter of fact. I'm expecting a repeat performance, you big oaf."

"You think I was apologizing for that?" He chuckled. "Hell, no. You'll definitely get that repeat performance. I was apologizing for tasting your blood. I should've had more restraint."

"Well, Wolf, I certainly hope you don't find that restraint." A shiver passed her shoulders. "Oh, hell, I don't even know how to describe what that did to me. Next time you think you might want to try biting? I promise not to tell your friends."

Grigore tipped his head and laughed, his mirth shining in his eyes. "Sunshine, you have no idea the pleasure you're in for."

And she didn't, not until after the third orgasm and several small bites later.

"You fucked her." Anger and accusation flared in Anton's gaze. "Don't even try to deny it, Wolf."

Grigore grumbled, unable to deceive his brother. The scent of what had transpired in the suite the night before, including the blood play, was impossible to conceal from one of his own. Caitlyn was fortunately still in bed, his bed, sleeping. Grigore didn't want her to witness the heated discussion he knew was coming.

When sleep had eluded him earlier, he had gone downstairs to the hotel's computer room to download and print the concert venue's layout. He hadn't been back in the room more than fifteen minutes before Anton had come through the fire escape door. Suddenly, Grigore was regretting giving any of his MC brothers the damn keycards.

"You want coffee, asshole? I could certainly use a cup before you chew my ass out."

"Might as well call for room service and order a few carafes." Anton's taut jaw spoke of his disapproval. "It won't be long before the rest of the crew head up."

Grigore grabbed the house phone and asked for several pots to be brought to the suite.

Anton paced the large room, stopping in front of the wrecked chair. Splinters of wood from the shattered arms lay scattered about the tile.

"You'll no doubt have to pay for that," he said dryly. "I suppose it means you showed a little restraint with Caitlyn. How the hell did she take seeing the vampire come out?"

Grigore said nothing, prompting Anton to comment further, "I fucking hope you hypnotized her from remembering that part."

He hung his head, not able to form a good lie.

Anton shook his head and sighed. "What the fuck am I supposed to tell Viper and Hawk?"

Grigore's lips thinned, his own anger itching up his spine. "You won't tell them a damn thing, Rogue. You let me decide what the fuck to do with the mess I created."

"It sure in the hell is a fucking mess."

"And it's my mess to contend with. This isn't any of your damn business, Rogue."

"The hell it isn't. You broke club rules, Wolf. You drank from her. And don't fucking deny it. I can scent her blood all over this damn suite."

The fire escape opened, Bobby and Grayson joining the party. Just fucking great. It wasn't as if he didn't expect his brothers to find out, he just wasn't ready to be called on the carpet. Grigore wasn't the first to break rules, and he doubted he'd be the last. Hell, even Kane broke their own fucking rules when he met his mate, Cara. Unfortunately, he paid the ultimate price by giving up his seat as club pres at that time.

So be it. When the time came, he too would pay his penance. Right now, though? They needed to focus on Caitlyn. Because if they fell short of their mission, this whole conversation would be a moot point anyway. Failure wasn't an option.

Grayson turned his nose upward, then chuckled. "Smells like someone's been doing the naughty."

"Don't start, Gypsy. I already got a verbal lashing from Rogue. I don't need it from you two wise-asses as well."

Bobby held up his hands. "Whoa, dude. I'm not one to pass judgment. What you do behind closed doors isn't any business of mine. And it's not like Tena and I didn't break a rule when we got together."

Anton crossed his arms over his chest and leveled his glare at the lot of them. "Club rules, boneheads. If he breaks them, then it becomes club business."

Bobby shrugged. "I'm just saying, P and VP aren't here. When we get back, it will be soon enough to sort out what went on."

"We can always use hypnosis when we leave," Grayson suggested. "She won't remember if we erase all of the horizontal memories."

Or vertical, Grigore thought, recalling fucking her up against the wall. Anton had hypnotized Kimber into not seeing the vampire side of him when they had made love. After the fact? Grigore wasn't sure they could erase only that aspect, or if it would have to be a complete memory scrub of the act itself. Taking those memories from Caitlyn wasn't going to happen. Christ, if he had to leave her behind again he wanted her to recall. Every. Damn. Waking. Moment. Just as he would.

"How about you guys let me worry about the end result? For now, we need to focus on tonight's show, make sure we don't have a repeat performance from the last one. I'd love to stay alive long enough to see this through."

"And Caitlyn as well," Anton said. "We have your back, Wolf."

"Rogue is right," Bobby said. "We aren't about to let anything happen. This fucker must go through us. You have numbers, Wolf. Something you didn't have then."

"Thanks, Preacher. I appreciate all of you being here." The elevator dinged, announcing the arrival of the car. "That would be our coffee."

A man dressed in a white uniform rolled a stainless-steel cart into the room. Four steel-gray carafes sat in the middle, surrounded by white stoneware mugs emblazoned with the hotel's logo in black.

"Do I smell coffee?" Tena asked, as she entered through the fire escape. "You're reading my mind, Wolfy."

Grigore grumbled at the nickname, not a fan of the added character. Tamara and Kimber followed her through the door, the three heading for the cart. Grigore reached into his pocket, withdrew a twenty for a tip and handed it to the man, thanking him. Once everyone was served they all gathered around the conference table situated behind the sofa, where Grigore had spread the papers with the venue's blueprint.

He pointed to a spot behind the stage. "I'll be here. It's the closest spot I can be without actually being on stage with Caitlyn."

The door to his bedroom opened and Cait walked through, tightening the white sash of the oversized terrycloth robe around her waist. "You didn't tell me we were having company."

Cait ran a hand through her bed hair, attempting to smooth down the silky tangles. Grigore had been the cause.

She glanced at him, offering him a timid smile before taking in her guests.

"If you'll excuse me, I'll need a shower before I'm fit to entertain."

"Girlfriend, you take all the time you need," Tena said, a knowing smile on her face. As soon as Caitlyn crossed the space and closed the door behind her, she looked back at Grigore. "Are you going to make her a mate? Because, Wolf, not cool! She's famous. I sure in the hell hope you made certain she didn't know about your freaky side."

Grigore mentally slapped himself right upside the damn head. In hindsight, he should've used a conference room downstairs to meet with his brothers. But truthfully, fucking Caitlyn wasn't something he thought would happen, nor was sipping from her arteries. His willpower had taken its leave. Anton and the rest had a right to be angry. His careless actions could cost them all exposure.

A quick glance at the clock on the wall told him they had plenty of time to put a solid plan into place before they had to head for the venue for a soundcheck. Once they got the big picture in hand, he'd present it to Ryan and Josh, right after he had a few words with Josh for his disappearing act.

Not fucking cool.

CHAPTER ELEVEN

DEA SPECIAL AGENT JANELLE FERRARI FLIPPED OPEN HER badge, showing her credentials to the police officer manning the door. What she found when she entered the premises sickened her. Blood splattered the walls and floor, looking like a bad movie set. Four men lay haphazardly scattered about the room. She didn't have to feel for their pulses to know they were dead. The evidence technicians worked diligently triangulating the room, taking pictures, and gathering evidence.

The detective who appeared to be in charge stood next to the window, speaking on his phone. One hand was jammed into his dress slacks. His gaze traveled the room until it stopped on her. He quickly ended his phone call and approached.

"Special Agent Ferrari."

"Detective Barker."

"To what do I owe the pleasure?"

Janelle hid her disdain. She had run into this detective before. She hadn't liked him then, and the feeling hadn't changed much since the last time she saw him. Something about the man rubbed her the wrong way. Could be his arrogance; he was the kind of guy who wouldn't tolerate a woman having jurisdiction over what he deemed to be his case.

Unfortunately for him, when one of the murder victims was a well-known drug lord, it became the DEA's business. Janelle had had eyes on the deceased son of a bitch for the past year. She had been building a good case against him, aware of his ties to the La Paz cartel. The kingpin, Raúl Trevino Caballero, had turned up dead about a month ago. Now one of his lieutenants?

That made it her business.

Janelle had a stinking suspicion someone might be going after cartel members, executing them one-by-one. She had heard Mateo Rodriguez had taken over as kingpin. Certainly, he wouldn't be guilty of taking out his own men … unless they had refused to follow him as the new self-appointed leader.

"Joseph Flores. This is his flat, no?"

"I believe that's a *was*." The detective's gaze fell to one of the dead men lying face down in a pool of blood. "His apartment will be back on the market once we finish and the cleaning crews clear out the stench."

"Cold even for you, Barker." Janelle bit her tongue from calling him more colorful names. "I've been looking into Mr. Flores's criminal activity over the past year."

"Then I'd say your case is now closed, Special Agent Ferrari. I can handle the mess from here."

This time she didn't hide her dislike. She sneered. "Sorry, Barker. I'm not going anywhere until I get answers. I'm interested in who came in here and cleaned house, just as much as you are. So unfortunately, looks like we'll be working together on this case until we close it."

He cursed her under his breath. Apparently, he wasn't a fan of her either. Good.

"Who were you just on the phone with?"

"The coroner, not that my phone calls are your business. He's on his way over."

"Have you ID'd the other three?"

"No, but I'm sure they're friends of Mr. Flores, no doubt."

Janelle nodded. "We can agree on that. Once you ID them, I'd appreciate you forwarding me that information."

"You got it. I'll make sure you have access to everything we gather here today as well. Now if you'll allow me to do my job—"

"Of course. I wouldn't want to stand in the way of police work."

"Detective work," he corrected as she turned away, leaving him standing there staring after her retreating back.

Retrieving a pair of rubber gloves from her jacket pocket, she snapped them into place. Kneeling next to Joseph Flores, she was careful not to disturb any of the blood congealing near his head. Something didn't sit right with her. Placing two fingers against his neck, she met cool dead skin and no pulse. No surprise. She turned his head slightly to see how deep the neck wound went, and if the unknown subject, UNSUB, had used a gun or a knife. She was betting a knife, being the more personal of the two. Joseph had no doubt made enemies in the drug world.

What she found shocked her, leaving her gasping.

Detective Barker moved quickly to her side, keeping his hands to himself. "What did you find?"

A large, ragged chunk of flesh, savage enough to tear the carotid, was missing from his neck. But it wasn't a knife that had done the job. No, it appeared someone had fucking ripped a huge chunk from Flores's neck using their damn teeth.

"Jesus!" Barker exclaimed. "What the fuck?"

"That's exactly what I was wondering."

"JUST GREAT," CAITLYN MUMBLED as she entered her room, effectively closing out the Sons of Sangue members and their significant others now using her penthouse for strategizing.

She'd need to have a conversation with Grigore later. Nothing like doing the walk of shame in her own damn hotel room. Miffed? Absolutely. Grigore could have warned her. So much for keeping their physical relationship under wraps. By the look on some of their faces as she passed by, Cait was certain they knew exactly what Grigore and she had been up to the night before.

Good enough for his sorry ass.

Let him do the explaining.

If they were supposed to keep it a secret, Grigore was doing a bang-up job. Opening her closet door, she withdrew a forest green peasant-style top and a pair of dark blue skinny jeans, tossing them to the bed. Cait grabbed a clean pair of black lace panties and a matching bra, then headed for the tiled shower. She adjusted the water temperature, preferring it on the hot side. Steam filled the room. Stepping beneath the rain showerhead, Cait raised her face to the water. The warm spray worked its magic, washing away her anxiety and easing the soreness from her muscles.

Memories of Grigore's mouth and capable hands from the night before had her body heating for an entirely different reason than the water now sluicing down her curves. She'd need to get a handle on her self-control if she didn't want the entire room of vampires privy to the rise in her libido every time Grigore entered the room.

Lord, what a conundrum.

Cait wanted to stay mad at the big oaf for his mishandling of the entire situation. But after the night spent in his bed, she was finding even that difficult. She traced her fingers over the smoothness of her neck, unblemished flesh greeting her touch. How in the world had he managed to heal the wounds where his fangs had fed, make them disappear altogether? Another vampire mystery.

What other skills might they possess?

Obviously, being sexually pleasing was top on that list. Grigore had certainly spoken correctly about the pleasure to be had from a vampire feeding from her artery. Cait couldn't remember ever having an orgasm so intense. No wonder these donors Grigore spoke of readily offered up their veins—probably their bodies too. Sleeping with a vampire definitely had its perks.

Turning the faucet handles and shutting off the water, Cait stepped onto the white Egyptian-cotton bath mat. She grabbed a large towel and began drying off when she heard the door to her outer room open.

Had she forgotten to lock it?

In her haste, she must have. Cait quickly wrapped the towel about her center and was just tucking it between her breasts when Grigore stepped into the room, consuming the space and the oxygen.

She sucked in a breath. "What are you doing in here?"

Grigore's gaze slowly traversed her body, his eyes damn near blackening in appreciation and hinting at his vampire humming just beneath the surface. Her flesh warmed as if his hand had done the perusal. He reached out to grip her waist, but she batted his hand away.

"Don't even think about it, Wolf."

He chuckled. "You didn't seem to mind my touch last night."

"Last night you hadn't paraded me in front of your friends. You don't think they know what we did? I was a total mess coming out of your room. Talk about bed-head."

His eyes twinkled with merriment. "Of course, they know, Sunshine. Not much gets past a vampire."

"And the fact you drank some of my … my blood?"

He nodded.

"You said it was against their rules."

Grigore shrugged. "It is. They know. And I'll be dealt with … later. For now, all we need to worry about is keeping you safe. That's why my friends are here. Not to pass judgment."

She rubbed her forehead, tension building. "How can I face them?"

"Easily. You get dressed and meet us out there, so we can discuss tonight's plan."

"Have you brought in the authorities?"

"No need." He framed her face with his palms and tenderly kissed the spot she had massaged. "There is nothing more formidable than a pack of vampires watching your back."

Caitlyn wasn't so sure. Last time, Grigore took a bullet to the chest. "You already proved to have a vulnerability. What about bulletproof vests?"

"You worry too much. We got this." He patted her terry-cloth-covered rear as his gaze landed on the black lace lying atop the vanity. "Definitely looking forward to taking these off of you later tonight. Now, get dressed."

Grigore turned and left the bathroom, leaving her staring in his wake, open-mouthed. Now that she allowed herself another taste and the sex had been off-the-charts, she was pretty sure there wouldn't be any turning back for her. The man was too sizzling-hot for her own good. He would be her downfall.

Losing him again was going to annihilate her.

Caitlyn finished drying off, then stepped into her lace panties and matching bra. Applying a bit of blush and mascara, she kept the cosmetics minimal. Later, her makeup artist would complete the look for her performance. Quickly finishing dressing, she exited her room and joined the Sons of Sangue crew in the main seating area. Grigore looked her way and winked, before bending his head over the papers they had laid out on the conference table. Leaving them to their discussion, Caitlyn sat on one of the leather sofas, her gaze falling on the ruined chair. Heat rose up the back of her neck and warmed her cheeks.

Yep, she was more than a tad bit embarrassed.

One of the women, whom Cait remembered as Tena, rounded the sofa and sat beside her, crossing her legs and smiled. "I'm really sorry for our intrusion."

Cait's cheeks further heated. At least her humiliation was keeping her libido in check. It would only add to the awkwardness should anyone scent her reaction to Grigore when he was in close proximity.

"It's fine … really, but thank you." Cait smiled at the young woman, who seemed to be several years younger than her. "I know you're all here to offer me protection. Grigore seems to think there is no one better."

Tena laughed. Cait found she liked the sound and the young woman. "There really isn't. We'll find who is threatening you. He'll be dealt with."

Exactly how did vampires deal with their enemies? Caitlyn didn't want to be responsible for anyone's murder. Even if that someone had threatened her life.

"Relax." Tena patted her knee. "We won't eat him."

"What will you do with him?"

"It depends on what's he's doing when we find him. If it comes down to your life or his, we'll choose yours. No mistake about it."

"And if it's not a life or death situation?"

Grigore's hands settled on her shoulders from behind. "He'll be handed over to the police, Sunshine. You won't have to worry about this blood-thirsty pack of vampires draining their prey. We only take the sustenance we need to survive, unless duty calls for it."

"We only take out those we deem a necessity." Bobby leaped over the couch and settled behind Tena, wrapping his arms about her middle. Tena leaned back against the man's barrel chest. "Bottom line, we protect our own by any means."

Caitlyn wasn't sure if she should be thanking them or be aghast. She presumed the former, but when it came to a room full of menacing men and women who could change at the drop of a hat, she couldn't help but be a bit alarmed as well, even if they were there to protect her.

Grayson sat in the broken chair, folding his arms across his chest since the armrests were nonexistent. His long hair was left unbound, damn near rivaling the length of hers. He was one of the more handsome of the bunch, aside from Anton. That man was model pretty. Grayson's girlfriend, Tamera, was stunning, her fiery red hair cascading over her shoulders. She stood to the left of the seating area, conversing with Anton and Kimber.

One look at the lot of them and she no longer worried about their abilities to protect her. "I should thank you all for coming here."

"When one of our brothers needs help, we're here," Anton said.

"I wish you would take payment—"

"You listen to Wolf," Anton continued, "Do as he says when it comes to your protection and stay alive. Keeping my brother happy is the only payment I require."

Caitlyn couldn't help but ask. "And when this is over? If Wolf is no longer happy?"

"If you're alive, then our job is done. What you and Wolf decide to do is your own business." Grayson's icy blue gaze pinned her. "What you're left remembering is ours."

Caitlyn didn't doubt Grayson's word. She recalled the fact they could hypnotize people into not remembering all the facts. If she was no longer with Grigore, they'd make sure she forgot every intimate detail between them, and the fact she currently sat in a room full of vampires.

It would certainly make his leaving more tolerable. But forgetting what was transpiring between them wasn't an option for her. She wanted to recall every detail, even if it brought her to her knees when he walked out. And he would. He had made that part abundantly clear.

CHAPTER TWELVE

"WHAT THE FUCK, MAN?" JOSH ASKED, HIS VOICE GOing an octave higher. "Seriously? We don't need your fucking motorcycle club's help. We got this. It's what we get paid to do. You can pack up your silly motorcycle vests and go home. You're not wanted here."

The man squealed when Grigore wrapped his fist around his throat and slammed him against the far wall, his cranium bouncing off the cement. The little fuck was lucky he didn't break his skull for the last stunt he pulled, or for the irreverence shown his MC.

No one disrespected the Sons of Sangue.

"Then where the fuck were you when I got shot?"

Josh gritted his teeth, his hands attempting to alleviate some of the pressure from Grigore's fist. "I told you at the last show, man, my walkie went dead."

Grigore released the jerk, who stumbled, nearly losing his footing. "So you said. And I don't believe it any more now."

"I don't give a damn what you believe, *Wolf*," he hissed. "I'm not here to save your sorry ass. I work for Caitlyn. That's more than you do. Last I heard, you weren't getting paid to be here."

"By *my* choice. That makes me better than you. I don't need her money. I'm here to make sure she stays alive, something you're doing a lousy job of."

"What's your story, anyway? It's not like she'd fuck someone as ugly as you. Why stick around?"

"He's here because I asked him to be. I suggest you stop harassing those big enough to kick your ass and get back to work," Ryan said as he joined the little soiree. "You should be thanking Wolf. If it wasn't for him, you'd be in the unemployment line because your boss would have been six feet under."

"I can get a job anytime in this business. I've already proven myself."

Ryan's brow inched up. "You want to start tomorrow?"

Josh's face turned red. Tony, a man Grigore remembered as one of the quieter from the crew, grabbed his co-worker's arm. "Don't make waves, Josh. It won't end well, dude."

Josh shook off Tony's grip, turned and stomped down the corridor. Tony began to follow when Ryan called out to him.

"What's his problem?"

Tony shrugged. "He doesn't like taking orders from the new guy, feels his authority is being challenged."

"His walkie," Grigore said "Was it not working when I called for him the night I got shot?"

The crewman's face reddened.

"The truth," Grigore growled. "I can smell a fucking lie."

"He left it on the charger. Said he didn't need to take orders from you."

Grigore nodded slowly, his anger on a slow simmer. "And you?"

He raised his hands. "I'm here to do my job. Josh isn't a bad guy, not really. Until you arrived, he seemed perfectly happy with his job. I'm not sure what his deal is."

"Go finish setting up," Ryan said. "I'll deal with Josh later. He best get his act together or I'll make sure he's looking for that other job he's so positive he can get."

Tony turned and jogged down the hall. Grigore placed his fists on his hips and wondered what to do with the crew manager. Not like the son of a bitch was going to start following his say-so any time soon. The last thing he needed was to contend with a spoiled little roadie who wanted to sleep with his boss.

He turned back to Ryan. "Josh have a thing for Caitlyn?"

"What makes you ask?"

"He said I was too ugly to fuck. The only reason I can think he'd even care is out of some fucked up form of jealousy."

"It's possible, though I can't say I've ever seen him treating Caitlyn as anything other than his boss."

"Keep an eye on him, Baxter. Something about him makes my skin crawl. He touches Caitlyn and I'll deal with him, you can be certain of that."

"I have no doubt. You want me to let him go?"

Grigore shook his head. "Just make sure he does his damn job and stays the hell away from Caitlyn."

"You got it. We good for the night? Doors open in an hour."

"Where's Cait?"

Using his thumb, Ryan pointed over his shoulder. "Her dressing room. I believe her makeup artist is in with her."

"You need me, I'll be outside her door."

Ryan nodded and traveled down the corridor toward the stage where the crew was finishing up last minute details. The soundcheck had gone well. Another half hour and her VIP meet-and-greet would happen. Grigore wondered if her super-fan Tyler would make another appearance.

"What's up, bro?" Anton asked. Grigore scented his arrival before he stopped a few feet behind him. "I have everyone in place. Any new details I should know?"

Grigore greeted him. "The plan stays. Keep Josh in your crosshairs. I still don't trust the son of a bitch. He's refusing to follow my direction and I doubt he'll use his walkie again tonight. Fucker thinks he's got more authority than I do."

"That's why you took a bullet." Anton's gaze darkened. "I've volunteered to stay with the crew leader. Everyone else is watching the exits. It's a big venue and we can't possibly cover every inch of it. We have most of the crew being our eyes as well. I've assigned each of us a team to manage. You stick by Caitlyn. We'll keep an eye out from afar."

"You should be able to scent gunpowder if you get close enough to a loaded gun. Let's hope that helps us."

"There are metal detectors at every entrance."

"We had that last time and yet someone still got a rifle into the venue."

Anton took a deep breath, then let it out slowly. "Let's hope that doesn't happen again. Otherwise, I'm thinking we have an insider taking matters into their own hands. Anyone who might be upset enough with their boss they'd want to take her out?"

"There's the celebrity named Tyler I told you about, who gave Caitlyn a bit of trouble during her meet-and-greet, same night I got shot. He disappeared after confronting her, didn't watch the show. He might have enough clout to get one of the venue employees to let him come into the arena ahead of time."

Grigore slid the screen open on his phone, brought up the photo of Tyler from the Internet and showed it to Anton. "If he shows up, he'll no doubt use the meet-and-greet to get close to her again. If he turns up, I'll alert you."

"I recognize him from some of his movies, though lately, I have to say his roles have been sucking. Must be on a downward spiral."

"Caitlyn accused him of wanting to use her to get back in the eye of the media."

Anton held up the walkie Grigore had given them all. "Keep in touch, bro. You see anything, we're here for you."

Grigore patted his shoulder. "Thanks, man. I can't thank you enough. Taking that bullet opened my eyes. Had I not been there, Cait would be dead. I can't let my ego think I could do this on my own, take the chance again with her life. I feel more at ease having you here."

"Glad you called."

Anton took the stairs to the left, leaving Grigore to head in the opposite direction. Arriving outside Caitlyn's dressing room, he knocked, tested the knob, and opened the door. Her hazel eyes greeted him. He doubted he'd ever get used to the jolt his heart felt when she blessed him with her warm smile.

"Why wasn't the door locked?"

"Ryan just left. Said he saw you down the hall."

"Next time lock it. I don't want you anywhere unsecured in these venues. Someone could have slipped by me. And don't tell me I'm being paranoid. I already took a bullet."

"How could I forget? It's not Ryan's fault. When he said you were down the hall, I told him to leave it unlocked for you."

The makeup artist finished with her last minute details. Caitlyn thanked him and left him to pack up his brushes and makeup. The man had his long black hair wound up in a messy-style bun.

Before leaving, he tipped her chin up and studied his handiwork. "Sei bellissima. Beautiful."

"Thank you, Roberto. I'll see you tomorrow."

He bowed his head, but not before Grigore caught a glimpse of Roberto's distaste as he glanced his way. The man shut the door quietly upon his leave.

Caitlyn stepped around the dressing screen to get changed, bringing his focus back to her. "All set?"

"I should be asking you the same thing."

She came back into view, a black, beaded ensemble hugging her every curve. Holding the top to her breast, she asked, "Zip me?"

"I'd much rather take it off. Damn, you look hot." Grigore whistled. "Too bad you have to go on stage or I'd bend you over right here."

Her cheeks reddened. "You're bad."

"Sunshine, you haven't seen anything yet."

"I'll admit last night was pretty fantastic." Cait pinned him with a glare. "But next time you invite your friends up, make sure I'm not leaving your room looking like I was well-used."

Grigore chuckled. "Sunshine, you were. And I appreciate every damn moment of it."

"How about we keep it between us from here on out. Doing the walk of shame in front of your friends was a bit of an embarrassment."

He reached out and caught one of her roller-made curls, letting it slide between his fingers. "Too bad we only have about five minutes before you meet your super fans or I'd show you how to get lucky without messing your hair or makeup."

This time Caitlyn laughed. "I have no doubt you could."

"Don't tempt me. On a serious note, do I need to worry about Tyler showing up tonight?"

"I wouldn't think so. After Cleveland, I bet we've seen the last of him."

"What about Josh?"

Her brow furrowed. "The crew manager?"

"I'm thinking he's got a wee-bit of a crush on you."

"What makes you say that?"

Grigore shrugged and stepped away from her, shoving his hands into his jean pockets to keep from touching her. "Apparently, he thinks I'm too ugly for you to fuck."

"He said that?"

Grigore nodded and smirked.

Her eyes twinkled as she attempted to contain her merriment. "Seriously?"

"Yep."

"Then Josh doesn't know me very well."

"You're known for parading around pretty boys. Tyler—"

"Ugh! Enough about him." Cait walked over to the chair where her black shoes with silver studded five-inch heels were, and slipped them on. He'd make sure she left those on for later. "Trust me, he's more into himself than me."

"From where I stand, any man would be blind not to be into you."

"If we weren't pressed for time, I'd show you the only man I'm currently into."

A knock sounded before Grigore could respond. What he wanted to do was pull her into his embrace and make her forget about tonight's damn show.

Ryan opened the door. "They're ready for you in the VIP room."

"Thank you, Ryan. I'll be there in a sec." The door closed and she looked back at Grigore. "Ready?"

"After you, boss."

She turned and batted a hand at him. Grigore jumped back, leaving her swatting at air. "You said yourself I don't pay you. That means I can't be your boss."

"Good thing."

"Why's that?"

"Because you probably have rules about fucking the employees."

Caitlyn opened the door and laughed all the way down the hall, leaving him smiling in her wake.

THE MEET-AND-GREET HAD been uneventful. No one seemed other than what they were, huge fans of the gorgeous lady now out there singing her ass off. With only about half a set left before the encore, Grigore was happy everything had gone according to plan. No monkey wrenches thrown into the mix and no psychos aiming a rifle at Caitlyn's head. The show was almost in the bag and then the crew would start prepping for tomorrow night's concert.

Soon, Grigore would have Caitlyn back at the hotel and he'd finally be able to breathe easier. His senses had been on high alert all evening, but nothing had seemed out of the ordinary. Caitlyn was giving her fans a stellar performance, looking sexy as fuck out there in her little black, beaded dress. He'd take great pleasure taking her out of it later.

Tyler hadn't shown up, which was just as well. Seeing the pompous ass again would be too soon for him. Maybe, the B actor had given up on hoping for a second chance and they'd seen the last of him.

Josh had been his usual non-communicating self, but doing his job nonetheless. Anton kept a close eye on him and his crew, reporting that he'd seen nothing unusual. The rest of the Sons hadn't alerted Grigore to anything out of sorts either.

The evening as a whole had been pretty uneventful. Just the way Grigore wanted it. Keeping his perch side-stage didn't afford him the opportunity to see much of anything beyond the backstage, leaving him to rely heavily on his brothers and their mates. Why he hadn't factored that in and taken their offer to help earlier, he didn't know. Had he not seen the red dot on Cait's forehead, he would've been left burying her. He would never have forgiven himself if he'd failed her.

Caitlyn's song about finding love again caught his attention. She had the voice of an angel, one to rival some of the best in the biz, including the late Whitney. The song hit close to the bone for him, and he couldn't help wishing for more time with Cait. They had been dealt a bad hand from the get-go. Too bad finding their way back to the love they once shared wouldn't be in their future. He had always known she had star quality. Who was he to stand in the way of that? Although Cait had argued in favor of him staying, Grigore still stood by his reasons for leaving.

Now, even though it was obvious their feelings hadn't diminished over the past years, the fact remained he was a vampire. Being with her could not only destroy her life and career should humans discover his secret, but also put his

MC brothers and fellow vampires in jeopardy of being exposed. If they were found out, it was liable to ignite a war
between humans and his kind, and he'd be the one to blame.
He couldn't ask her to give up her career.

It would have been selfish to keep all of that talent to himself.

A talent like hers needed to be shared.

One more hour and he could get her back to the hotel …
beneath him. Hell, Grigore could think of little else as he
watched her sway in her tight dress. Her legs seemed to go
for miles under the short hem. He couldn't wait to wrap them
around his waist while those black and silver five-inch heels
dug into the cheeks of his ass.

Grigore could hardly focus on the job at hand, not after
the night they had spent. But feeding from her? That had
been a huge fuck up on his part, one that he couldn't allow to
happen again. Not that he hadn't enjoyed it. Hell, no. He
thirsted for another taste of the sweet honey flowing through
her veins the way an alcoholic craved wine, but it wasn't going to happen. Hell, he had broken enough rules since his
arrival. He needed to get his head in the game and out of the
front of his jeans. He had been doing too much thinking with
the wrong head as of late. He deserved whatever retribution
the Sons doled out, and then some.

Besides, the more he fed from her, the harder it would be
to leave her behind when this gig was up. He'd still need to
feed, but to find a mate? There would be no one else for him.

The problem was what to do with her memories when it was time to head back to Oregon. Anton and his brothers wouldn't allow him to walk away, leaving her recollection intact. Christ, if he were honest with himself, he would feel much the same way should another member be in the same predicament. Rules were put in place for a reason, to protect vampires from discovery. Grigore had fucked up and his brothers knew it. It pained him to know that his best option would be to take away her knowledge of vampirism as well as the time they spent making love.

He couldn't argue that it would make the transition easier for her when he left. She wouldn't recall anything other than his protection. There would be no reason to mourn his loss.

Too damn bad they couldn't wipe his memories as well.

While the Sons all had their mates, he'd be left living life alone, taking an occasional donor to his bed. And it would have to be enough. Because there was no way he could ever take on a life partner other than the one woman he loved … would ever love.

Cait hit a high note and finished her latest hit before looking to side-stage and gifting him with a smile. Damn if it didn't warm his cold heart. He was going to miss the hell out of her. Even more of a reason to take what she offered before he was forced to hypnotize her.

But blood play? Was off the fucking table, even if it killed him to abstain. Normally when he fed, even if it was in the middle of having sex with a donor, his heart never entered into it. It was just sex and feeding, nothing more. With Caitlyn, it left him raw, vulnerable even, because he couldn't keep his big dumb heart out of it.

For the first time, he knew what his brothers felt with their mates. They didn't get sustenance from their mates' vampire blood, but the act of drawing blood during the sex took it to a whole different level. And if they fed off each other at the same time, it was possible to bring another little blood-sucking vamp, a true blood, into their world. Although he could see Cait carrying his baby, desired it even, it could never happen as long as she remained in the spotlight.

The one thing he had pushed her to achieve.

Funny how years ago he thought it had been the right move. Without him having left her, she wouldn't have worked so hard to realize her dreams. Now it was the very thing that damned him and kept him from taking her as his mate.

"Everything okay?" Grayson asked as he stopped beside him.

"Yeah." Grigore hoped his brother didn't note the hoarseness of his reply. "Why wouldn't it be?"

"I worry about you, Wolf."

"Well, don't. I'll be fine."

Pity filled Grayson's gaze. Damn, he hated anyone looking upon him in sympathy. He was a big boy and he paid the consequences for his decisions. End of story. Grigore supposed, though, there were times he looked upon Grayson in the same manner when he was going through his own personal hell with Tamera.

"Until we walk away and you leave her behind," he said. "You know we can't allow her to remember, right?"

Grigore hung his head and jammed his hands into his pockets, hoping Grayson didn't see the moisture gathering in his eyes. "I know, bro. Let's just get through this. One day at a time. And then … I'll let you take away her memories. I thought I could do it, desired to be the one even. But man, I'm not sure I can go through with it."

"It's for all our good. You have to know we wouldn't do so if there was any other way."

"Yeah. Doesn't make it suck any less, though."

Grayson patted his shoulder. "I'll be there for you, Wolf. Anytime you want to talk, you come out to the coast and hang with me. I'll even teach you to surf."

"I'd like that, Gypsy."

"You hang in there. We'll get you through this. You aren't alone."

"Thanks, bro. I know you guys have my back."

Grayson fist bumped Grigore, then strode down the long hall. When he turned the corner, Grigore's gaze went back to Caitlyn. Yeah, losing her was going to destroy him.

CHAPTER THIRTEEN

V LAD paced the lobby of the Lane County Sheriff's Office, waiting for an impromptu meeting with the sheriff. He had arrived fifteen minutes prior and was asked to take a seat. Feeling much like a bug caught in a pickle jar, he could hardly stand immobile, let alone sit. He wasn't used to taking orders, but rather being the one who issued them.

After hearing about the slaughter of the four young drug runners in Eugene, Oregon, he couldn't help but wonder if it wasn't the handiwork of Mircea and his newly mated Nina. His brother was no doubt hoping to draw out Vlad, which of course worked like a charm.

Someone had to do damage control.

The bloodshed of the La Paz cartel soldiers had been splashed all over the news. The commentator mentioned the mortal bite wounds and blood loss as being the likely cause of death. The news clips showed a DEA Special Agent being interviewed, although she seemed quite closed-lipped about the details of the case.

Fucking Mircea.

It had to be him. He doubted there was another psychopath running around tearing holes out of the necks of his victims. When he caught the son of a bitch, and he would, Vlad would show him no mercy this time. He and Nina would be swiftly dealt with, giving the pair no time for explanations. He didn't care about their reasoning for his latest stunt. Mircea had been reckless, bringing unwanted attention to the possibilities of vampirism.

Too bad Vlad no longer impaled those foolish enough to cross him, or Mircea's head would be gracing his property back home alongside his disloyal servant. Nina had no doubt been wooed with the promise of immortality, unaware his brother's vow would bring her nothing but an early grave.

The dispatcher opened the window and stopped him in his pacing. "Mr. Tepes? Sheriff Ducat will see you now."

About fucking time. Lord, he was annoyed. No one kept Vlad Tepes waiting. "Thank you."

Vlad approached the heavy steel and glass door. The sounding buzz indicated it could now be easily pulled open. Not that the lock could have stopped him from opening it before, but he wasn't about to make a scene by yanking it from the steel framing. Grabbing the handle, he opened it and passed through, where he was then escorted to the sheriff's office.

A rotund man with a balding pate sat behind a large oak desk. As he entered the room, Sheriff Ducat stood and shook Vlad's hand. "What can I do for you, Mr. Tepes?"

"You're aware that I am the grandfather of one of your detectives. Cara Brahnam?"

"Yes. She's one of our finest."

"Then you're also aware of the need my family and I have for discretion."

Kane had already told Vlad about the club's relationship with the sheriff. The man had kept their secret and had their backs over the years. The alliance worked and the man could be trusted.

He stood from behind his desk, walked to the door and closed it.

"I'm aware of the Sons of Sangue." He leaned on the corner of his desk, crossing his arms over his barrel of a chest. Age and laziness had added the extended belly beneath. "What can I do for you, Mr. Tepes?"

"Please, call me Vlad."

"Then what can my office assist you with, Vlad? I'd be happy to help in any way I can."

"The young Special Agent on the news."

"From the DEA? What about Special Agent Ferrari?"

"The case she is studying, the men who were killed. This brings me great concern."

"Because of the bite marks? I would hope that's not the work of the Sons."

"No. And I need you to make that part of the investigation go away."

The sheriff chuckled, stood and walked back around the desk to retake his seat. He folded his hands in front of him on the desktop. "I assure you that's not possible. Once the DEA gets involved, it's really out of my hands. Not to mention it isn't our case. This belongs to the Eugene Police Department, not the Lane County Sheriff's Office."

"Should I have gone to Cara? I thought by contacting you, you would have more clout with this woman."

"I do. But what do you expect me to say? Again, it's not my jurisdiction."

Vlad shrugged. "Say whatever you can to get the focus off the neck wounds."

Ducat laughed. "That's like you asking me to get rid of the smoking gun. It's not possible. Too many people know how these men died. It was on the news, for crying out loud."

Vlad couldn't argue the fact, and hypnotizing them all wasn't feasible. He'd need to come up with another angle.

"Then make it sound like a cult, devil worshippers. A ritualistic type of murder. I don't care. Plant the seeds in her head. Just make sure the word 'vampire' never enters into it."

"I'm sure that would be a much more believable explanation than a pack of vampires descended on the foursome."

"You would think. Make some noise and make sure your theory goes as viral as the news report did."

"You know the murderer?"

"Why do you ask?"

"Because otherwise, I doubt you'd be in here pleading your case. An election year is coming up. Detective Joseph Hernandez is running unopposed. I'm stepping down. It's time for my retirement. I'm getting too old for all of this. I'm sure you can understand that I'd rather not get involved in this messy case."

Vlad nodded. "Of course. But you're still sheriff, therefore this is in your, I hope, very capable hands. I need this to be handled quietly and efficiently."

"Why?" His gaze narrowed. "Although, I've had Kane's back over the years, if you're lying to me and Kane's crew got messy, I'm not about to help you cover this up. These men were murdered, regardless of what they did for a living."

"What I want, Ducat, is you to keep the suspicion of vampires living among the population out of the news."

He laughed again. "You must think I have more power than I do. You should be talking to your grandsons. They aren't bound by the law. Surely, there is something more that they can do."

"Perhaps they'd be better at getting certain elements to be, let's say, forgotten. And if I must, I'll go that route. But I wouldn't need Kane or Kaleb to do it for me."

"Then why are you here if you can do this task yourself?"

"I was hoping to persuade you into talking to the special agent. Shed a different light on the case, get the focus off the bite wounds. But since that seems impossible for you, I'll need an introduction to this woman in charge of the case."

"What exactly would you like me to tell her the reason is that you wish a meeting with her? You're not exactly law enforcement and I'm assuming you'd rather keep Cara out of this, or you would have gone to her instead of me."

"Let me put it this way. I have an idea who the culprit is."

"Then why the hell are we even talking? Give me the name and I'll take it to Special Agent Ferrari myself."

Vlad sighed heavily. "Exactly the reason I'm here trying to get this swept under the rug a bit. I believe my brother Mircea is sending me a message. I heard it, loud and clear. Now, I must keep my family from being exposed due to his recklessness."

Ducat sat back in his chair and crossed one ankle over his knee. He grabbed his cup of coffee and took a sip before balancing it on the arm of the chair. "What will you do to your brother if you find out this is true?"

"Trust me, he will be dealt with. There won't be any more trouble from him. Until then, I need to contain this situation. Are you going to get me the meeting?"

The sheriff nodded. "I'll put a call in to her office."

"You don't have her direct line? The fewer people who know about my meeting with her the better. I need this to be a private meeting."

"I'll call her. Promise me you won't make me regret this. I just want to retire peacefully."

"Duly noted."

"As soon as I have a meeting set up for you, I will give you a call. I assume you have a number I can reach you by."

Vlad took a piece of paper from the sheriff's desk and scribbled a number on it. He slid it across the desk. "Time is of the essence, Ducat. Don't dally. I fear my brother won't quit until I stop him."

Ducat rubbed his brow. "Just my luck he'd pick my county to exact his revenge on you."

"Of course." Vlad stood, his dark gaze pinning the sheriff. "I'll expect that call shortly."

"Of course, you would. But if you don't hear from me, my request to get you that audience fell on deaf ears."

Vlad smiled, then turned and left the room. Hopefully, he'd get that meeting soon with the lovely Special Agent Ferrari. He couldn't help but wonder if her blood was as sweet as she looked.

CAITLYN WALKED INTO THE penthouse more nervous than a virgin bride on her wedding night. There was no doubt where this evening would lead, that much was apparent in the hot gaze of the additional passenger in the limo ride back to the hotel. Grigore's eyes had been nearly black, telling her the vampire in him simmered beneath the surface as he sat quietly across from her. They had spoken very little, making her wonder what was on his mind, if anything other than sex. She, of course, had thought of little else. Though Caitlyn was still getting used the vampire idea, she'd also found it sexy as hell.

So why was she so nervous? It wasn't as if they hadn't made love the night before. What made tonight any different? She supposed it was because it had been spontaneous. What had transpired between them came as naturally as drawing breath. Tonight there had been underlying sexual tension between them from the moment he helped her get seated in the back of the vehicle. Grigore had held her hand a bit longer than necessary as he assisted her, his skin hot against hers.

Her show had gone according to plan, with no issues and thankfully no one getting shot. While the crew had begun setting up for the next night's concert, the rest of them had headed for the hotel. The Sons of Sangue had followed the limo on their motorcycles, keeping an eye on traffic and making sure their ride from the venue was just as uneventful. Following their arrival at the hotel, they had all gone their separate ways.

She tossed her dress bag onto the sofa arm and dropped her black pumps to the tiled floor, the thump echoing in the spacious room. Cait collapsed to the sofa and slipped off her flip-flops before plopping her tired feet onto the coffee table. Her gaze went to the ruined chair, or what had been, now replaced by a new one with cushioned arms. A smile crept up her cheeks with a reminder that she would have to apologize to the staff and the hotel before they checked out the following day. The damaged chair would be added to her bill.

Grigore traveled the room, looking around furniture, behind curtains, before clearing each room, making sure she was safe and the penthouse had not been disturbed in their absence. Seemingly satisfied, he returned to the main room and sat on the chair opposite her, his dark gaze dropping to the black heels at the corner of the sofa.

"I was hoping you would've worn them home."

She laughed, trying not let her nerves show. Leaning forward, Cait rubbed her tired feet. "Are you kidding? I can't wait to get out of the heels. They may look good on, but they are killer on my toes."

He raised a brow, the heat in his eyes evident. Lord, Grigore oozed charisma. Caitlyn shifted in her seat, desire skyrocketing and taking over her case of nerves. Surely, there was a *Wanted* poster with his picture on it. He definitely brought out the naughty.

"Will you wear them for me?"

She licked her lips, drawing his gaze down. Reaching for the shoes, she snatched one off the floor and slid her foot into it.

He shook his head, leaned forward and clasped his hands between his spread knees. "With nothing on."

And just like that, the temperature in the room shot up, making it hotter than Hades. Caitlyn could have refused him. But if he wanted to play, who was she to deny? Feeling a bit mischievous, she stood barefoot, grabbed both heels, and padded across the space separating them. She stopped just out of his reach.

Dropping the heels with a thud, she then slid her hands up her sides to the peasant-style top she wore. Gripping the hem, she slowly pulled the material over her head, shaking out her blond hair, letting it cascade over her shoulders. Her fingers went to the front of her jeans, slipping the button free of the hole, before the zipper's rasp filled the silence stretching between them.

The Adam's apple bobbed in Grigore's throat as his black gaze fixed on her fingers. Hooking her thumbs in the waistband of the jeans, she shimmed out of them, leaving her nearly naked aside from her matching black lace panty set. Turning around, she bent forward to retrieve the heels, pushing her backside in his direction as she stepped into the black shoes with the silver-studded heels and fastened them.

Grigore cleared his throat. "I believe I said wearing *nothing*."

Ignoring his request, Caitlyn stood and turned to face him again. She ran her hands over the lace covering her breasts and moaned, then ran her tongue over her lower lip. Grigore's features slowly morphed into vampire. Razor-sharp fangs dipped beneath his upper lip; his nostrils flared. Knowing her actions increased his desire only drove her own to inferno level. Gone was the nervous woman who had entered the suite. Making love to Grigore was as natural as self-gratification, but much more intense.

No one had ever excited her the way he did. Just looking at him now, she was a hairbreadth away from orgasm. Placing two fingers against his lips, he sucked them into his mouth, thoroughly wetting them. She withdrew the digits, then ran them down her belly, beneath the thin scrap of lace, and finding her center already wet.

His eyes widened and he sucked in a breath. Cait circled her tiny knot of nerves, eliciting a shallow intake of air.

"Christ Almighty," he hissed.

Tugging her lower lip between her teeth, she worked her fingers, her own breath hitching. Using her free hand, Caitlyn tugged on her taut, lace-covered nipple.

Grigore cursed, his hands tightly gripping the soft arms of the new chair, whitening his knuckles. He continued to watch her play as he ran his fangs over his lower lip. Her gaze dropped to his lap where an impressive-sized bulge pressed against the front of his jeans.

Noting her obvious focus on him, Grigore released the chair, reached for the fastening of his jeans and wasted little time withdrawing his cock. He double-fisted the thick erection, slowly pumping the steel-like staff. A shiver passed down her spine, only seconds away from a climax.

"Is this what you want to see, Sunshine?"

She didn't want it this way. No, Caitlyn wanted him thick and hot inside her when she came. Withdrawing her hands, she reached for him.

"Fuck me," she said, causing him to chuckle.

"My pleasure."

Grigore stood. He took two steps to reach her and had her bent over the arm of the chair in the blink of an eye. One of his large hands splayed across her back, anchoring her, ass in the air. He gripped the lace panty with his free hand, easily ripping it and tossing the ruined material to the side.

Shoving his jeans and boxer briefs further down his hips, he ran his cock along her center, coating it, making it easier to slide in. She damn near stopped breathing in anticipation, looking back at him from over her shoulder. Caitlyn had never wanted something more; she quivered from need. Her thighs shook.

"Oh, Wolf, I can't—"

He thrust into her, her words dying in her throat. Never had she felt so full. Grigore paused, giving her time to acclimate to his incredible size. Her breath came in shallow pants as he slowly withdrew.

"Fuck…" He hissed. "I don't think I can go slow, Sunshine, but I don't want to hurt you."

"I'm not going to break," she said, before another shiver wracked her, rendering her speechless.

Her hands tightly gripped the other arm of the chair as Grigore slammed into her. Her backside tilted at just the right angle, thanks to her heels. Grigore growled, bucking into her, rocking her against the chair, the legs screeching against the marble floor. It was all she could do to keep the chair from sliding out from beneath her. His fingers bit into the cheeks of her ass as he held her firmly in his grip. He impaled again, his breath sawing out of him, eliciting another moan from her. One more…

"Damn it, Sunshine, I need you to come. I'm not going to last."

His words had her tumbling over the white-hot edge and screaming his name. Seconds later, Grigore tensed behind her, his release spilling into her as his hands tightened on her backside, no doubt leaving bruises. Caitlyn collapsed over the arm of the chair. He had ruined her for anyone else. How in the world would she ever go on without him?

Seconds passed as their breathing evened, before they both composed themselves. Standing on shaking legs, Cait managed to reach down in an effort to remove the heels. His large hand gripped her forearm, stopping her.

"Leave those on, Sunshine. I want you wearing them with nothing. You still owe me."

A soft laugh breezed out of her. "I'm pretty sure that just happened."

Grigore reached over and unhooked the front clasp of her bra, her breasts spilling out. He wet his lips, his gaze hungry, as she dropped the lace to the floor.

"Now that's more like it. Those heels are killer on you. Last night we christened my bed; tonight, it's yours."

Caitlyn raised a brow. "Seriously? I'm still catching up on my sleep from last night."

He grinned, the humor present in his marble-like gaze. "Who said anything about getting sleep?"

She laughed. "You're incorrigible."

"Sunshine, when it comes to you, I'm incapable of being restrained."

Grigore gripped her by the waist and tossed her against his shoulder, heading for her bedroom, her derriere in the air. He slapped her hard on the ass, causing her to squeal.

"Ain't no one getting any sleep tonight."

Well into the night, he finally took mercy on her and allowed her to cuddle against his chest to watch the sun come over the horizon from the large picture window overlooking the city, where her black heels now lay on the floor beneath it. She might just have to wear them more often, Caitlyn thought with a yawn, then fell promptly to sleep.

CHAPTER FOURTEEN

G ABRIELA TREVINO CABALLERO ENTERED THE BLOOD AND Rave, followed by her best friend Adriana Flores. The two had been house hunting along the coast just outside Florence when they decided to pay her childhood friend, Brea Gotti, a visit. Gabby had called ahead to make sure Brea would be there, being that it wasn't normal operating hours for the Rave. They were told the main entrance would be left open for them. Entering the darkened club, they skirted the line of empty tables with upturned chairs near the dance floor and headed for the back. The bar was illuminated by five canister pendant lights hanging over the polished wooden surface, lending them a dimly lit path.

Brea sat on one of the stools while her mate Draven stood on the other side, no doubt preparing for the opening of the club later in the evening. The man was certainly drool-worthy with his longish hair pulled back in a messy bun and a pair of round, blue-tinted sunglasses perched on the end of his straight, slender nose. He wasn't overly muscular like most of the Sons, but more on the slender fit side. She could see why her friend had fallen for him. From what Gabby had been told, Brea had helped turn Draven's life around. Apparently, he had been running drugs from his club for the Devils and the La Paz cartel for many years before turning informant for the DEA.

The Sons of Sangue had a vested interest in the club and its dealing since Draven provided the donors, the vampires' primary source of nourishment. Gabby had quickly put a stop to Ryder's need for one, being his exclusive source of sustenance. Of course, that would change once she agreed to become his mate. After her turning, her vampire blood could no longer be a source of food for him. She wasn't sure how she'd handle him sipping from another woman's artery, especially since all her life she had not once had to share since she'd lived a privileged life.

The Sons' mates seemed to handle their men taking their fill from another woman's neck rather well, though she'd heard teasing about equal rights and stocking men donors at the club for the female vampires to feed from. So far, Kane and Kaleb Tepes and the rest of the Sons had not yet given in to the request, leaving it to fall on deaf ears. Gabby was on the women's side. If Ryder was going to sip from another female's artery, then she should be able to partake from the opposite sex as well.

Latching onto a neck that wasn't Ryder's, though, held little appeal. She supposed it was the reason the mates of the Sons of Sangue didn't raise a bigger stink about the whole practice. Drinking from an artery that didn't belong to their mate was no more appealing than drinking a meal replacement shake. There simply was no enjoyment other than appeasing their hunger.

It wasn't as if Ryder hadn't asked her to be his mate, or at the very least hinted at it, but he had promised to wait for her until she was more comfortable with the idea. This whole vampire thing was still too foreign and drinking blood wasn't something she was ready to consider just yet. With the Sons' permission to allow her to remain with Ryder unmated, yet know about their vampire existence, Gabby wasn't in any rush to join their lifestyle. From what she heard, it had taken Anton Balan's Kimber sometime to join their ranks as well.

"Gabby." Brea broke into her musings as she jumped to her feet and folded her into her petite embrace, her friend barely standing over five feet tall. "So glad to see you again. I am loving that we've reconnected. Please tell me you found a house nearby so we can hang out more often."

Gabby stepped back and smiled. "We've lost so much time because of our families."

"You stick with Ryder and we'll have many years to rectify that."

Gabby noted that Brea hadn't mentioned becoming a mate or the immortality that came with it, as Adriana knew nothing about vampires. Like the rest, Gabby had been sworn to secrecy and that included her best friend who had followed her from Mexico, leaving behind her fiancé. Mateo Rodriguez had taken over her Uncle Raúl's cartel when the Sons had ended the kingpin's life.

Losing her uncle still cut deep and probably always would. After all, he had been the one to raise her when her own father's life had been cut short. But the fact was he had lived a double life and had caused or ordered the deaths of thousands. There weren't many men more feared or evil than Raúl and that side of her uncle wouldn't be missed.

"Any luck on the house hunting?" Brea asked, once again drawing back her focus.

Gabby clasped her hands in front of her. "I think so. There's a beautiful four bedroom house with two master suites, a gourmet kitchen with white shaker cabinets, four and a half bathrooms, and over three-thousand square feet on an acre of ground overlooking the ocean. Adriana would have her own wing, that is until we can find her a little bungalow nearby. Or maybe I'll have a small cottage built for her on the back of the lot."

Adriana's cheeks reddened. "I promise not to get in the way or overstay my welcome."

"Oh, please." Gabby placed her arm over her shoulder and drew her into her side. "You can stay with us as long as you want. After all, you helped me through the death of my uncle, the selling of his estates, and transferring my money here. I couldn't have made the move without you. I told you I would buy you a home and I intend to do just that. It's the least I can do."

"I wouldn't think of taking it."

"Of course, you wouldn't." Gabby dropped her arm from Adriana's shoulder and grabbed her friend's hand, squeezing it. "You'll take the offer and you won't argue or be offended. What better way to use some of my uncle's money? I couldn't possibly spend it all in my lifetime."

Adriana's cheeks reddened. "I can't thank you enough either."

Gabby knew Adriana referenced helping her get away from Mateo. The man was bad news and always had been. She would've spent a small fortune to get Adriana away from him and his lifestyle. They were both starting over and leaving the cartel behind. Good riddance.

"Is it close?" Brea asked.

"Actually, not far from here. I know Gypsy and Tamera have a place up the coast, but I don't think this is as far out or quite as remote. It still has a Florence address. It's just down the highway a couple of miles on the outskirts of town. Not sure what Ryder will think of it, as he hasn't yet seen it. It may be too close to Florence for his liking. The Sons seem to like more remote locations."

"If you love it, I'm sure he will as well. Plus, I'll get to spend more time with you if you are just down the road." She glanced over at Draven who paid them little mind as he finished restocking the liquor shelves. "Isn't that awesome, Draven?"

"Whatever makes you smile, sweetheart." He leaned over and kissed her cheek. The love he carried for his mate was evident in his dark eyes as he glanced at her over the rim of the blue glasses. "If you ladies will excuse me, I have some paperwork to do before we open the doors tonight. I have a big name DJ booked. Should be a packed house. The tickets have been sold out for weeks. You two should stay."

Gabby smiled. "Thank you, Draven. I appreciate the invite."

"I can set up the VIP room if you like."

"Please don't go to the bother. I need to get back to Ryder, so I can show him the estate I found."

"Any time you girls want to use the VIP room, it's yours. Just give Brea a call," Draven said, then leaned down and kissed Brea on the lips. With a quick rap of his knuckles on the wooden surface, he turned and exited through the door behind the bar.

Gabby glanced back at Brea, her face sobering. "I have another reason for stopping by."

"I'm just super stoked you're here." Brea's smile lit her blue eyes, speaking of her happiness at having Gabby around again. "So what's up?"

Gabriela sat on one of the bar stools, the other two women following suit. "I'm sure you heard about the recent slaughter in Oregon."

Brea's lips thinned, but she said nothing, only nodding. Adriana worried her lip, clearly already knowing what Gabby was about to ask. Seeing how she and Brea had only recently reunited, she wasn't sure she even had a right to ask.

"I heard on the news that the hit might be cartel-related."

"Not that I try to get involved any longer," Brea said with a sigh. "But I do believe the four men who were slaughtered were from the La Paz cartel."

"The deaths themselves concerned me, but the brutality of the way they died was particularly disconcerting. You don't think the Sons are still…"

Brea glanced briefly at Adriana, already knowing she had no knowledge of vampirism. "Why not ask Ryder?"

"Because I don't want to draw him into this. We've only recently reconnected since my uncle's death and I'd hate to throw my accusations at him."

"Why would you worry about the death of four drug runners, Gabby? They are no longer your problem."

Gabby's gaze widened. "Really? You of all people should know that all of those running drugs for the cartel aren't bad. Take Draven, for example."

Brea cleared her throat, her lips turning down. "He's changed and he no longer works for the Devils or the cartel. Why the sudden worry?"

"Because I don't want to see Ryder hurt due to some vendetta he has against the cartel. The Sons may be many, but the number of soldiers Mateo has far outnumber us. This is a fight we can't possibly win. Riling up the cartel will only bring them north of the border."

Laying a hand atop Gabby's knee, Brea offered her a tentative grin, understanding in her eyes. "I'll see what I can find out, Gabby. I understand your concern. You and I both came from that world and know how dangerous it can be."

"Not to mention how crazy Mateo can be," Adriana spoke up. "He's out to prove he belongs at the head. He won't stop until every Sons of Sangue member is dead if he thinks they took out the four men in Eugene."

Brea tilted her head. "Then why didn't he order a hit on the Sons for killing Raúl?"

"Because Mateo considered that a favor. He dreamt about taking over Raúl's position. Without Raúl dying, he'd still be the kingpin's 'yes' man. But this? Taking out four of his soldiers? He'll take that personally and will want to send a message."

"And you know this because?"

"Adri was engaged to Mateo," Gabby said. "She left him when he took over for my uncle. Was this the work of the Sons?"

"I can't honestly say, but I'll see what I can find out. I'm sure a few of them will be in tonight."

The women stood and Gabby gave Brea a quick hug. "Thank you. I was hoping to find out so I wouldn't have to do damage control with Ryder. I'm sure he wouldn't appreciate my meddling. After all, my number one priority is finding a house for us, or so he thinks."

Brea laughed. "You consider that your priority, Gabby. I'll let you know what I find out. You and Ryder need to think about taking your relationship to the next level."

Gabby knew Brea referred to her becoming a mate. And one day she would. Just not in the immediate future, not until she could stomach the idea of taking blood from another's neck. A shiver passed down her spine. The idea still made her queasy. Lord, how would she ever express as much to Ryder without outright offending him?

"Thanks, Brea."

"It's not so bad, you know," Brea said as if reading Gabby's mind.

She always had been very intuitive when it came to her. It was like they had been twins separated at birth.

Gabby leaned forward and kissed Brea on the cheek. "I'm sure you're right. I best get out of your hair. You have a club to run and it sounds like a busy night ahead."

"You two aren't staying then?"

She shook her head. "Adri and I are going to be showing Ryder the house I found. With any luck, we'll be moving out of the cramped little bedrooms at the clubhouse soon."

"Good luck, and don't be a stranger."

"Are you kidding? I just found you again; no chance you're going to get rid of me now."

Brea laughed. "Good to know. And nice seeing you too, Adriana. You guys are always welcome here. I'll get back with you when I find out anything."

"Thank you, Brea. I owe you."

Brea waved her hand. "It's what we do. We help each other out when needed. I'll be expecting an open invite to your new house overlooking the ocean once you get settled."

"I can't wait to have you and Draven over."

Gabriela bussed Brea's cheek again before she and Adriana made their way to the club's exit. She prayed the Sons weren't involved in the latest bloodshed in Eugene. Gabby had been around the cartel business long enough to realize that Mateo would want payback in the way of each one of the Sons' heads, including Ryder's. If she had to, she'd quickly take his offer as mate and become strong as a vampire if it meant helping the Sons and keeping her man alive.

THE NIGHT'S SHOW HAD ENDED in a standing ovation and without cause for concern. Grigore wasn't sure if he felt more blessed or disappointed that the son of a bitch hadn't surfaced. Caitlyn hadn't been used for target practice and had remained unhurt, which was his primary goal, but it also meant this threat continued to loom over her. Not knowing who they were looking for made this a damn near impossible task night in and night out. And the longer this menace went unresolved, the longer Grigore stayed by her side which would make it all the harder to leave in the end.

Sleeping with Cait had certainly complicated matters, getting their emotions wrapped up where they had no business being. No matter how much either of them tried to remain detached, it wasn't working. Grigore had never truly stopped loving her and leaving wouldn't change that fact. Caitlyn may not have said as much, but he was pretty sure she had never stopped loving him either. She may have hated him for the way he left, but that spot in her heart had never truly iced over or she would have never invited him back into her bed.

Caitlyn's ex, Tyler, had thankfully not shown his face since the first sighting. Grigore would rather it not be someone she had been emotionally involved with at one time. Less messy that way and easier to keep everything out of the tabloids. Josh, on the other hand, remained somewhat closed off. He had used his walkie tonight and answered his calls, but continued to act like an asshole whenever he had to deal with Grigore. Ryan must have had a chit-chat or a "come to Jesus meeting" with the crew manager to get him responding on the walkie, but that didn't make him any more cordial. Grigore didn't give a rat's ass how the man acted as long as Josh worked with him when it came to keeping Cait safe. The bottom line was about Caitlyn's safety and not the pissing match between the two of them.

Grigore had spent little time with Caitlyn, other than shortly after her makeup artist Roberto had finished with her stage look. The truth of it was Grigore preferred her more natural look. Caitlyn was more beautiful without the added extra. She was naturally stunning.

Opening the door to her dressing room, Grigore stepped in while Ryan and Cait finished their discussion about the upcoming shows. They were headed to New York next with a few days off in between. It would be nice to get some downtime again, and a little less stress. He was certainly partial to the laid-back Cait.

They had a little over a five-hour bus ride in front of them, with her crew taking a different bus. Tena had volunteered to ride Bobby's motorcycle to New York while he took Grigore's so that Grigore could ride inside the bus with Caitlyn this time, giving them a bit of alone time on the road.

Ryan excused himself when Caitlyn walked behind the dressing screen to change out of the night's ensemble. Grigore had yet to tell her he'd be riding in the bus with her. There was plenty of room in that king-size bed for two, and if Grigore had his way, there wouldn't be any sleeping being done until they arrived at the next destination.

"You ready, Sunshine?"

"As ready as one can be," she said, coming back around the screen.

She donned a long baggy, hooded sweatshirt over a pair of what looked to be buttery soft leggings. He couldn't wait to run his hands over the material to see if it was as soft as it looked.

"Tired?"

"Exhausted."

So much for his plans, he thought with a chuckle. Grigore would be just as happy to hold her while she slept. He'd wait until they arrived at the hotel to get inside her. Which he looked forward to. Every. Damn. Time.

"I'll be riding with you tonight."

"What about your motorcycle?"

"Bobby will be driving it while Tena takes his."

Her eyes lit. "She knows how to ride a motorcycle? That's so cool. Will you teach me?"

Grigore chuckled. "Maybe someday. Right now, you'd be a moving target with this nutcase chasing you."

Cait yawned, covering her mouth with the back of her hand. "We can have a little fun on the trip to New York City if you want."

Grigore walked over to her and pulled her flush against him, his hands squeezing her ass. "Sunshine, it can wait. You look ready to drop."

She yawned again as if laying proof to the fact of how tired she was. "You're probably right. It's been a long, stressful day. So glad Tyler didn't show again, but worrying about who this unknown person is who wants me dead is taking a toll on me. And then there is you to worry about. You already took a bullet for me once."

"Stop stressing. I'm here to see that nothing happens to you. And me? The fucker needs better aim."

She drew in her lower lip, her gaze filling with moisture as she laid her palm over his heart. "I could have lost you."

"You didn't. Now, let's get this show on the road and get the hell out of here while the crowd is still dispersing. Hanging around here too long makes me nervous. I'd rather have the distraction of your fans leaving the building."

"And the rest of the Sons of Sangue?"

"Watching our backs. Once we are on the bus, they'll be following us to the hotel."

"Let me gather my things and I'll be ready."

Caitlyn made quick work of packing her belongings, then handed the garment bag to Grigore. She stepped into a pair of flip-flops, then picked up her wristlet wallet before scanning the room.

"I think that's everything."

"Good. Two more tour dates down without incident. Another win for the good guys."

Caitlyn's smile turned saucy. "Let's get on the road. The sooner we get to New York City, the sooner I can give you your reward."

Grigore growled as he stepped behind her, gripping her ass. "That's one reward I'll be looking forward to."

He stepped around her, opened the door and looked down the empty hall. Satisfied, he led her from the room and down the concrete corridor. Bobby was stationed at the corner. They bumped fists before heading toward the back of the venue where Tena and Kimber stood watch at the exit, which was held open for them. Outside they'd found the rest of the Sons lining the walk and keeping a close eye on the surroundings. The bus was no more than a few hundred yards from the back door. They'd make quick work of getting onto the bus, then Grigore could finally relax.

Tena, Bobby, and Kimber followed them into the inky-black night. No moon showed as the impending storm covered the sky in low-hanging clouds. The rumble of the bus's engine cut through the sounds of the fans spilling from the stadium to find their vehicles and head home. Grigore's hearing easily picked up on their excitement, loving the night's concert and the show Caitlyn had given them.

Due to the threat, no fan was allowed anywhere near the buses and the back of the venue. Caitlyn had first argued, knowing that some fans waited hours to try and get an auto-graph, which she was happy to oblige. But given the crappy situation, she understood Grigore's insistence to keep every-one from the rear of the building, not only for her safety but theirs as well.

Halfway to the open door of the bus, a barely audible clack caught his attention, something whizzing by his ear. His gaze, as well as the other vampires', went to the roof of a five-story building just beyond the back parking lot. There at the top was a lone figure dressed in black with a long-range rifle aimed at Caitlyn. The fire flashed from the end of the barrel, right before the sound of the bullet being fired had reached his ears.

With lightning speed, Grigore took the few steps separat-ing him from Cait, attempting to shield her with his body and spinning her around to put him in line with the oncoming bul-let. Even with his vampire speed, he couldn't tackle her fast enough.

The bullet grazed his shoulder, hitting Caitlyn in the back. They both went down hard. Not only did he worry about the bullet's damage, he feared his heavy weight following her to the ground broke a few bones. Bobby, Anton, and Grayson were already in pursuit of the hooded figure while the women stayed, circling Caitlyn and Grigore.

He quickly rolled off her. "Cait?"

When she didn't answer, his heart sank. Agony clawed at him for failing to protect her. Blood blossomed from beneath her shoulder blade, just left of her spine, the red circle grow-ing larger by the minute. Fangs emerged from his gums as the vampire tore through him. The scent of her blood beck-oned at him.

"Jesus, Mary, and Joseph. Sunshine!"

Grigore rolled her over, his fingers going to the weak pulse at her neck. Thanks to the good Lord, she still had one, but her complexion had gone deathly white. Tearing her hoodie from her shoulder, he caught sight of the ugly wound. He quickly licked the puckered hole, hoping to slow down the flow of blood with his salvia. Giving her his blood to heal wasn't an option. He could no more break the rule of the Sons by turning her without permission than to force vampirism onto her. But giving up on her wasn't an option either.

Grigore pulled his phone from his pocket and punched in 911.

CHAPTER FIFTEEN

THE SHOW IN NEW YORK CITY HAD BEEN CANCELED WITH the possibility of more dates put on hold. Caitlyn had yet to wake up following surgery as she lay in the hospital bed with wires and tubes hooked up to her. The wound to his shoulder had been superficial and had already healed. The would be assassin had gotten away, giving Bobby, Anton, and Grayson the slip. Grigore wanted to find this asshole and now, rip him to shreds right after he drained the motherfucker dry. He paced the tile flooring, while the rest of the Sons waited in the small room down the hall, taking turns keeping vigil outside of the door.

The doctor-on-call had said the bullet hadn't hit anything major. It had been easily removed without further blood loss. Caitlyn also had a few broken ribs, along with a slight concussion from when Grigore had tackled her to the ground. The doctor thought it might be contributing to her failure to awaken, though he expected a full recovery as a CT scan showed no damage to the brain.

Cait now sported a big, ugly lump and purple bruising on her forehead, compliments of Grigore. His chest ached at having been the cause. He rubbed the area over his heart as he approached the second-floor window of her room. The sky was filled with low-hanging clouds, all that was left from the late-night downpour. Dark and dismal, matching his mood.

A quick glance at the black-and-white clock on the adjacent wall told him it was just after nine in the morning. Caitlyn was expected to awaken at any time.

So why was it taking so damn long?

The more drawn-out her recovery, the worse he felt. Had he done a better job and not let his defenses down following her performance, she wouldn't have taken the bullet in the first place, nor would he have tackled her to the cement, leaving her with a bump the size of a small egg. Fuck, he was too damn big to be wrestling Cait to the ground.

He turned and approached the bed again, gripping her cool hand in his warmer one. "You need to wake up, Sunshine. Give me hell. Just laying here isn't an option."

A knock sounded on the door. Grigore was expecting one of the Sons or their mates, but what he found was a couple of detectives in suits from the city.

"Can we ask you a few questions?" The shorter of the two spoke and offered his hand. Grigore shook it. "I'm Detective Miller and this is Detective Beckett. We're with the PBP, Pittsburgh Bureau of Police."

Grigore stepped back, shoved his hands into his jean pockets and rocked back on his heels. He wasn't thrilled with their appearance. After all, the Sons took care of their own, even if he was doing a bang-up job. It was only a matter of time before the detectives handling the case showed up anyway.

"We gave our statements last night. I'm pretty sure they haven't changed since the sun rose."

Detective Miller's gaze darkened as he briefly took in Cait's supine body. "I'm not here to ask you to restate or clarify what you told my officers last night. Surely, you must know we take it personally when someone shoots a high-profile star such as Ms. Summers here. We'll do our best to see the culprit is found and brought to justice."

"All due respect, I appreciate that, but I fail to see how you think you can catch this son of a bitch when we haven't."

"Has he struck before?"

"Once. At a show in Cleveland a few nights ago. You can contact their PD if you need the details."

"We'll be sure to do that. Was Ms. Summers shot then?"

Grigore shook his head. "The bullet tagged me. Flesh wound."

"Anyone else hurt?"

"Nope."

"And was the bullet fired from out back of the stadium as well?"

"No. It was done from inside the venue."

"Interesting. I wonder how the gun had been smuggled in."

"I'd like the answer to that too."

Detective Beckett began typing into his phone what Grigore figured was specifics of their conversation. Detective Miller turned back to Grigore. "Any idea why Ms. Summers would be targeted?"

"As I told the officers last night, I haven't a clue. I'm here to protect her. Unfortunately, last night, I did a damn poor job of that."

"You couldn't have known."

"It was my job to." And Grigore meant that. "I failed and I take that personally."

One of Detective Beckett's brows rose as he spoke up for the first time. "Meaning?"

"Meaning you better get to him before I do."

Beckett cleared his throat. "No offense, but we'll take it from here, Mr. Lupei. The PBP doesn't need your help. You wearing that MC vest doesn't make you judge, jury, and executioner. We'd appreciate it if you'd stay out of our way and let us do our jobs."

Grigore stiffened his spine and growled. "You do your job and I'll do mine. My MC cut has nothing to do with my promise. I swore I'd keep Caitlyn safe, and I'll do just that. Either within the law or outside of it. I really don't give a damn." He pointed to Beckett's pad. "Write that in there while you're at. So if this son of a bitch comes up dead, you'll know who to come looking for."

"I'll pretend you didn't just issue a threat." Detective Miller's stare hardened. "That's all we have for now. When Ms. Summers wakes up, we'd like to talk to her before she leaves the city."

"I'll see that she contacts you."

Miller reached out and shook Grigore's hand again, followed by Beckett. "We look forward to hearing from her."

The two men turned and quit the room. Grigore supposed he just insinuated himself into the investigation as a number-one suspect should this asswipe turn up dead, not that he cared. Once Grigore was done with him, the motherfucker would become a missing person. Hard to prove anything if there's no body to be found.

Bobby walked into the room with one arm draped over Tena's shoulders. "How are you holding up, man?"

"I'm good. I'd be happier if she'd wake up."

"I'm sure. You need anything, Wolf?"

Grigore shook his head. "I don't think all of you need to be sitting around and wasting a good day, although I appreciate your support. One of you can stay outside the door, but the rest of you can head out. Maybe take turns manning the post. Besides, I'm pretty sure Lefty and Chad could use some relief from their babysitting duties."

Bobby laughed. "No doubt in that. I'll be glad to stand vigil first round and send everyone else back to the hotel."

"Sounds good, bro. And thanks to you as well, Tena. I appreciate you being here."

"Glad to help." She laid a hand on Grigore's tattooed forearm, taking a brief glance at Caitlyn. "You need anything, just ask. We're all here for you."

Grigore nodded, thanking them before they left the room. He turned back to Caitlyn, pulled a chair over to the side of the bed and sat down. He rubbed his large palm over her arm, wishing he had the power to wake her. When she did, she'd likely have one hell of a headache, he thought, as he again took in the goose egg. Lord, he always seemed to make a mess of things.

Looking toward the floor, he leaned forward and clasped his hands between his spread knees. Who the fuck could possibly want her dead? And more importantly, why? If he could come up with the answer to the last question, he might just figure out the first. Other than her crew and Tyler, Grigore had no clue where the fuck to even start looking. Never had he ever felt so helpless. Twice now, Caitlyn could have gotten killed on his watch and that scared the hell out of him.

A moan caught his attention. Grigore looked to the bed, standing and gripping her hand again. This time, to his elation, she squeezed back. Her eyes fluttered open, before taking a glance around the room. She licked her dry lips as she looked up at him.

"What happened?" Her voice was but a whisper.

"You were shot, Sunshine. I fucked up."

Caitlyn closed her eyes, shifted in the bed and moaned again before looking back at him. "Did you ... shoot me?"

"No, but—"

"Stop ... blaming yourself, Grigore." She groaned again. "Can you lift ... my head?"

"Are you sure? I don't want to hurt your shoulder where the bullet was lodged."

"Other than this ... damn headache, I'm fine." She kept pausing for short breaths. "Please lift the headrest. I'll let you know if it ... causes me pain."

Grigore pushed the button on the side rail, elevating her head until she motioned with her free hand to stop.

"I need to let the nurse know you're awake." He pushed the call button on the rail.

"Can I help you?" came across the speaker.

"Caitlyn is awake."

"Great. I'll let the doctor know and then I'll be right in to check on her."

Moments later, the nurse came through the door, checked her vitals, and let them know the doctor would be in later. Grigore thanked her before she turned and left. He gave Cait back his attention. Other than the ugly knot and her very pale complexion, she'd never looked more beautiful.

"When can … I get out of here?"

Grigore laughed. "Not until the doctor gives the okay."

"This bed is awful. Every part of me hurts."

"I'm sure. You've been through a lot."

Her free hand touched the bump on her head, causing heat to rise up Grigore's neck, damning him. His actions hadn't saved her from the bullet anyway. Although, had he not thrown her out of the way, it might have hit something more vital.

"What exactly happened? Last I … remember was leaving the venue and heading for the bus, then I hit the pavement and you telling me … I had been shot."

"I tackled you. I'm sorry. I'm the one at fault for your head-ache and broken ribs."

"You big ox." She tried to laugh, but groaned instead, grabbing her side for her effort. "It's okay, Grigore. Had you not … played running back, I might not be alive to feel the pain. Thank you."

Grigore leaned down and placed a chaste kiss on her forehead. Caitlyn winced, then tried to move her shoulder, earning her another moan.

"I'll expect a better kiss than that when I get out of here."

"You won't need to ask me twice."

"Where's Ryan?"

"He's back at the hotel, changing show dates and moving things around. You won't be singing for a while."

Her gaze widened. "How long?"

"The doctor told Ryan at least a month." He placed a finger over her lips, stopping her from arguing. "Your fans will wait. No dates are canceled, they're just being moved. Besides, you really want to go on stage looking like that?"

She touched her forehead again. "How bad is it?"

Grigore slid the bed cart over to her, careful not to bump her, and lifted the tray where a mirror was concealed. Caitlyn looked into it, touching the area gingerly.

"I guess it could be worse."

He raised a brow. "Are you kidding me? Much worse. You're here and able to look in the mirror. Besides, you can't look bad."

Cait chuckled, then grimaced. "You aren't a good liar. I can see what I look like. Hopefully … I'll heal with no visible scars."

Grigore touched the long scar cutting across his forehead into his eyebrow. "Yeah, no doubt it will. Don't worry, you won't turn out as ugly as my sorry ass."

Her smile fled her face. "I didn't mean—"

"Relax, Sunshine. It was a joke."

"But your scar."

"It's nothing more than a reminder to stay away from a man wielding a knife."

"It adds character, you know."

This time Grigore laughed. "Exactly what this ugly mug needs. You rest. We'll get you out of here and back to the hotel as soon as the doctor gets here."

Her face sobered. "Grigore?"

"Yes?"

"I'm scared."

That admission tore at his heart more than anything because, yes, he had failed her not once, but twice. He leaned down and kissed her forehead again.

"I know, Sunshine. But next time, I won't be found lacking."

CAITLYN WALKED FROM HER suite, tired of lying around. Her migraine had diminished to a dull ache, but her shoulder and ribs still hurt like hell. Wrapped in the white terry cloth robe the hotel had provided, she padded over to the sofa and sat down, grabbing the remote from the coffee table and flipping on the television. Finding a DIY program, she stopped surfing through the channels. As far as she could tell, she was alone in the penthouse. Had Grigore been anywhere near, he'd likely have given her hell for leaving the bed. He had been watching her like a hawk since her release from the hospital yesterday afternoon.

Her heart went out to him. It wasn't his fault she had been shot, and yet he acted as though he had been the one to pull the trigger. Nothing she said had made him feel any better. Ryan had moved three weeks' worth of concert dates out, giving her a brief hiatus. But if Grigore had his way, he wouldn't allow her to go back at all.

Not an option.

She had fans who were waiting to see her live, having paid hard-earned money for it, and she'd be damned if she disappointed them by canceling the rest of her tour. Spotting a bottle of ibuprofen on the side table, she grabbed it, opened the cap and shook out two tablets. A water bottle sat on the table behind her, making her debate whether she wanted to make the trek to get it or swallow the pills dry. Maybe leaving her bed hadn't been the best idea. Now that she was on the sofa, she had little energy to get back up. Sitting here the rest of the day, though, wasn't an option.

Suck it up.

Just as her feet hit the floor, the elevator door opened and Grigore strode into the room, a scowl on his face, no doubt at having caught her out of bed.

"What the fuck are you doing?"

Cait put up a hand, stopping him from giving her more hell. "I can't lie in there a moment longer. I was going stir-crazy. Getting up and moving around will keep my muscles from going to shit. Can you please hand me that bottle of water?"

Grigore walked over to the table, picked it up and gave it to her, still not looking happy at seeing her in the living area.

"You should be resting."

"I can damn well rest right here, Wolf. I'm not going to break."

He sat heavily next to her. "You're under my watch."

Tossing the two tablets into her mouth, she then took a large swig of the water. Cait screwed the cap back on and set it on the side table next to the bottle of ibuprofen.

"That may be but I'm an adult, capable of making the decision if I want to sit out here or in there."

"You took a hell of a hit to your forehead." His cheeks reddened at the mention. "You could have fallen. Look, Cait, I need you to take it easy."

"I am."

He pointed at the open door to her room. "Not out here, in there."

She let out a deep sigh. "I'm perfectly fine out here, Grigore. Look, we need to talk."

"About?"

"I want to head home. Spend the next few weeks in my own bed."

He raised a brow. "And?"

"Let you guys go home. It will be a while before I go back on the road and I don't want to keep your friends here. And that includes you."

Grigore jerked as if she had slapped him. "No fucking way. You aren't getting rid of me until this son of a bitch is caught."

"If no one knows I went home, they won't know where to find me. There's nothing you can do."

"That's it?" His dark gaze blackened. "You fuck me, and now that I'm at fault for you getting hurt, you want me gone?"

"No." Damn, she was making a huge mess of things. This wasn't going at all how she imagined it earlier while she lay in her bed. "That's not it at all. I just think I'll heal better if you're not there."

"Like hell."

"Ryan can take care of me."

"No one"—he growled loud enough for the entire floor below to hear—"and I mean no one will take care of you but me. Not until this fuck is found."

"Ryan—"

"Might be involved in this. You ever think that?"

"What?" Her voice rose. "Surely you're jesting. Have you lost your effing mind? Ryan wouldn't want me dead. Who the hell do you think found you to come and protect me? Does that seem like someone who wants to hurt me?"

"What better way to cover it up?"

"What the hell, Wolf? You're delusional."

He grabbed her smaller hand in his large one, sending heat sizzling up her forearm from his mere touch. Even hurt she couldn't seem to control her libido around him.

"Look, Sunshine, I'm not trying to upset you, but I don't trust anyone at this point. Other than my brothers and their mates."

"What possible motive could Ryan have?"

"I haven't figured out why anyone would want to harm you, let alone kill you. When we left the venue, where was he?"

She shrugged, wincing from the sharp pain it caused her wound. "He left before we did."

"Exactly. I don't know where he was, or Josh, or anyone else who works for you. Any one of them could have left ahead of time and waited for you to exit."

"Anyone could have done that, including an outsider."

"Which brings me to Tyler."

Her brow creased. "What? I haven't seen him since Detroit."

"That doesn't mean he hasn't been keeping tabs." He squeezed her hand. "Cait, I have no clue who wants you dead or why. It's driving me fucking nuts. I've been racking my brain over this and I keep coming up empty. At this point, I can't properly protect you. I'm doing my damnedest and yet you still got hurt … almost twice. If you go back out on the road, what's to stop this from happening a third time?"

She reached up with her free hand and cupped his whiskered cheek. "I know, I'm scared too, but none of this is your fault. You took every precaution."

"That's just it. I brought my brothers here, and although we kept a good eye out, you still got shot. Next time we might not be so lucky."

"Send your friends home, Grigore. At least for the three weeks while I recover. Once I'm home and I get some rest, then we can talk about it. I'm tired, I hurt, and I just want my own bed."

"I'll talk to them."

"And you?"

"I'm staying, Sunshine. I'm not going anywhere until this son of a bitch is caught. End of discussion."

She nodded, secretly happy he agreed to stay on. The truth of the matter was, she had been scared to death ever since receiving the threat. Having him at her side eased those fears, even if she had gotten shot. Had he not been there, Caitlyn doubted she'd still be sitting here. He looked at it as if he had failed her twice. Cait looked at it as if he had saved her life. Had he not reacted, the killer's aim would have been dead-on.

"Fine. We'll fly home tomorrow. I'll have Ryan make the arrangements."

"I'd rather you let me book the tickets."

"You really don't trust him?"

Grigore shrugged. "I don't trust anyone at this point. Where's home anyway? With your mom?"

Caitlyn smiled. She supposed he would think that. "Crescent City. Just off of South Pebble Beach Drive. I've lived

there for five years. It made more sense than staying in Detroit."

"California?"

She nodded. "It's closer to L.A. where Ryan is from and
my recording studio. Besides, I love the coast. There are less
than seven-thousand residents in Crescent City. I love the
small-town feel. I have a nice little beach house overlooking
the ocean and if I need to get to L.A., it's a beautiful two-day
drive down the coast."

"Florence is just up the coast. A hell of a lot closer than
L.A. You've lived within three and a half hours from me for
the past five years?"

"It looks that way."

Grigore rubbed his chin, deep in thought. Caitlyn wished
she could read his mind.

"What?"

"Going back home is a good idea. But instead of your
home, we're going to head to the clubhouse. If someone is
coming after you, they'd look for you at your home. No one
would possibly think to look on my home turf. No more hiding
among the masses. If they want to come to get you, they may
think you're easy pickings out on the coast, when in fact the
opposite will be true."

"How would they know?"

"You're going to tell them."

Caitlyn chuckled. "And how am I supposed to do that if I
don't know who I'm looking for?"

"Easy, you're going to tell someone from the media."

CHAPTER SIXTEEN

THANKFULLY THE CLUBHOUSE APPEARED EMPTY AS GRIG-
ore exited the cab. He reached out and took Cait's
hand, helping her from the backseat. Reaching in his pocket,
Grigore pulled out enough bills for the fare, including a generous tip, and paid the cab driver for the ride from the airport.
The man set their bags on the gravel, pocketed the money,
and wished them well before he hopped back into his vehicle
and headed out of the parking lot.

"Well?" Grigore smiled nervously at Caitlyn. He couldn't
help wondering what she might be thinking of his humble
abode. Surely, it couldn't possibly compare to her beach
house overlooking the Pacific. "This is home for the next
three weeks."

She looked around, took in the wooded area and the river
out back before returning her attention to him. "Nice."

He chuckled. "You say that now, wait until you get in-
doors."

Grigore picked up their bags and headed for the door. Before they reached it, Cara Brahnam swung it open, with Suzi
Stevens close behind. He should have known there would be
a welcoming party. Not that he minded. He got along with all
of his brothers' mates, but at the moment, he wasn't in the
mood for company.

209

Taking a deep breath, he nodded at the two women. "Are there more?"

Suzi's brow furrowed. "More?"

"I thought the clubhouse would be empty. I didn't see any other vehicles."

"My car is out back." Cara laughed. "What kind of friends would we be if we didn't clean this place up for your return? Well, maybe I should say Caitlyn's arrival? You may be used to this, but she needs clean linens at the least. Ryder and Gabriela are still staying here, with Rocker occupying one of the other rooms. I hope it's okay if Caitlyn stays in yours, Wolf. You can always take the couch."

"The hell you say. She sleeps with me."

Caitlyn's cheeks reddened. "It's fine. Thank you both for going to the trouble."

"No trouble," Suzi said. "We just knew that ... well, that it's Wolf. He doesn't know the first thing about hospitality."

"Is there anything else you two need?"

Cara rolled her eyes. "No need to be rude, Wolf. Where's the thank you?"

"Thank you," he grumbled, barely audible. He supposed he was irritated because he didn't have Caitlyn to himself. There would be time to socialize after he had her settled in. "Caitlyn, this is Cara Brahnam and Suzi Stevens. They belong to the twins."

One of Cait's brows rose. "Twins?"

"Viper is the club P, that's Cara's mate. And Hawk belongs to Suzi. He's club VP."

"Oh, don't let him hear you say he belongs to me." Suzi laughed, mirth gathering in her eyes. "Although, I do like the sound of that."

Their son, Stefan, came running up, wrapping his tiny arms around one of Suzi's legs. "And this little guy is Stefan, future club P."

Grigore reached down, picked up the toddler and positioned him in the crook of his arm, bringing the boy eye-level. Grigore held up a hand. "High five," he said, and the boy promptly slapped, finishing with a giggle.

Setting him back on his feet, Grigore watched as the boy ran back to the center of the room where wooden building blocks were stacked on the coffee table. "Come play."

"You play for now, Stefan. Wolf is busy settling in his new friend, Cait."

"Cait," the boy repeated as the stack of blocks he was building toppled over. "Uh oh."

"I'm told there are congratulations in order?" Grigore asked Cara.

She smiled, one of her hands going to her abdomen. "If you're speaking of Viper's and my recent news, then yes. We can't wait to meet our son."

Cait's eyes widened in response, her gaze following Cara's hand movement. "You know the gender already? You're not even showing yet."

"Genetics only allow for true bloods, vampire babies, to be of the male gender."

"Are there other children?" Cait asked. "I mean aside from Lucian and Stefan?"

"India is pregnant. That's Xander's mate. You'll meet her later. And if I can talk Hawk into it, I want to give Stefan a brother," Suzi said, before turning to Grigore. "Why don't we get out of your hair so you can get settled?"

"Please, do." Grigore groused.

"Grigore!"

Cait's tone shamed him, leaving him to wonder if it was such a great idea bringing her here. For her safety it certainly was, but not so much otherwise. "Sorry, ladies. Caitlyn needs her rest from her stay in the hospital. And I need to get us unpacked."

"Of course." Cara smiled at Cait. "How insensitive of us to keep you."

"No really, Wolf is just being an ass. Thank you for cleaning up. I appreciate you thinking of me."

Suzi walked over to Stefan, tossing the blocks into a wicker basket and storing them under the coffee table. Both women finished grabbing their things, then met back at the entry.

Grigore supposed he needed to add his gratitude. If he didn't, Cait would likely give him hell once the ladies left. "Thank you, Cara and Suzi. It was nice of you to stop by." He refrained from saying, "*Now, get the hell out.*"

Cara laughed. "That wasn't so hard, now was it?"

"No problem, Wolf. You need anything, give us a call," Suzi added.

"Where's Ryder?" Grigore asked.

"He and Gabby are house hunting." Suzi placed her backpack containing Stefan's things on one shoulder while cradling him with her free arm. "Not sure where Rocker is, probably out with Viper and Hawk, something having to do with Grandfather. For now, you have the place to yourselves."

"Can you give Viper and Hawk a message? Tell them the rest of the Sons should be here tomorrow."

"Sure. You two get settled." Cara gripped Cait's hand briefly. "Nice to meet you. You have nothing to worry about. You're in our territory. We won't let anything happen to you."

"Thank you. Nice meeting you both as well. Come by any time."

The door closed behind the women and Grigore let out a heavy sigh, followed by Caitlyn swatting his shoulder.

"What was that for?" he asked, rubbing the area.

"You need to be nicer."

Grigore growled, grabbed both their suitcases and headed for his room. "*Women.*"

CAITLYN HUNG THE LAST OF her shirts in Grigore's closet. He had insisted that she get in bed while he did the bulk of the work, no matter how she tried to convince him she had been hurt but wasn't helpless. If they were going to be stuck here for the next three weeks with no concert shows to distract them, then they needed to learn to get along, which included him not treating her like an invalid.

Her gaze took in the freshly made bed. They certainly had no issues when it came to intimacy. Sleeping in the same room wouldn't be a hardship. Sex was the least of their worries. Once Caitlyn had made the decision to crawl back into his bed, the sparks of attraction had ignited into flames. Their problems didn't include being sexually incompatible. If nothing, they were more than on the same page, leaving her thinking of little else when Grigore was near.

No, their struggles stemmed from getting along on a day-to-day basis. Cait had yet to completely forgive him for walking out, even if his motivation had been big-hearted and selfless. Grigore should've given her the choice. Although, in all honesty, Cait would have chosen him and he knew that. Love had blinded her to seeing and reaching her full potential as an artist. Grigore knew what she was capable of, and by walking away, he had given her the career most strive for but few achieve.

The cost had been too high.

Losing Grigore had never been an option. She would give up everything to have shared a life with him, had a family together. Now? Grigore was a vampire, which she was still having trouble wrapping her mind around. Not that it made her love him any less. He was still the same man beneath it all. Except now, he drank blood to survive. And as much as she'd like to think he could fit into her public life, it wouldn't work. Not without risk of exposure. The Sons of Sangue members would be hunted, and if not killed on sight, become lab rats.

When this threat to her life was no more, Grigore would leave her again, this time for an entirely different set of reasons. Ones she couldn't begin to argue with. The media hounded her. There was no way his lifestyle wouldn't eventually be discovered.

Caitlyn couldn't ask him to stay, knowing it would put everyone here at risk. This time, she would let him walk away even if it crushed her. They had no other options. Even when lying low, the media had eventually found her.

The door opened and Grigore walked in, damn near swallowing the room with his presence. "Done?"

"Almost. I have just a few more things left to put away."

"How are you feeling?"

"I've been better."

His gaze swept over her, heating her along the path his dark eyes took. "You need to lie down?"

"Honestly, I could use something to eat. It was a long flight."

"I was just checking the fridge and it looks stocked. Either Cara and Suzi made sure you had everything you could want, or it's because Gabriela is living here."

Cait couldn't help feeling a bit elated at the possibility of not being the only human staying in the clubhouse. "She's not a vampire?"

Grigore shook his head. "I'm sure she'll be one day ... when she's ready."

"She knows about you and what you are?"

"The same as you."

"I thought it was against the rules?"

He chuckled. "It is. There are extenuating circumstances."

"What if she leaves?"

"She won't. She loves Ryder but should that change then she'll be made to forget. She'll have no memory of vampires."

"You'll make me forget too, won't you?"

His lips thinned. "I'll be left with no choice, Cait. When it's time for you to go back to your life, one of us will be forced to erase your memory. Gypsy has offered to do the honors."

Her heart beat heavily. Anxiety fluttered in her chest. She didn't want to forget Grigore. "What if I refuse?"

"It won't matter what you want, Sunshine." He ran a knuckle down her cheek, causing her to shiver. "When the time comes, the only thing you'll remember is the fact that I'm an asshole."

Moisture gathered in her eyes. She refused to let the tears fall. "And the time we spent making love?"

Cait could see the momentary heartbreak in his eyes before he blinked it away. "I can't allow it, Cait. Walking away won't be easy for either of us. I'll spare you the pain of me doing it to you a second time."

Clearing her throat, she said, "But you'll remember."

"Every last detail." He took in a deep breath. "I'll go fix you something to eat."

When he turned and left the room, Caitlyn sat heavily on the mattress, feeling the weight of despair settling on her chest as if it were an elephant. Grigore had no choice, and she being made to forget what was growing between them was for the best and the least painful option. So why the hell did it hurt so damn much?

Tears slipped down her cheek, tears she wouldn't allow Grigore to see. Cait refused to cause him further pain, knowing he wouldn't have the luxury of forgetting. If he'd have to remember, then she planned on giving him memories to last a lifetime. Yes, she was that damn selfish. No woman would ever replace her in his heart.

Cait swiped away the moisture from her cheeks, finished unpacking, then left the room and headed for the bathroom. Glancing in the mirror, she didn't like what she saw. A sad, haggard woman looked back. What if she left the music industry behind? What if she made this her last tour? Caitlyn had made more money than she could spend in her lifetime. Eventually, the media would dry up and forget about her. She could then disappear from the public eye and live out her days with Grigore.

Could it work?

She would give it all up in a heartbeat if it meant having the one man she had never stopped loving. Of course, Grigore would reject her idea. He'd never accept the sacrifice of her career for him. She needed to come up with a plan, a way to get him to see her life would be better without the stardom. She didn't know how she'd accomplish it, but with her mind made up, she knew she'd figure a way because life without Grigore was not an option. Nor was forgetting all that had transpired between them these past couple of weeks.

With renewed hope, she splashed cold water on her face, brushed her unruly curls, and left the restroom. The scent of eggs, toast, and bacon wafted to her nose, making her stomach growl. Grigore had set a plate on the counter by an empty stool, across the island from where he prepared her meal.

He poured a cup of coffee and set it in front of her. "I hope this is okay. Not close to the cuisine you're used to, I'm sure. But I'm afraid my cooking skills are rusty. I haven't had to cook in a long time."

Cait watched his muscles move as he worked around the kitchen. Damn, but he really hadn't aged a day since they had been together fifteen years ago. He still looked as if he worked out daily at the gym and yet she hadn't seen him enter one even once since they've been together. Vampire genetics?

"Thank you. This is perfect, really." She picked up the cup of coffee, steam rising from the rim, and took a sip. "Oh, this is Heaven."

"And here I thought I brought you to Heaven with you calling me 'God' and everything."

Cait laughed, tossing her napkin at him. "*Men*. It's all about sex with you."

"Not always." Although his smile said it was exactly where his thoughts had been. He used the spatula to serve up a good-sized heaping of eggs and bacon that she couldn't possibly finish, then grabbed a couple slices of toast. "Eat. You won't die of malnutrition on my watch."

She used her fork to move around the contents of her plate before she took a bite of the fluffy scrambled eggs and moaned. "I guess I was hungrier than I thought. This is delicious. Thank you."

Grigore leaned forward on his elbows, clasping his hands before him on the counter and smiled. "Seeing you happy is thanks enough."

"Then why make me leave?"

His smile fled his face as quickly as it came. "Stop, Cait. This isn't a discussion we're going to have. Life gave us choices and we are who we are because of them. We can't change that now."

Cait had been correct. Grigore would never accept or allow her to walk away from her career by choice. She needed to come up with a damn good course of action. One he couldn't possibly argue with. One where they could both win.

"What's the plan to catch this guy?" she asked before taking a bite of bacon.

"You'll contact the media, let them know you're taking a few weeks off and lying low in Pleasant, Oregon. The town isn't that big and knowing my MC cut has been seen while I was employed by you, it won't take long for this psycho to find you. We're on Sons' territory now. He won't be able to hide among the masses. And when he shows his face, we'll get him. You leave the details to us."

"Meaning?"

"Meaning, how we choose to take care of this situation doesn't include you knowing the details."

Cait thought about that, knew without a doubt Grigore wouldn't likely allow this threat to walk away. "You can call the authorities."

"I could. But I told you before, we take care of our own."

She nodded slowly, not really wanting to know exactly what that meant. "And that's why you'll make me forget about you and vampirism when this is all over? You'll be taking care of your own?"

Grigore reached out and covered her small hand with his larger callused one. He loved her, that much was evident in his gaze, fueling her desire to find a way for them to stay together. "If there was another way, Sunshine, I'd take it. But there isn't. You have a responsibility to your fans to continue doing what you do, and I can't be a part of that."

"I know. But—"

"Eat. This conversation is over. Once we take care of your threat, you go back to your life. End of story."

"And you?"

"I'll go back to mine."

Lord, he made her angry. "Yes and remembering everything we did. Do you know how unfair that is?"

"You want the fucking truth?" Grigore righted himself, his face etched with anger. "You may think it's unfair. But the truth is I'll be missing you every fucking day. I won't forget one detail of your face as I brought you to orgasm, or how it felt to slide into your heat. I won't forget your smile when I did something to warrant it, or your laughter when something struck you as funny. But most of all, I won't forget that you love me. Because, damn it to hell, I know you do. Just as I'm in love with you. I always will be. No matter what happens, that won't fucking change. But it won't work, Cait. You and I both know it. When it's over, you'll go back to the hatred you had for me from walking out on you fifteen years ago. And knowing that will damn near kill me. So don't fucking talk to me about the unfairness of it."

Moisture again filled her eyes, but she refused to let him bring her to tears. The stubborn ass wouldn't allow her to give up her career for him, or find a way to make it work. Damn him for thinking he had to control everything, right down to choices that were hers to make. Damn him for knowing she loved him but refusing to accept it. And damn him for still wanting to walk away … again.

He may think he had the last word, but not this time. Once she figured a way out of this mess, she'd prove that. The last word would be hers. Love wasn't something you walked away from and she meant to prove it. Damn his stubborn hide anyway.

She rose from her stool, took her unfinished plate to the sink and set it down. "I'm tired, Wolf. I need to go lie down. You keep your bullheaded ass out here while I nap. When I wake up will be soon enough for me to contact the media. I've heard enough of your plans and opinions for the moment and I'd rather be alone."

Cait turned and stomped off to their shared bedroom, slamming the door.

CHAPTER SEVENTEEN

V LAD OPENED THE DOOR MARKED "SPECIAL AGENT JANELLE Ferrari" unannounced. Since his meeting with Sheriff Ducat hadn't resulted in getting him an audience with the special agent, he had to take matters into his own hands. In his way of doing things, he had scrambled the minds of those who had witnessed his entrance as well as the multi-camera feeds catching him in their lenses. Once he left there would be no recollection of seeing him and the cameras' feedback would be nothing but static.

He had spent years honing his skills, discovering new talents. In time, Kane and Kaleb, along with their brethren, would discover on their own new endowments with which their vampire genetics had gifted them. The mind was a powerful thing, most of which humans couldn't tap into. Vlad had learned long ago there were no limits to his vampire DNA.

There were certain abilities he kept to himself, aiding him in being not only the strongest but the most cunning living vampire. Not even his brother could hope to take him down. He hadn't lived this long by being foolhardy. This was one battle his brother wouldn't win. This time, Vlad meant to make his penance a permanent one.

"Excuse me?" The stunning woman he had first seen on the news stood from behind her desk and peered briefly over his shoulder, then turned her attention to him. "I'm sorry. Did we have an appointment? Apparently, someone failed in their job to announce your arrival. My afternoon was clear, so forgive me for being dumbfounded on how you arrived in a secured area."

He hadn't missed the fact her right hand drifted to the butt of her gun, holstered at her side. "At no fault of theirs. I let myself in."

One of her brows raised, her hand remaining where it was. "Funny. Normally, no one comes into this building without clearance. I fail to see how you got all the way back here on your own."

"Trust me, *iubi*. I'm far from normal."

"What did you call me?"

"*Iubi*. It's Romanian for love."

"I assure you I am not your love and you need to address me as Special Agent Ferrari. Now who the fuck are you and what do you want?"

Vlad slowly stepped forward as not to cause her further alarm and reached out his hand, which she ignored. Shaking his hand would have required her to remove her grasp from the butt of her pistol. *Smart woman.* He sat in one of the white leather chairs, flanking her large oak desk. Crossing a booted ankle over one of his knees, he leaned back and laced his fingers over his chest.

Janelle removed the gun from her side holster and laid it on her desk, keeping her hand firmly wrapped around the grip. Little did she know, Vlad could take the pistol from her before her finger so much as twitched on the trigger, and there wouldn't be a damn thing she could do to stop him. He saw no harm in allowing her the false sense of security. He'd much rather hold an amiable conversation. It certainly wasn't a hardship being in her presence. She was far more gorgeous than he originally thought, not to mention one of the most beautiful women he'd had the pleasure of meeting in over a century.

Vlad certainly wouldn't mind a few romps between the sheets with her. Or bent over this desk, for that matter. Too bad she was more focused on why he was here and not what he could do for her. Vlad wasn't one to beg but for her ... he might just make an exception.

"Who I am isn't important, it's the why that counts. You have a case you're working on. I'd like to know what information you've gathered."

Janelle laughed, most likely taking him for a flake. Since she wasn't about to share, he'd need to use a little *persuasion*. His eyes heated, allowing the blackness to consume them, not allowing the rest of his genetics to take over.

The special agent blinked and her brow pinched over the bridge of her nose. "What the hell?"

"Hear me now, Special Agent Ferrari. You'll answer my questions, and when I'm satisfied, I'll take my leave. You won't remember I was here. If you understand, nod your head."

Instead of doing as told, she narrowed her gaze. "What are you trying to accomplish? You certainly are special, aren't you? Get the hell out before I call security."

Dumbfounded, Vlad sat forward, bracing his palms on his knees. Never in all his years had his hypnotism not worked.

"What kind of information do you hope to get from me? Just so you know, I'm seconds away from calling security and having your ass arrested."

Vlad rubbed the stubble on his chin. "I am Vlad Tepes."

One of her brows raised. "As in, the Impaler? That's rich. Did you escape a psych ward or something? Maybe I should check the area hospitals for a missing patient."

He leaned forward, decreasing the space that separated them and placed a hand on hers, the one holding the gun grip. She tried to remove it, but found it impossible. He held her stare.

"You'll do no such thing."

Janelle shook her head, her free hand going to her temple, Vlad having used the scrambling technique this time. "I'll … ummm, what was I saying?"

Keeping his hand on hers, he prompted, "Tell me about the case involving the four cartel members missing their throats. What do you know?"

She blinked, attempting to shake the hold he had on her mind. "Nothing. Other than someone tried to tear their throats out. We have no finger prints, no suspects."

"You need to close this case."

"But—"

His grip tightened on her hand. "Close this case, Special Agent Ferrari."

"I … can't. It's not entirely in my hands."

"Then make a believer out of whoever needs to be convinced. This is obviously the work of a rival cartel. Let them fight amongst themselves. Am I clear?"

Blinking again, she repeated, "A rival cartel."

"Close this case."

"What about the media?"

"Convince them it was a vicious act by a rival."

Janelle tugged uselessly against his grip. "You're hurting me."

Her hand would be bruised, though it couldn't be helped. He could've scrambled her thoughts without touching her, as he had the others upon his arrival, but he worried about its effectiveness since hypnosis hadn't worked on this woman. Contact made his summons more effective.

"The four dead cartel members were committed by?" he asked.

"A rival cartel."

"You know this because?"

Bewilderment filled her gaze.

"An anonymous tip," he prompted.

Janelle repeated his words.

"You'll search no further because…"

Again, her gaze became befuddled.

"Not enough tax dollars. Move on to your next case."

She rubbed her temple again. "I need to move on."

"And me?"

"Who?"

"Exactly. I'm going to release your hand, get up, and walk out. You won't remember my being here."

Janelle took a deep breath, staring at the file in front of her. She closed it and set it aside. Vlad took the opportunity to rise and walk from the room. Once he was a safe distance from the building, he released the control he held over the people and the cameras. No one would know he had been there. The only thing Special Agent Janelle Ferrari would have as a reminder would be her sore gun hand. She likely wouldn't be able fire her weapon for a few days.

Vlad stepped among the throng of people until he reached the end of the building. No one would witness his racing through the streets, and into the trees at the end of the long drive. The human mind couldn't process anything faster than the speed of light.

Vlad had trouble shaking Janelle from his thoughts, or the fact she had been immune to his hypnosis. Although it would be foolhardy to pay her another visit, he wouldn't mind running into her again. Vlad wanted her beneath him in the worst way, his sporting of an erection laying proof to that.

His best bet would be to avoid Ms. Ferrari in the future, though a small part of him thrilled at the idea of going head-to-head with her again.

————

WHAT THE HELL HAD JUST happened? Moments ago, she had been looking through the case file of the deaths of the four LaPaz cartel members and then...

What?

She searched her memory, coming up empty-handed.

Janelle rubbed her temples, her gaze falling on her pistol lying on the desk. Hadn't that been holstered? She punched the TALK button on the speakerphone, connecting her with her administrative assistant.

"Special Agent Ferrari, can I help you?"

"Did anyone pass by your desk moments ago?"

"No, ma'am."

"So, no one came to my office?"

"I'm pretty sure I would've noticed someone."

"Huh... Okay, thank you."

She could swear that someone had been there. Janelle ended the connection and sat back, steepling her fingers beneath her chin. The case in the manila file she had been looking at was now shut, sitting at the corner of her desk. It was obviously the work of a rival cartel if her anonymous tip had been on the up-and-up. Her caller had known far too many details not to be trusted.

Funny, she couldn't remember the actual call. She pulled the file forward and flipped through the graphic pictures and annotations, noting nowhere had she documented the call.

Fingers back at her temples, she tried hard to tap into her psyche to help her recall the conversation, though to no avail. She couldn't completely deny the fact that she had received a tip either. This case was the brutal actions of one cartel disputing over another's territory.

Closing her eyes and breathing in deeply, she tried to pull forward her visions. Instead of recollecting the call, a man came to the forefront of her mind. One with long black hair and equally black eyes. He was large, muscular, standing nearly six-and-a-half feet tall. Maybe evidence had come in the way of this person.

She opened her eyes and zeroed in on the chair sitting across from her, where the man had been sitting according to her vision.

Something about him excited her in ways a man hadn't done in years. He was confident, sexy, and not intimidated by her in the least. Whoever he was, she meant to find him and get to the bottom of his visit.

Punching the intercom again, she asked, "Can you get me the camera feed for the last couple of hours?"

"I'll have security get you the clearance."

If the man had been here, he'd be on those feeds. No way had he gotten into the building unseen. Vlad the Impaler came to mind, though she had no idea why. Janelle trusted her visions as they were rarely wrong, but the freak show had been dead for centuries. Grabbing her laptop, she flipped it open and punched in her password. Typing into the Internet browser 'Vlad the Impaler,' the image that came up had the breath freezing in her throat. The man from her vision could be a twin to the ancient ruler, but looking as though he belonged in this era.

Her administrative assistant walked into her office, gaining her attention. "Security said they sent you the feeds from all of the cameras over the past hour. Funny thing? They're nothing but static."

CAITLYN LAID HER CELL PHONE on the scarred wooden bar, taking in a shaky breath. Anxiety had her strung tighter than a bow. Being proactive wasn't always the right move and poking the bear could have adverse effects, even if Grigore promised her his protection. She couldn't help it. Getting shot had made her more skittish than a rabbit staring down a python.

Looking up from the counter, she offered Grigore a tentative smile. "I don't suppose there's any turning back. I let my contact know I was taking time off in Pleasant, Oregon. It shouldn't be very hard to find us."

It wasn't only the phone call hinting her whereabouts to the media, but the fact that once this threat was dealt with and gone from her life, the man standing across the bar from her would be too. She tried not to think about it, knowing it would only bring more tears, tears she refused to allow Grigore to see. It was damn unfair of him to consider erasing her memories of them together, along with their resurfaced feelings. They hadn't slept together since their return to Pleasant. As a matter of fact, Grigore had been sleeping on the sofa since the night she stomped off to his bedroom like a two-year-old throwing a tantrum, slamming the door and effectively shutting him out of the room and her good nature.

Two days had gone by with them barely speaking to each other while the rest of the Sons seemed to be keeping their distance, no doubt giving them privacy. She supposed his MC brothers figured they had a lot to sort out, and they did, but not conversing was getting them nowhere. Looking at Grigore now, black T-shirt stretched over what she knew to be solid muscles, made her want to wrap herself around him and beg him for what they both wanted.

Sex, which had never been their issue.

This time around, it had been mind-blowing, and yet she wouldn't be left with enough memories in which to pleasure herself later, with him in mind. Sex with anyone else held no appeal, never really did. Grigore had officially ruined her for any other man, damn his sexy hide to hell and back.

Forget the media, forget the threat.

If that were even possible.

Not having sex with Grigore was becoming the immediate issue. He had barely touched her since they arrived, and now the phone call had become the elephant in the room, taking over her thoughts on the lack of intimacy.

"I'll let my brothers know we'll need to be on high alert. Someone will always be here with you and watching the club-house. We also have security cameras inside and out. After the place was bombed—"

"Bombed?" Her gaze widened. "Jesus! And you brought me here?"

He raised a palm. "Relax, Sunshine. That threat has been dealt with. Trust me, he's ash. Xander was offering India refuge when her ex came calling. He thought he was sending us a message by planting a bomb that put a pretty big-sized hole in the clubhouse, damn near taking Xander out in the process. When we rebuilt, we added the extra security. No one will sneak up on us again."

"Meaning we have no privacy."

Grigore ran a hand down his beard. Where she once saw heat, fire, and desire, she now only saw sadness. "It's probably for the best."

"For who? You?" Her tone raised in pitch. "Because I won't fucking remember anyway."

"Cait—" He reached for her hand but she jerked it away. "I'm not about to argue with you on this again. It won't change the end."

"I know, you've made that very clear." She hardened her jaw, angry with Grigore, angry with the Sons of Sangue and their stupid rules. "I don't get why Gabriela gets to know, why Kimber was allowed, and I'm not. It's not fair, Grigore. The thought of forgetting what've we've found again—"

"Stop it, Cait. I'm not about to rehash this with you. It is what it is. And it's best for you, whether you want to admit it or not." Grigore braced his hands on the bar, biceps bulging as he leaned in. "In both cases, the women stayed here in Pleasant. Kimber moved in with Rogue. Gabby lives here with Ryder. We've talked about this, Sunshine. You'll be leaving and the Sons can't allow the liability."

"So I'm a liability."

Hope died in her chest. They might as well hypnotize her now because the idea of forgetting Grigore was slowly killing her. Regardless of what she remembered or didn't, she knew she'd never love another. Grigore was it for her.

"You would be the only outsider who knew that vampires exist, Cait."

"Then I'll stay." Cait wasn't above begging. She loved Grigore, damn it. In truth, she'd never stopped. "I'll live here with you."

Grigore chuckled, though no humor reached his eyes. "The media would find you. Fuck, we just gave them your whereabouts. It wouldn't be long before one of my brothers or their mates were caught feeding, and then what?"

"You wouldn't have to hide anymore."

Caitlyn knew it was impossible, knew exposure would bring them nothing but harm. The human race would never allow vampires to live peacefully among them, their fears outweighing common sense. Leaving Grigore, though, wasn't an option for her. There had to be another way. She may have started this journey hating Grigore for leaving, but her re-emerging love for him nearly crippled her at the thought of returning to her old life without him in it.

"You know that's not possible, Sunshine. We'd be slaughtered. Not only would you have to go on without me, but you'd do so with the knowledge I was dead and you'd feel somewhat responsible. The Sons won't live in fear of being exposed. Rules are no outsider can know about us and for good reason."

Her cell phone chirped from the counter, thankfully interrupting what was sure to become another argument. Caitlyn picked it up and glanced at the screen. "Well, that certainly didn't take long."

"What it is it?"

She turned the screen so Grigore could read the text.

I know you're lying low. I was given your whereabouts, but I'll need your exact location when I land. Don't give up on our love. Let's talk.

"Looks like Tyler's on his way. I didn't give my insider at the magazine any specific information, but like we said, it won't take long for them to follow the Sons' tracks here. I suppose Tyler is too lazy to connect the dots and believes I'll be his guide."

"Funny how he's the first one to take notice. Do you suppose your person called him? If so, I'd refrain from using them in the future for any newsworthy events."

Caitlyn chuckled. "I suppose you're right. Tyler doesn't exactly have my best interests at heart. What should I tell him?"

"That you'll meet him after he lands. Don't give him any information about where you're staying. If he comes here without your direction, then I'd be hard-pressed to allow you to see him. If he's on the up-and-up, he'll wait for you to pick a location."

Of course, Grigore was right. Meeting Tyler in a public place was for the best. The only other person who knew exactly where she was staying was Ryan, whom she had yet to hear from. Caitlyn had to believe anyone else coming to the clubhouse didn't have good intentions. She typed out a quick response.

Text me when you land. I'll provide the meeting place.

Caitlyn hit send and glanced back at Grigore. "Now what?"

"We wait."

CHAPTER EIGHTEEN

T HE HAIR AT GRIGORE'S NAPE RAISED. FROM HIS VANTAGE
point in a corner booth of a coffee shop near the airport, he watched as Tyler walked through the door. Even had
he not seen the man, Grigore's senses would have picked up
that he was near. Caitlyn caught sight of him as well, her reaction evident in the stiffening of her spine. Grigore resisted
the urge to drape an arm across her shoulders and tuck her
into his side. In appearance, he was her bodyguard, nothing
more. Tyler wasn't supposed to think of him as a threat in the
romance department.

Seconds later, her ex spotted them, acknowledging Cait
with a tip of his fucking chin. Instead of heading straight over,
he approached the counter and stepped in line, waiting his
turn to order a cup of java. Grigore bet he took it with plenty
of cream and sugar. Nevertheless, Grigore was happy they
had a couple of minutes before the pretty boy injected himself
into their conversation.

Grigore placed his hand on one of her thighs, which were
covered by a pair of cream-colored slacks. He gave her a
squeeze. "You going to be okay?"

Cait drew in a deep, steadying breath. "You know, when I
broke up with him, I had hoped I'd never have to see him

again. He was that much of an ass. And yet, here we sit, wondering if he's the one who has the balls to pull a trigger."

The thought of this pantywaist doing so, let alone pointing a gun at someone, left him chuckling. "I doubt you'll find a pair of balls in those fancy studded jeans of his. If he's guilty, I'll bet my left nut he hired someone. What we witnessed at the last show took skill and planning, something pretty boy over there is no doubt lacking. If you want to get out of here at any time, just say the word. I can always interrogate him later."

As a matter of fact, Grigore would love a few minutes alone with the fuck. Then he'd bet Tyler wouldn't be bothering her again.

The corner of her eyes turned up at his suggestion. "He'd likely piss himself."

"You're probably right."

"What is she right about?" Tyler set down his mud-colored coffee and slid into the booth across from them.

"That you'd piss yourself." Grigore kept one hand flat on the table while the other stayed on Cait's leg, offering her support.

"Very funny, asshole." His glare turned to Caitlyn. "You had to bring him?"

"It's what a bodyguard does, Tyler. Follows me where I go. He's *supposed* to be by my side. You, on the other hand, are not."

"Then why agree to this meeting, if not to get back to-gether with me?"

"Seriously? Not happening, Tyler. Call it simple curiosity."

Tyler hid the anger filling his gaze by taking a sip of his coffee. Grigore was surprised his pinky didn't go airborne from the mug as he drank. Blinking a few times and pulling at the neck of his turtleneck sweater, he returned his focus to the woman he was hoping to get back in good graces with.

Wasn't going to happen.

"Look, Cait, can we at the very least have a conversation without the goon listening to our every word?"

Grigore hardened his jaw. He already abhorred this man without having been called a goon. For the life of him, he couldn't figure out what Cait had been doing with him in the first place. "Watch it, Tyler. Or I might be tempted to show you what a real asshole I can be."

"He stays." Cait drew Tyler's attention back and likely hoped to defuse the rapidly deteriorating conversation. "What has you traveling all the way to Oregon, Tyler, that couldn't be said on the phone?"

He reached across the table to grip Cait's hand, earning him a growl from Grigore. Tyler quickly withdrew. "I thought if you saw me, it would be much harder to turn your back on"— he cleared his throat, finger going back to the neck of his sweater—"us."

"There is no us, Tyler. And if memory recalls, there never really was. You were too busy fucking other Hollywood starlets while riding my coattails."

"I never—"

Her harsh laugh cut him off. "You can't deny what was all over the tabloids. Let me see, first there was Clara, from the romantic comedy you both starred in, which flopped. Then there was Bunny, whom your manager picked up and who is now a bigger star than you—that's got to hurt. And Ana, who kindly informed me she had fucked you backstage while I was on stage performing. Funny how none of them furthered their career by sleeping with you, well, other than Bunny, who, let's face it, has more talent than you."

"Jesus," Grigore muttered more to himself than to be heard. Why the hell had she put up with this ass? Not one, but three indiscretions. It wasn't as if his pretty looks were legendary. Maybe Tyler was better looking than him, but Cait's ex didn't hold a candle to half of Hollywood's leading men. Tyler was more famous in his own mind than he had ever been on the big screen.

"Excuse me." Tyler tapped a finger on the table aimed at Grigore. "No one was speaking to you. I suggest you keep your opinions to yourself."

"Look—"

Grigore squeezed Cait's thigh to keep her from going to his defense. He didn't need her singing his praises. "You're definitely looking for an ass whooping. And I'm about to hand it to you. I suggest you get back on topic, say what you came here to say, then take your sorry ass and head back to L.A. where you're barely tolerated."

The Adam's apple in Tyler's throat disappeared beneath the turtleneck line as he swallowed. As much as he tried to show bravado, Tyler's nerves were starting to get the best of him. Being subject of said ass-whooping probably didn't help. Grigore wasn't sure Tyler could be the one behind Caitlyn's threat. That took balls, which they had already established he didn't have. One thing was for damn sure, if he was guilty, he had hired someone to do the deed, which meant they could very well be sitting ducks. Something told Grigore, though, Tyler wouldn't want to be anywhere nearby when the trigger was pulled, further implicating himself in the possibility he wanted Caitlyn dead.

Tyler turned his attention back to Caitlyn and ignored Grigore's threats, that or he had actually decided to do as he was told. "Caitlyn, I'm sorry. I was young and dumb. I didn't know what we had at the time."

"Until it was too late." She huffed. "And it is. Tyler, if your only reason to meet with me was to talk me into getting back together, you've wasted your time."

One of his plucked brows rose. "You have someone new? I haven't heard that you're dating again."

Grigore again squeezed her thigh, hoping she didn't mention what was going on between the two of them. Tyler would sing like a canary and Grigore didn't want the publicity that would come with the situation.

"I'm single and happily so. Unlike you seem to think, I don't need a man in my life to make me happy."

He looked down at his cup of coffee, tracing the rim with his forefinger. "So there's nothing I can say to change your mind about us?"

"No, Tyler. There isn't."

Grigore almost felt sorry for him. He looked damn near on the verge of tears as his Adam's apple bobbed again in his throat.

"Then I guess there's nothing left to be said."

"I don't suppose." Cait laid her hand on Tyler's. "I'm sorry."

He glanced back up. "You'll regret this, you know."

Cait's lips turned down, more out of pity than sadness Grigore guessed. "No, I won't."

Her ex stood, glared briefly at Grigore then stormed from the coffee shop.

Grigore looked at Cait. "You okay?"

She nodded. "You think he's the one behind me being shot?"

"Honestly? No." Grigore didn't know why, but even though Tyler was a complete fuck-up, he didn't think he had it in him to be a killer. "I think he's a jerk and I'm not sure what you saw in his pansy ass."

Cait chuckled, bumping her shoulder against his side. "I can't even give you an explanation other than I was lonely."

She looked at him, her face sobering. Damn him to hell for not being able to offer to fix that for her. A woman as beautiful as her shouldn't be alone. But the idea of her with another man set a fire burning in his gut that he wasn't about to extinguish. When he walked out of her life this time, it was going to damn near kill him.

——

CAIT SAT ON A BARSTOOL fidgeting, her nerves getting the best of her. Grigore had picked up on her obvious jitters, evident in his frequent glances in her direction. But he kept his observation to himself, talking strategy with Ryder and Alexander, just a few yards away in the living area. Grigore meant well; she knew his number one priority at the moment was keeping her alive, which obviously was on the top of her list too. But they had completely different outcomes once the death threat was in the rearview mirror.

Cait wasn't having it. She'd be damned before she allowed him to send her away. She had already called her manager, Ryan, laying out her course of action. Caitlyn was planning on leaving the music business and retiring after the tour. This would be her last hurrah before disappearing from the public eye. The money she had made was more than enough to last a lifetime. What good was it if she were lonely and full of hate, missing the man who had stolen her heart?

Gabriela laughed at something Adriana said, shaking Caitlyn from her musings. India stood among the three of them, a warm glow about her, pregnant with Alexander's child. Grigore had told Cait about India's crazy ex and the path they had traveled to get here. They both looked so happy. If the two could overcome the obstacles put in front of them to find a forever love, then it was certainly possible for her and Grigore. Gabriela and Ryder as well had weathered a hell of a storm.

Caitlyn wasn't about to let her music career stop her from getting her forever with Grigore. Hell no. The man had another thing coming if he thought he could walk away from what they both desired. He tried to control her future, and at one time accomplished it, but no more. She could only imagine what it would feel like to bring a child into the world with the man she loved. Caitlyn wanted what India and Alexander had.

The house. The kids. The whole nine yards.

Grigore didn't know it yet, but he was going to be the one to give it to her, even if she had to shove the damn idea down his throat. Cait rubbed the area where the bullet had gone through. Hopefully, she lived long enough to make that happen.

From what Grigore had explained, the only way he could get her pregnant was if they were both vampires. India, having been turned, didn't appear any different from the other two women, Adriana still unaware that vampires existed. Would Gabriela have to leave her best friend, Adriana, behind once she agreed to become Ryder's mate? Adriana would note Ryder and Gabby didn't appear to age, making her wonder. Becoming a vampire meant leaving behind those you loved. Hopefully, Caitlyn wouldn't need to walk away from her mother, crushing her in the process. There had to be a way to keep her mother oblivious.

Glancing over at Grigore, he looked a few years older than the other two Sons, having come into his vampirism a little later in life. Caitlyn loved that about him, the slightly graying sides of his long hair to the white in his beard. It gave him character. He had always joked about her falling for an older man, though she cared little about the age difference. Cait loved the crow's feet accenting his eyes, the laugh lines surrounding his mouth partially covered by his whiskers, and the furrow lines on his forehead slashed by a scar that bled into his eyebrow. It all pointed to a life well-led and his fun-loving personality, that was before he fixated on sending her away.

Telling him she was leaving the music industry wasn't going to be easy and he'd likely try to shut her down. *Wasn't going to happen.* Caitlyn would wait until the others had gone home or retired to the other bedroom before she brought up the topic. Hopefully, he'd see reason. Either way, Caitlyn was more than ready to go to battle. Another glance at India and Caitlyn knew she would fight him tooth and nail for what she wanted, the one thing he had denied her so long ago.

My forever with Grigore.

"We'll be moving once we close on the house. Since no one is living there, they promised us it would be quick. Ryder loved it and there's a second master suite on the other end of the house for Adri. She's stayed in the hotel long enough."

"I don't mind." Adriana shrugged and took a sip of red wine. "There's free breakfast every morning."

Gabriela laughed. "Seriously? You can get free breakfast at Ryder's and my new coastal home, too, and wake up to a fantastic view every morning. What are you looking at from your hotel room?"

Adriana raised a brow and grimaced. "A parking lot."

"Exactly." Gabriela turned her attention to Caitlyn. "I do hope you're sticking around, Caitlyn. We'd love for you and Grigore to come by for dinner one night once we're settled."

Caitlyn smiled. With any luck, they'd be taking Gabriela up on her invitation. "I'd like that. Now, all we need to do is eliminate this threat against me so we can move forward."

"Let's hope that's soon. No more bloodshed."

"Speaking of…" India drew Gabriela's attention. "Xander told me you were worried the Sons might be involved in the slaughter of those four men in Eugene."

"I spoke to Brea about it, but I had hoped Ryder didn't know I was poking around in his business."

India chuckled. "You should know there are no secrets with the Sons. They gossip more than any women I know."

Gabriela looked briefly over her shoulder at Ryder. "I worry about the Sons butting heads with Mateo's men. And you should too, India. The Sons can't think to win if Mateo decides to go to war. They far outnumber us."

"We have our … strengths, but I understand. Just so you know, though, Xander said it wasn't their doing. Viper and Hawk fear it's the work of Vlad's brother, Mircea."

"Why on earth?"

"Because Mircea hates his brother and wants to hurt Vlad. Long story, but Vlad took his step-daughter from him." India's lips turned down. "You're right to worry, Gabby. Mircea could get the Sons and the cartel warring against each other because of his vendetta against his brother."

"Then he needs to be stopped. This is insanity."

"I couldn't agree more. Viper and Hawk are well aware of what could happen. They're working with their great-grandfather to find him. Vlad, Viper, and Hawk will find Mircea. He can't hide forever. He'll be eliminated."

"Let's hope you're right, India, and before Mircea stirs up the hornet's nest."

"Anyone speak to Gunner?" Adriana's cheeks blossomed red in her curiosity. "You know, in case the Sons need help from the Washington chapter."

Gabriela smiled and patted her best friend's hand. "You, my girlfriend, have it bad."

"It's a fair question." She wasn't able to look Gabby in the eyes. "I couldn't care less what that man is up to."

Leaning sideways, Gabby bumped her shoulder into Adriana's. "You keep telling yourself that."

India laughed, the humor twinkling in her eyes. "I could get Xander to call him for you, Adri."

"No." She wagged her finger at India. "Don't you dare."

Caitlyn smiled at Adrianna's razzing. Cait might not know who this Gunner was, but Adriana had an obvious thing for him if her reddened cheeks were any indication. Maybe Gabriela wouldn't have to leave her friend behind after all. If Gunner had a pair of eyes, no way he wouldn't find this Latina beauty stunning, making her another great addition to the Sons of Sangue family. Caitlyn hoped she would be around to see it all unfold one day.

Ryder stood and walked over to the group of women, his hands resting on Gabriela's shoulders. "Who wants to make a trip to the Blood 'n' Rave. I could use a little snack and some entertainment."

Caitlyn wasn't sure what a vampire thought of as a snack but she had a good idea. It wasn't long before all the women and men were headed down to the shores to Draven and Brea's nightclub, leaving the clubhouse to Grigore and her. Her jitters returned tenfold.

Grigore approached, bracing a hand on the bar on either side of her, hemming her in. "Spill."

"What on earth are you talking about?"

He chuckled, leaning down until their noses nearly touched, amplifying her own kind of hunger. They still hadn't made love since arriving in Oregon and it was getting damn maddening. If it wasn't for the need to tell him her plan, she'd be dragging his ass to that big bed of his they had yet to share.

"You've been sitting here stealing glances at me all night. Had I scented your desire then, as I do now, I wouldn't be so worried. But you look jumpier than a virgin in a prison rodeo. So spill. What the hell has you all tangled up, Sunshine?" He used one of his hands to brush a stray hair from her messy bun behind one of her ears. "Anything to do with your earlier phone call to Ryan?"

"It does." She wet her lips, drawing his gaze downward. His gaze heated, which might go a long way in ending their dry spell. "I have an idea on how to fix this situation."

"Really? How do you plan to catch this guy?"

"Well, actually … I'm leaving that to you and the Sons. I was speaking about something else." She twiddled her fingers in her lap, having no idea how Grigore would react. She hoped he'd be thrilled and see beyond the immediate threat. "I'm leaving the music industry."

"What?" He stepped back, his scarred brow inching up. "Like hell."

"Grigore, please—"

"I didn't leave you behind fifteen years ago for you to throw it all away now that you're at the top of your career." He jammed his hands into his hair and stepped back. "You have fans, responsibilities."

"But I don't have you."

"I won't be the reason you later regret losing all of this."

"Don't you see? You gave me fame and fortune by leaving, even if my choice would have been different. This time, I'm the one making the choice. And I choose you. I'm leaving behind my music and nothing you say will change my mind, Wolf. I love you. I never stopped."

Grigore gripped her biceps, pulling her from the stool. He leaned down, his face precariously close to hers. "I. Will. Not. Be the reason. Cait, this is non-negotiable."

"It's already done."

"You can undo whatever you've done."

"No, I won't. I already told Ryan. He's keeping it on the down-low until this tour is finished. Then we'll make an announcement on my retirement."

"It won't fucking matter, Cait." His grip tightened, though not painfully. "The press will still hound you. You'll still be in the spotlight."

She squared her shoulders. "I will, for the time being. I can't deny that. But they'll eventually tire when there is no news. We can see each other in secret. When it all dies down, I'll return here and become your mate."

"I didn't fucking ask you."

That hurt. Deep down she knew he loved her, even if he didn't say it back moments ago. Grigore was still trying to do what he thought was right. Not this time. "You didn't ask, but you will."

He shook his head, released her and stalked around the bar, putting it between them. Cait turned and braced her hands on the top.

"You will not dictate my life, Wolf. I'm retiring, no matter what you say. When the media quiets down, I will come back and you damn well better not have found another girlfriend."

A small grin inched up the left side of his beard. "Jealous much?"

"Damn straight."

"You don't know what you're giving up. I can't let you."

"Not your choice this time, big guy."

He took a deep breath and let it out slowly. "I should've gone to the Rave with the rest of the guys."

"Why? So you can avoid any conversation that ends with how you really feel?"

"And what's that, Sunshine?"

"That you love me."

"Not an issue. You want me to say it? It's never been my problem. I love you so damn much there will never be another woman for me. Happy?"

"Don't push me away."

"It's for your own fucking good. You don't want this life, Cait. It's not all cocktails and parties. We're an MC. Life can be dangerous. You heard the talk about the MC getting mixed up with the cartel. Or did you somehow tune that out?"

"My life isn't worth living without you. I don't care about any of that, I care about being with you."

"I live a quiet life, Cait. The media—"

"—will get bored," she finished for him. Cait walked around the counter and placed a hand on his cheek. "Don't send me away, Wolf. My heart won't take it."

"Your heart won't know if I erase your memory."

Cait gritted her teeth, stomping her foot. Yes, she did. "Damn you, Grigore. I'll get my way, you son of a bitch. One way or another."

And she would, Caitlyn was determined to make it happen. If she had to, she'd enlist the other mates to help. This was one fight Grigore had no shot of winning.

CHAPTER NINETEEN

THE FULL MOON CAST ITS EERIE GLOW OVER THE NEARLY empty parking lot. Two safety lights were situated on either side of the asphalt, one bulb either burned out or broken at the far end. Kaleb, Kane, and Ryder hunkered down behind a half wall hemming in the lot of the little coastal motel just off of Highway 101.

The quaint inn wasn't much in the way of fancy facilities and definitely not Mircea's style, nor a place they'd have thought to look for the ancient vampire and his nefarious sidekick. Thankfully, luck had been on their side. The Sons' Prospect, Lefty, following his return from Pittsburgh, had been bar-hopping with Chad, a co-worker of Kimber's, when they had come across the primordial and his mate.

Lefty had spotted the pair, taking nourishment from a couple of drunken sots in the alley outside one of the seedier taverns in Florence. Since Lefty had yet to be turned, there wasn't a vampire scent to cause Mircea concern. Lefty had followed Mircea and Nina from afar to the motel and promptly called Kane with the pair's whereabouts. Mircea and Nina inhabited Room 10 at the farthest end of the building where, according to Lefty, they were still in residence.

Waves crashed against the shore across the highway, a strong breeze rustling Kaleb's overlong hair. The motel rooms faced the Pacific, and with the three of them standing downwind, Kaleb hoped the winds carried their scent away from Mircea. Chances were, even with the air current aiding in their cover, Mircea might already be aware of their presence. There wasn't much they could do to hide the vampire scent from a primordial. Kaleb tipped his nose, catching the slightest whiff on the coastal breeze of both Mircea and another, whom he expected to be Nina, telling him Lefty had been correct. The two were still within the dwelling.

"They're definitely here," Kaleb said as he looked at Kane and Ryder.

"We can't waste our time chit-chatting then, Hawk. We need to move before they give us the slip."

"You're right, Ryder. But we can't go in all Hell's blazing either. It could be a trap." Kaleb's jaw hardened. "Too bad we don't have Lefty to scope out the unit."

"I stand by my reason for sending him and Chad on their way," Kane said. "It would have been too dangerous. We couldn't chance their human lives. Mircea and Nina are lethal and not to be trusted."

"Agreed, Viper. Vlad might not be happy about leaving him out, but we didn't have time to alert him."

Ryder chuckled. "You never know what that old man is up to."

"Don't let him hear you say that." Kane shared in the humor. "He'd likely clock us all. Besides, Hawk is right, we can't chance losing his brother by waiting for his arrival. Vlad stopped me from ending the motherfucker's life before. No one will stop me from taking it today."

"What's the plan?" Ryder asked.

"Mircea will be expecting Viper and me, that is if he has scented our arrival," Kaleb said. "I doubt you're on his radar. No offense, Ryder."

He smiled. "None taken."

"Viper and I will walk right up to the fucking door. No sense trying to sneak up on the cagey bastard when he'll probably be waiting on us. He'll think he and Nina can take Viper and me. His ego won't allow him to believe otherwise. Once we get them outside and in the open, you grab Nina. Take no chances, Ryder, take her swiftly. She may have his primordial blood, but it won't be a match for you being a true blood primordial. Besides, she's newly turned."

"Got it, Hawk. I'll come around from the backside. You lure them out the front. She'll be dead before she even knows I'm there."

"I get Mircea, Hawk." Kane's eyes darkened. "This isn't up for discussion. Vlad deprived me. He's mine."

"You got Raúl, you get Mircea." Kaleb raised his hands. "You get all the fucking fun. Fine. He's all yours, brother. Unless you need my assistance, of course. It wouldn't be the first primordial I took out."

"Let's hope it's our last, Hawk. We don't need more rogue vampires forcing us to do damage control."

"On the count of three, Viper and I'll head that way." He pointed to the nearly empty parking lot. "Ryder, you circle around back. We'll lure them to the side of the building and out of sight from traffic and onlookers. There is a large brush to the side of the building we can use for cover. If this goes our way, we should have two dead vampires in very short order. We'll call Lefty, get him to bring around the box truck, and load their bodies to be ashed back at the clubhouse."

"Sounds like a solid plan," Kane said. "Let's go get us a couple of primordials."

Kaleb ticked off the count of three on his fingers. Ryder turned and headed for the back of the motel, while Kane and Kaleb jogged toward the door marked with the number 10. By now, Mircea was well aware of their presence. These units had no windows on the backside, so they either had to come out the door and greet Kaleb and Kane head on, or slip through the side window, at which they'd encounter Ryder. There was no other way out except to drive straight through the fucking wall.

The closer they came to the unit, the stronger the vampire scent became. Kaleb was happy to know they weren't going to have to chase down the sons of bitches. His only fear was walking into a trap. Mircea was lethal and shouldn't be taken lightly.

Before they reached the door, it swung open. Nina stood in the doorway, fangs bared, eyes black. Her white dress flowed about her ankles, making her look like an angel from Hell. Her hands looked like talons, her red fingernails sharpened to points. She wasn't about to go down without a fight. Kaleb caught her attention, hoping to coax her from the door and give Kane a clean line of sight into the interior. Mircea had yet to make an appearance. The coward had sent Nina out for the slaughter, maybe hoping to draw their attention from him.

Like lightning strikes, Kaleb reached out and gripped her by the wrists, but not before her claws raked his cheek, drawing first blood. Kaleb yanked her back against his chest, anchoring her with his forearm, holding onto her with primordial strength. Nina was stronger than he had anticipated, newly turned or not.

She kicked at his shins, her heels thumping hard enough to fracture one of his tibias, damn near causing him to drop. Kaleb hissed. Her claws sank into his forearm, making mincemeat of his muscles. Fuck, she was a wild one. He tugged her to the left of the building, hoping to find Ryder before she did any more damage. He needed to get back to Kane, fearing Mircea would either outsmart or out-strengthen his twin.

Ryder waited behind the brush, eyes feral, muscles lethal and waiting for the hellcat. He could have her. Kaleb'd had his fun. Ryder wasted no time, grabbing Nina by the sides of head and twisting. Bones snapped, blood spurted. Nina screamed just before her head snapped free of her body. Her skull and hair dangled from Ryder's fist while her body went limp against Kaleb's forearm. Both were covered in her blood but the bitch was dead.

Kaleb dropped her body, turned and headed for Kane. Just as he and Ryder cleared the corner, Mircea jumped through the window, sending glass shards tinkling to the asphalt. The tick of a clock could be heard seconds before an explosion sent both of them flying back through the parking lot, the smell of burnt flesh wafting to their noses.

"Motherfucker." Kaleb struggled to his feet, his gaze taking in the nearly obliterated unit. Not much was left standing of what was once Room 10. "Viper!"

Before Kaleb could get to the rubble, Kane crawled out from beneath one of the walls, stumbling as he tried to stand. Ash floated around him in a cloud of smoke. But Christ, he was alive.

Blood ran from Kane's ears as he shook his head. "Did you see which way Mircea went?"

Kaleb rolled his eyes and slapped his brother on the shoulder. "He lives to see another day, bro. We need to heal before chasing him down."

Ryder wiped the soot from his hands on his jeans, though it did little good. "Well, at least I held up my end of the bargain."

Kane chuckled. "That you did, brother."

"Smart ass." Sirens sounded in the distance. Kaleb attempted to take in a deep breath of oxygen, only to cough from the toxic fumes. "Let's get the bitch's body back to where we hid the motorcycles and get the hell out of here before the authorities arrive. Once we get back to the bikes, we call someone to bring the box truck."

"I'm not so sure I can ride my bike back." Kane held his side. "I'll put my motorcycle in the back of the truck and ride back to the clubhouse with them. We might not have caught Mircea … this time, but we got his bitch."

"What's this we?"

Kaleb clocked Ryder against the back of his head, causing the three of them to laugh as they gathered up what was left of Nina.

"RYAN'S COMING OVER."

"Good, then you can let him know you ain't quitting," Grigore grumbled, his lips turning down. A black T-shirt stretched across the muscles of his back, his spine stiff and his shoulders straight. It was pretty apparent he wasn't thrilled with the news.

Stubborn like an ox.

Funny, Grigore thought he could order her around. Trouble was she wasn't listening. Her mind was made up and nothing Grigore said or did would change the end result. When the tour was complete, she was walking away and she didn't need his permission to do so. It was about time Caitlyn got her way.

In no mood for an argument, she asked, "You think you can make yourself scarce?"

Grigore turned on his barstool and folded his arms over his chest, leveling his unyielding gaze on her. "Come again?"

"You heard me, Wolf. This meeting has nothing to do with you and is none of your concern."

"The hell it isn't." His bark echoed about the empty club-house. No doubt the man was used to getting his way. Well, not this time.

"You're my business, Sunshine." His tone brooked no argument.

Annoyance itched up Caitlyn's spine, heating her face and ears. Grigore could be exasperating at times. Not one to stand down either, she said, "Ryan has some things he wants to discuss with me in private. You think you can give me that?"

"I haven't left your side since this began, Sunshine. And until we catch this piece of shit, I'm not budging. You can talk about whatever the hell you want, but it will have to be done with me here."

Hard—fucking—headed.¬

"Stop being so inflexible. I'm only asking for an hour."

"I'll go to my bedroom and you can have the rest of the clubhouse."

Not happening, because, with his enhanced hearing, he'd catch every word said. If Caitlyn tried to reason with Ryan about her retiring while Grigore listened, the two of them would gang up on her. She needed to talk to Ryan alone where Grigore couldn't insert himself into the conversation.

"Why not go to the Blood 'n' Rave you told me about? You haven't fed since our arrival. You have to be starving."

"We don't necessarily starve or have hunger pangs. We take on the death chill. Our skin pales and becomes more translucent."

Grigore held out his hands in front of him, his veins very much visible through his ash-colored flesh. Pale didn't begin to describe the pallor of his skin. He was already taking on the death chill by the looks of his hands. Hopefully, he'd take her suggestion, leaving her in Ryan's care for the time it took to get to the Rave and back. Caitlyn didn't like the idea of him sucking on another woman's neck, but it would buy her time to talk to Ryan without his interference.

"You need sustenance, Grigore."

A growl rumbled up from deep in his chest. "Nice try, Sunshine. I'm still not leaving."

"Grigore." She stomped her foot.

"If something were to happen—"

"I'll be fine with Ryan here."

"I'll call Lefty—"

"I don't need a babysitter and I couldn't be safer anyway with all of the security and cameras you have around here. It's like Fort Knox. Besides, I have my cell should anything come up. And … I promise to keep all the doors locked."

Grigore's cell rang. He pulled it from his pocket and hit the answer. "What's up, Viper?"

Caitlyn couldn't hear the conversation on the other side of the call, but considering Grigore's deep scowl, she could tell it wasn't good. "Jesus! Where the hell is Lefty? … Give me fifteen minutes and I'll be there."

"What's wrong?"

"Is Ryan coming alone? No Josh?"

Grigore had mentioned his mistrust of her crew manager in the past, but Caitlyn had never really encountered any problems with Josh until Grigore's arrival in Detroit. If Josh had a problem with his ego or some weird fixation on her, he wouldn't likely have been happy with her newly hired body-guard.

"No Josh. Just Ryan. Why?"

"I need to get the box truck over to Kane and Kaleb. It appears they can't get a hold of Lefty. There was a bombing."

Caitlyn sucked in a breath. "Is everyone okay?"

He nodded. "Viper took a pretty good hit, can't ride his motorcycle. I need to take the box truck over and bring back Viper and his bike. I won't be much more than a half hour."

"I promise not to open the door for anyone."

Grigore scrubbed his beard, no doubt considering leaving Caitlyn alone with Ryan. Obviously, he wasn't about to feed now, so she hoped he might later use her for nourishment, likely ending their dry spell. The stubborn ass seemed hell-bent on avoiding her and sleeping on the damn sofa.

"When is he arriving?"

Caitlyn looked at her wristwatch. "Any minute."

"I'll wait until he gets here. I won't be long."

Not that she wished any of his MC brothers harm, but this accident worked in her favor. No one in the Sons of Sangue needed to be privy to her business, not even Grigore.

A knock caught both of their attention. Grigore stood, his booted feet clomping on the wood-planked floor as he made his way to the entrance. Opening the door, he stood back and allowed Ryan to pass, but not without a glower. Caitlyn could see the argument in Grigore's gaze before he yanked a set of keys from the hook beside the entrance.

"Go, we'll be fine."

"Don't fucking open the door for anyone other than a Son or one of their mates."

One of Ryan's brows inched up. "Mates?"

"Sorry … wives." Grigore scratched his nape. "Old MC term. I'll be back in less than an hour. Lock the deadbolt and stay here—"

"Go. Your MC brothers need you. I'm not going anywhere," Caitlyn shooed him out the door. "I promise to follow all of the rules: lock the door, don't allow anyone to come in, call if I need you. We'll be fine, Grigore."

Grigore scowled at Ryan, though Caitlyn wasn't sure why. The two had always gotten along until today. "She gets hurt, I'm holding you responsible."

"Duly noted." Ryan's reply seemed cold. Had something been said between the two she wasn't aware of? "I won't be long."

"Stay with her until I get back."

Ryan gave a brief nod and Grigore walked out the door, shutting it behind him. Caitlyn padded across the floor and turned the deadbolt, no doubt Grigore waiting for the sound of it to click into place. Shortly thereafter, the old box truck engine rumbled to life.

Ryan stood with his hands stuffed into his jacket pockets as he rocked back on his heels. "What did you say to get him to leave?"

Caitlyn waived her hand in the air. Ryan didn't need to be privy to their argument. "Not much. Now, what did you want that couldn't be discussed with Grigore present?"

Ryan smiled, though not his usual jovial one. This one seemed a bit hostile. The hairs rose on her forearms. Suddenly, she wasn't so sure she should've sent Grigore on his way without her. Caitlyn shook off the trepidation. Surely, she was just being paranoid due to all of Grigore's worrying.

Caitlyn cleared her throat. "Is something wrong, Ryan?"

"Why would you ask? Could it be because you're fucking me over for a lowlife?"

Her brow furrowed. "Excuse me?"

Ryan pulled his right hand from his pocket, holding a pistol aimed at her chest. His lips thinned and the mask of familiarity fell from his face. He no longer looked like the manager she had worked with the last two and a half years, but a man filled with malice.

She took a step back, toward the entrance. "What the hell, Ryan? What's going on here?"

"Stop where you are." Ryan pulled his other hand from his pocket, and with a loud clack, pulled back the slide and chambered a bullet. "You're no longer calling the shots, sweetheart. From here on out, I'll be the one in charge and you'll do as I say."

Her heart doubled its beat. "What are you going to do? Kill me?"

"That depends on you. You do as I say and you'll live."

Caitlyn pinched the bridge of her nose, trying to ward off the hysteria bubbling up from her chest. Rising panic would not help her reason with Ryan. She needed to stay calm, focused if she were to outsmart him.

Taking a deep breath, she looked back at him. "Put away the gun and let's talk like a couple of adults."

"Place your cell phone on the bar." He used the barrel of the gun to indicate her action.

Doing as she was told, she took the phone from her pocket and laid it face down on the surface.

"Grab your purse." He motioned to her handbag on the table near the sofa. Caitlyn did as instructed, slipping the strap over her shoulders. "Shoes next."

She slipped her feet into her flip-flops left by the door. Maybe the cameras had microphones and she could at the very least get a destination out of him. The more she kept him talking, the more Grigore would know when he found her missing.

"Where are you taking me?"

"Open the fucking door."

"Not without you telling me—"

Ryan grabbed her by the throat with his free hand and pushed her back against the wall. "Open the fucking door, Cait!"

Once he dropped his hold, she gasped for air. Terror gripped her gut. If she didn't do as Ryan said, she feared he'd end her here, giving her no chance to reach Grigore. Cait flipped the deadbolt, turned the knob and opened the door. The warm evening breeze greeted her, doing little to heat the chill freezing her insides.

"Get in the car."

Caitlyn spotted a blue Ford near the door, no doubt a rental. She approached the vehicle and opened the door. A quick glance around the parking lot told her she had gotten what she had asked for ... they were completely alone.

Why did Grigore have to pick now to actually listen to her?

Ryan motioned with the pistol again. "Get in the fucking car, Cait, the driver's side."

She circled the vehicle, opened the door and slipped into the leather interior, shutting herself inside. Her opportunity for action was running out. If they left the clubhouse, Grigore would never find her in time. Grabbing the steering wheel with both hands, she focused on breathing, hoping to keep her wits about her. Cait knew this man, worked side-by-side with him. Surely, he'd listen to reason. Ryan slid into the passenger side and shut the door.

"Start the car."

She glanced at him, swallowing the mammoth-sized lump threatening to cut off her oxygen. "Ryan—"

"Shut the fuck up, Cait!" He jammed the barrel of the gun against her temple. "Drive."

Reaching with shaken fingers, she turned the key and started the engine. Grabbing the gear shift between them, she placed her foot on the brake and put the car into reverse. Her blood pounded in her ears as her heart raced. There didn't appear to be an ounce of sanity left behind Ryan's insidious gaze.

What have I gotten myself into?

Grigore would no doubt give her hell for forcing him to go against his better judgment. She hoped she lived long enough to hear it. He had been correct to trust no one ... including the one person who was supposed to have her back in business and most aspects of her life.

Putting the car into drive, she pulled onto the road, heading away from the coast and farther away from Grigore.

CHAPTER TWENTY

GRIGORE PARKED THE BOX TRUCK TO THE BACK OF THE clubhouse and cut the engine. The blue Ford Ryan had arrived in was gone, making him wonder why Ryan hadn't stuck around for Grigore's return as requested. He wanted to give Caitlyn's manager a beatdown for the disrespect. What the hell was up with Ryan anyway? Before today, they had seemed on the same page and got along well enough. If Ryan thought he was out to steal Caitlyn away from her career, he couldn't be further from the truth.

Two motorcycles sat near the entrance, telling him Kaleb and Ryder had beat them back, leaving him feeling better about her manager hitting the road. At least he hoped Caitlyn had been taken care of in his absence. If anything had happened to her, Ryan's life wouldn't be worth spit when Grigore got done with him.

He hadn't been happy about leaving Caitlyn in the first place, but his brothers had needed him. The death chill had started to take over, but his need to feed was something that could wait. Maybe even using Caitlyn again for nourishment if need be, likely ending in the two of them in bed.

Not that sex with her no longer held appeal.

Hell no. He could think of little else, his desire plaguing him twenty-four-seven. Even cold showers weren't working,

269

nor was his nightly jacking off in them. Nothing could take the place of being wrapped by Caitlyn, heart, body, and soul.

Sending her away in the end, though, would be easier on them both if he abstained. Loving Caitlyn had never been the issue and he needed to do right by her. Grigore didn't belong in her life any more now than he did fifteen years ago. Apparently, he addled her brain whenever they were together and she made damn stupid decisions, like now and wanting to quit the music business. *Like hell, she would.* He didn't leave fifteen years ago so she could go and piss it all away.

Caitlyn had built an extraordinary life without him and she'd damn well return to it. With help of hypnotism, she'd go right back to hating him, even if the thought of it nearly killed him.

Grigore stepped down from the truck and slammed the door, heading for the clubhouse with Kane following close behind. Opening the door and striding in, he found Ryder in the living area, drinking whiskey.

"Where's Hawk?" Grigore asked.

"Hawk's in the shower. You drive that truck like an old man, Wolf. We beat you back by ten minutes." Ryder looked as if he had already cleaned up, his hair wet and slicked back. "It sucks Mircea got away, but damn glad his bitch didn't. One down, one to go."

"At least we won't have to worry about her," Grigore said.

"Someone call Vlad?"

"I did, Ryder," Kane said. "On the way here. Seems he was a bit pre-occupied, mumbled on about some DEA special agent that was becoming a thorn in his side. It wasn't much of a surprise to him that Mircea got away. On the other hand, I think he might have even been happy about it. No doubt Vlad wants to do the honors when it comes to his brother."

"I'm sure he does." Grigore looked around the otherwise empty clubhouse. He couldn't detect Caitlyn's scent, but that didn't mean she hadn't retired to his room. "Where's Cait?"

Ryder shrugged. "Thought she was with Ryan."

Grigore's heart battered his sternum. "She wasn't to leave with him. She's not here?"

Ryder stood, his expression darkening. "No one was here when we arrived."

Jamming a hand through his hair, he growled. "Fuck!"

Heads were going to roll, specifically Ryan's. He pulled the cell from his pocket, slid the screen to his contacts and punched on Caitlyn's name. Her phone started to ring from where it lay on the bar, drawing their gazes. Grigore hit END, then quickly selected Ryan's name from his contacts, which went straight to voice mail.

Kaleb exited the bathroom, rubbing his wet curls with a towel. "What's going on?"

"Caitlyn's missing." Anger, fear, and guilt sluiced through Grigore, damn near incapacitating him. "Why the hell would she leave without her phone? I told her to stay put until I returned. Ryan was supposed to be keeping an eye on her while I brought the truck to you guys."

Grigore caught his brothers up on the events leading to his departure, and his entrusting her to Ryan's care. Christ, he should have made her go with him.

"Something's wrong."

Ryder snapped his fingers, then glanced up at one of the new cameras installed in the corner of the room, aimed at them. "Let's check the feed. See what happened while you were gone. There's a camera facing the lot outside too. It should give us a time that they left and let us know what direction they headed."

Ryder circled the bar and opened the laptop on the counter. In short order, he had the video feed running over the past hour. Grigore watched as he left the clubhouse and Caitlyn dead bolted the door as directed. What happened next made his blood run cold.

"Motherfucker!"

Grigore listened to the feed and watched the scene unfold, until the point Ryan followed Caitlyn out the door. Ryder switched camera feeds and they watched the blue Ford pull out of the parking lot and head away from town.

Shutting the laptop, Ryder asked, "Any idea where they might have gone?"

Kaleb placed a hand on Grigore's shoulder. "Anything Ryan may have said in the past that might give you an inkling what he's thinking or where he might have taken her?"

"No fucking clue." Grigore ran both hands through his hair, pulling the long waves away from his face, every inch of him scared spitless. "I'm sure if he has a hotel room anywhere near, he didn't use his real name. Christ, I have no fucking idea... Wait!"

"What is it?" Kane asked.

"It's a long shot, but Caitlyn's home isn't in Detroit where we originally met. Her mother lives there, but Cait has a place in Crescent City, California. Cait told me it's just off South Pebble Beach Drive. Straight down Highway 101."

"If we leave now, we can get there in a little over three and a half hours," Ryder said.

"Or we can beat them there if we fly."

"Surely you don't mean catch a plane, Wolf."

Grigore backhanded Kaleb's shoulder. "I mean bury the speedometer needle, Hawk. If they're headed there, maybe we'll catch them before they arrive."

"Ryder, you go with Wolf," Kane said. "Hawk and I will take a different route down, just in case they didn't take 101. I'll get Lefty over here if I can get a hold of his dumb ass to clean up the box truck and make sure Nina's ashed."

"I got this. My screw up." Grigore picked up Cait's phone and pocketed it. "You guys can take care of Nina."

"No fucking way, Wolf." Kane leveled his gaze. "We're brothers first and we have your back. We're better off in numbers. More eyes on the road means bettering our chances of catching them. You two head out. Hawk and I won't be far behind."

"Thanks, man," Grigore said, meaning it.

He wasn't used to leaning on anyone, but he'd welcome their assistance. Finding Caitlyn before Ryan decided to use that gun he pulled on her was going to take all the help he could get.

CAITLYN DROVE ALONG THE COASTAL highway, heading for her home in Crescent City. Normally, she would've enjoyed the drive and beautiful scenery. Nothing was more tranquil than watching waves crash along the shore, but today she was anything but calm. She didn't suppose they'd be staying at her home overlooking the Pacific long enough to enjoy the views. The truth of it, she wasn't sure she'd ever see her home again after today.

Ryan was no fool. He had to know her house was the first place Grigore would look for them. They'd stop long enough to pick up her last will and testament that he had insisted she had her lawyer draw up about a year ago. The will had split her assets sixty-forty, with the larger share going to her mother. At the time, she had no other family and didn't see the problem investing in Ryan's future should something tragic happen to her. She had been a fool to trust Ryan, and because of that, he was about to inherit millions if he got away with her murder.

Good Lord, she was about to become a story on 20/20.

At the time Ryan brought up the subject of a will, she thought he had been wanting to protect not only her mother, but his future as well should something had happened to her, leaving him unemployed. Caitlyn hadn't seen the harm in giving him some of her amassed fortune, after all, he had been there with her the last couple of years, diligently working to get her the best contracts, new record deals, and setting up her world tours. Although she had already been a star at the time her last manager had tragically died in a car accident, she had considered it a blessing to have found Ryan so willing to quickly step in and offer his help and experience.

Too quickly. That should have raised warning flags.

Now she had to wonder if her last manager's car crash had been an accident after all. His brakes had given out going downhill on a winding road, where he crashed through the guardrail and into a large tree. He had left behind a wife and three kids. Although Caitlyn had made sure they were taken care of, money hardly made up for the loss.

What a fool I've been.

"You're awfully quiet over there. What are you thinking about in that pretty little head of yours?"

She briefly turned her glare on him. "Nothing you'd care about, I'm sure."

"Try me."

Even though it was foolish to ask, she had to know. What would it matter if she knew the truth? He planned to kill her, she was certain. "My last manager, did you mess with his brakes?"

"You wouldn't be where you are today if I hadn't, you ungrateful bitch."

"He had kids, Ryan. A family!"

"He was in my way," he hissed.

"In your way?" She glanced at him again. "Seriously? So you just tampered with his brakes?"

"Relax. I didn't do it. I didn't possess the skills to make it look like an accident. I paid someone else to do it for me."

Her heart damn near stopped. "Someone else is aware of your depravity?"

"After the deed was done, instead of giving him the promised cash, I shot him, then buried him deep in the woods, never to be found."

Her fingers tightened on the steering wheel, whitening her knuckles as she stared straight ahead. Why the hell had she not seen this side of Ryan? He was damn good at masking the crazy.

"That's cold, Ryan."

"I haven't gotten this far by thinking small, sweetheart. Worrying about someone else is a waste and does nothing to further my goals."

"Which are?"

He shrugged again.

"Why go to all this trouble?" Her gaze flicked back to him and the gun laying on his thigh, his hand still wrapped around the grip. "For the money?"

"Not at first." He began nervously tapping the flat of the pistol against his thigh. "I did it for you, for us. We are meant to be together."

Her brow furrowed. "Us?"

"There was supposed to be an us, Caitlyn. Aren't you listening? No, you never do. Apparently, you missed the memo about us because you were too busy parading around losers like Tyler, who didn't have your best interests at heart."

He slapped the gun so hard off his thigh, she feared it accidentally discharging. "I had your best interest at heart. I watched you for years but you never noticed me. I went to nearly every fucking show early in your career, spending all my hard-earned money. And for what? You didn't know I existed!

"That's when the plan formed in my head. I was tired of managing small-time local bands, wasting my talents. I knew I could take you places. Make you a ton of money. And it worked like a dream. I stepped right into the position vacated by your manager. Only you were supposed to fall in love with me... But you didn't, did you? I had to devise another plan."

What. The. Ever-living. Hell? "You sent the death threat?"

"When I realized you were never going to love me, yes, I talked you into the new will, waited a year, and then sent the threat. It was all supposed to go according to plan, but you fucked everything up by trying to quit the business, quit me. And for what? A loser, deadbeat biker?"

"How did you pull off shooting both of us? You were near us at the time of the first shooting."

"Just like before, I hired someone. Although, the fool wasn't worth paying him the money I owed. How do you fucking miss twice? Jesus!" He shook his head, clearly agitated. "I made sure he found the same backwoods, right next to the last guy. If you want something done right, you have to do it yourself."

"You killed three people?"

"Four when I'm done with you."

Who was this guy? Why had she not seen this side of him before? "You realize you'll never collect a dime from the will if they find out you hired someone to kill me."

"No one will know. Just like before." He cleared his throat, rolling his head to stretch his neck. They had been in the car for nearly three and a half hours. "Unfortunately, your biker friend has nine lives and you, you had to wake up in the hospital. Had your boyfriend not stayed by your side, I might have been able to inject air into your IVs and that would have been that."

Ryan was talking crazy nonsense. Bottom line, he had paid someone to kill her so he could collect the money from her will. Money she worked for. And all because she didn't love him? Talk about certifiable. She was a living, breathing *CSI* episode.

They weren't far from home, only a few more minutes down the coast. "How do you hope to collect money from the will? Grigore will figure out it was you who murdered me."

"He'll believe whatever story I tell him. He knows I care about you and would never let anything happen to you. After all, I hired him to protect you. He'll be too busy blaming himself for doing a lousy job."

"The clubhouse has cameras, Ryan. He'll see and hear our conversation."

At least she hoped the cameras had microphones. Even if they didn't, it would be hard not to see the gun pointed at her.

"What?" His head turned so fast it looked like a scene from *The Exorcist*. "You bitch."

"It isn't my fault that you couldn't see them."

"You should have told me." He slammed the gun against his leg again. "Damn it. Now you've gone and ruined everything."

"Calm do—."

He turned, jamming the barrel against her temple so hard she nearly saw stars. The car swerved toward the guardrail and the long drop below before she got it back under control. Her heart skipped a beat or three and bile rose up the back of her throat.

"Are you crazy? Wait, don't answer that."

"Shut up and drive. We're almost there. When we arrive, pull into the garage and close the door."

"Then what?"

"I don't fucking know. You were supposed to die, and then your mother and I would be very rich. There has to be a way to fix this without implicating me." He withdrew the gun from her temple and started tapping his leg with it again. "If Grigore knows you're here, he'll come to rescue you... That's it. I'll kill you both. No one will know I was involved at all and I'll still be able to collect."

"How do you plan to get away with this when you're right here with me?"

"I rented a room in Florence, where my car still is. No one knows that I even left."

"You rented this car…"

"Fake ID, paid in cash. A Bob Jones rented this car."

"How will you get Grigore here?"

"You know as well as I do, he'll come after you and this will be the first place he looks." He chuckled. "It's brilliant. A murder-suicide. I'll tell the authorities that Grigore was in love with you, but you were in love with me. And since he couldn't have you… Well, do the math."

"No one will believe you."

"Sure, they will, sweetheart. Who would believe for a moment you would take that ugly biker over me?"

Caitlyn pulled into the drive, fearing Ryan might just get away with his crazy scheme. After all, who would believe she'd go back to the man who left her fifteen years ago, shattered her heart into a million pieces, and made her hate him with every fiber of her being? Even her mother might be hard-pressed to believe it.

"Open the garage door and don't do anything stupid. I'm still holding the gun."

Caitlyn exited the car and used her code on the keypad. The door started its slow ascent as she got back into the car and pulled it into the empty bay. Caitlyn and Ryan both stepped from the vehicle and headed for the door entering into the house. She pressed the button, lowering the garage door behind them, feeling much like she was lowering the lid to her coffin.

CHAPTER TWENTY-ONE

THE TREK DOWN THE COAST TOOK LONGER THAN PLANNED. Wolf's tire on his motorcycle blew, nearly costing him a trip over the guardrail. A few skin abrasions and a new tire later, they traveled the rest of the way on foot, arriving at Caitlyn's house on the coast. Luckily, Ryder had done a little digging on the Internet before they left Pleasant and was able to find her exact address.

A quick sweep of the grounds, and a peek inside the window on the side door to the garage, told Grigore that Ryan and Cait were likely somewhere within the house. The blue Ford sat in the left bay, next to a sleek red Viper.

"What's the plan, Wolf?" Ryder whispered, following him around to the back side of the house, staying low and out of view from the windows.

"Plan?" He scowled. "Getting Caitlyn out of there and draining her fucking manager. Other than that, no plan. You have any ideas?"

"As a matter of fact, I do." Ryder smirked, clearly pleased with whatever scheme he had come up with. "Walk right up to the front door and ring the bell."

"Seriously?" Grigore planted his fists on his hips and shook his damn head. He needed to remind himself never to put Ryder in charge of missions. "That's your plan?"

Ryder placed a hand on his forearm. "Hear me out. Caitlyn knows me, but her manager doesn't. If I ring the doorbell, he'll likely send Caitlyn to get rid of me, leaving his back to the rear of the house, so he can keep a close eye on her. Caitlyn will know help has arrived, and while I hold their attention, you come in through the back and nab her manager."

It was an okay plan, and considering they didn't have a better one, he hoped to hell it worked. If Caitlyn wasn't sent to open the door, they'd tip their hand and Ryan would be made aware they had company. One way or another, Grigore needed to get inside the house before Ryan pulled the trigger.

Ryder tipped his nose skyward. "Cavalry has arrived. Kane and Kaleb are in the vicinity."

Ryder's primordial strength got the jump on him. Grigore detected the twins' scent a few seconds later. "Show off."

"No need to be jealous." Ryder winked at him. "Think of it this way, you couldn't ask for better help. You have three primordials at your beck and call. Let's see if Hawk and Viper have a better plan."

"Oh, that's rich," Grigore grumbled. "A moment ago you wanted me to follow your plan and now you're not so confident it's a good one."

He shrugged as Kane and Kaleb rounded the corner of the house. "Four heads are better than one."

Grigore quickly recounted Ryder's plan to the twins. "Think it will work?"

"Other than the fact Ryan's got a gun and could possibly shoot Caitlyn in the fray, this is child's play," Kane said. "We need to make sure he doesn't pull that damn trigger before we get to her."

"There are four of us and one of him. How about while she's at the front door with Ryder, I'll knock on the back," Kaleb added. "That will briefly draw his attention, giving Ryder time to pull her from the house and out of harm's way, allowing Wolf and Viper to jump through the floor-to-ceiling window and get to him before he flees. He'll be caught off guard and won't know what the fuck is happening."

"Why am I jumping through the window and getting cut up while you're knocking on the damn door?"

Kaleb grinned. "Because I thought of it, Viper."

"All jokes aside, it could work." Grigore took a deep breath. The scent of salt from the ocean did little to calm his fucking nerves. Something didn't sit right with him, but they had no time to come up with a better plan, and losing Caitlyn wasn't an option. "And Ryan?"

Grigore knew what he wanted to do with the son of a bitch, but he feared the twins nixing his plan in lieu of turning Ryan's worthless hide over to the authorities, especially since Kane's mate Cara tended to follow the book since she was one of them. Regardless of what the twins wanted, Ryan's chances of walking out of the house alive were pretty fucking slim.

"You contain the situation, then we'll decide," Kane said. "If he hurts Caitlyn in the process, it's your decision."

Grigore nodded. If Ryan so much as laid a fucking finger on her, he'd rip his damn head off. "Then let's go, time's awasting."

Ryder jogged around the perimeter of the large home. Once the doorbell rang and they had a clear shot of Ryan through the large window, he'd signal Kaleb to knock on the back French doors and get this party started.

Moments later, the doorbell chimed, giving Grigore and Kane the opportunity to peer through the window undetected. Just as hoped, Caitlyn walked to the front of the house, spine stiff and shoulders squared. She had to be scared spitless, but she seemed to be holding her own. From his position, he couldn't tell if she had been harmed. The motherfucker better pray not, or Grigore would become his judge and jury.

Ryan stood out of sight from the front door, pistol pointed at Caitlyn. When she opened the door, other than the slight softening of her spine, she thankfully didn't give away that the caller was an acquaintance. Grigore nodded to Kaleb, who began pounding his fist against the French doors.

What happened next hadn't been part of the plan, for fuck's sake.

As Kane and Grigore jumped through the thick glass, sending shards of glass flying, Ryan turned, aimed at Caitlyn, and fired.

A growl left Grigore's chest, but he felt none of the cuts and gashes caused by the breaking glass.

Caitlyn was no longer in the house, likely pulled to safety by Ryder. Grigore didn't know if the bullet had struck her, but he prayed she had been out of harm's way.

Enraged, Grigore stayed focused solely on Ryan Baxter and taking out the son of a bitch. Ryan aimed the pistol, pulling the trigger several times and lodging at least four bullets into Grigore's stomach and arms. Grigore fisted Ryan's plaid shirt, shaking the motherfucker. The gun flew from his grasp and skidded across the tiled floor.

Grigore sank his fangs gum-deep into Ryan's throat, his screams echoing around the house. He would find no mercy here. Grigore took his fill and didn't stop until her manager slumped in his hold and was drained of his life's fluid. Hell, Grigore hadn't even been aware he was alone in the house until he dropped Ryan's bloodless corpse to the floor.

"Jesus." Kane's voice came from somewhere out front of the house.

Grigore stumbled over the body and headed for the doorway. His blood roared in his ears, his heart almost jumping through his chest. What he saw when he reached the porch damn near stopped it.

Caitlyn lay in Ryder's arms, beautiful blond hair gone crimson, as one of Ryder's large hands covered her neck. A large pool of blood gathered beneath them and soaked their clothes, telling Grigore the seriousness of her wound.

His beautiful Caitlyn was pale, far too pale.

"What the fuck?" He dropped to his knees beside Caitlyn and took her from Ryder's arms, holding his palm secure against her artery.

He cradled her head against his already healing wounds on his own body and roared to the heavens. By all that was holy, if she died, Grigore swore he'd go with her. No fucking way was he going to live out eternity knowing he was at fault for her death. It had been his job to protect her and he had failed miserably. Tears rolled down his face unchecked. Tilting Cait's face so her dimming gaze held his, he placed a lingering kiss on her brow.

"Hold on, Sunshine. Help is on the way." The lie left a bitter taste in his mouth. No way would help arrive before she bled out. The bullet must have nicked her carotid before Ryder was able to pull her to safety. "Don't you fucking die on me. Stay with me."

"I'm sorry, man." Moisture filled Ryder's gaze. He was covered in Caitlyn's blood, looking nearly as miserable as Grigore felt. How had everything gone to shit? "So fucking sorry. I tried—"

"Give her your blood, Wolf," Kane interrupted, drawing their attention.

"The rules." He damn near choked on the last word.

"I'm sure we all agree, Wolf. You have my blessing. Do it before you run out of time."

"What if she hates me for this, Viper? She'll be a vampire, a bloodsucker. A life she didn't ask for. Hell, she'll be stuck with my sorry ass for eternity."

"Better to have her hate than her death. Now give her your damn blood already."

Grigore took his wrist to his lips and tore a large hole in his flesh. Blood immediately pooled to the surface and ran down his hand. He held it against her lips as the light in her eyes began to diminish. Time was nearly up and he had no idea if this would even work.

"Drink, damn it."

Caitlyn didn't so much as move her lips, already too weak to respond. Grigore pried open her lips with his fingertips, then placed his wrist against them, hoping that any blood that dripped in would be enough. Grigore prayed it wasn't too late, prayed she'd forgive him for making her a creature of the night. Prayed his love would be enough to see her through. Because now? Giving up her career was no longer an option but an inevitability.

FIRE TRAVERSED THROUGH HER veins, licking her flesh and setting her ablaze. Caitlyn tried to move, to find blessed relief from the sea of flames threatening to engulf her. An unmoving band across her chest held her immobile, her limbs pinned fast to her sides. Each indrawn breath seared her throat, delivering no relief.

What was happening?

Try as she might, her mind couldn't focus beyond the substantial pain, couldn't remember the events leading up to her physical suffering.

Have I died? Is this Hell?

Caitlyn fought the band across her chest, squirming in its hold to no avail. Her eyelids briefly fluttered, only to scald the cornea from the meager light streaming in the blinded window. Surely, Hell didn't have mini-blinds. Opening her eyes to mere slits, she noted the familiarity of Grigore's room, the dark painted walls, the satin comforter. Cait found a little comfort in knowing she wasn't dead, but lying atop Grigore's bed.

Fighting for deliverance, she managed to see the tattooed forearm banded across her chest. Grigore held her tightly, her back to his front, making her wonder why he would want her to suffer. She needed a cold shower, better yet a bath filled with ice. Anything to offer her relief from the excruciating pain. The flames continued to lick through her blood vessels, nearly teetering her back into oblivion.

"Grigore." Caitlyn opened her mouth, her tongue dry as ashes, though she couldn't be sure she had spoken at all until his lips caressed the top of her head.

"Shhh," he shushed, ruffling strands of her hair. Even the follicles stung from the modest stir. "Try to relax, Sunshine. Let me take away some of the pain."

"How?" she croaked, unsure of what he was asking from her.

Caitlyn wanted to struggle against his hold, to find release, but couldn't muster the strength to change her position. How the hell was she to relax?

"Focus on me. Let me absorb some of your pain."

Tears made watery treks down her cheeks. She was ready to concede to anything that might take away the agony. "Please, Grigore… Oh, God, help me. I feel as if fire is coursing through me."

Grigore leaned down and whispered, "Focus on me, Sunshine, not the pain. I can absorb some of the fire, but you have to trust in me and stop fighting."

"How can my trust possibly rid me of this pain?"

"Trust in my love and know that I won't fail you again."

"But—"

"Trust." His breathy reply fluttered over the shell of her ear.

Caitlyn snuggled into him, trying to find the comfort his hold offered. She closed her eyes and breathed out as she and Grigore seemed to meld into one. Her fiery agony receded and Grigore hissed, likely from her affliction he had somehow absorbed.

How is that even possible?

"Trust in me."

And she did. Her heart swelled with the knowledge, trusting he would always be there, trusting he would keep her safe, trusting he would love her for a lifetime. Caitlyn had no idea how Grigore managed to take away most of the misery, but he had.

"What happened?"

"You nearly died," he bit out, his hold tightening as he now fought through the fiery agony.

Caitlyn closed her eyes, sinking further into Grigore's offered comfort. Memories assailed her. Ryan holding her at gunpoint, driving to her house in Crescent City. Ryder at the door. The gunshot, the pain caused to her neck. Blood. Too much blood. The last thing she remembered was the tears wetting Grigore's cheeks as he took her and cradled her against his chest.

"How did I live?"

"Not now," he grunted.

"Please."

His colorful curse told her he'd rather avoid the conversation. She could feel his hesitation, feel his heartbeat as if it were in her own chest. They now had a connection that hadn't been there before.

"Grigore," she prompted softly.

"Christ, Caitlyn, this should wait until you're no longer feeling the fire burning within."

"You helped. It doesn't feel like I'm burning alive anymore."

She felt his chuckle rumble against her back. "Because it's now in my fucking body."

"I'm sorry."

"Don't apologize. I'd do anything for you."

"How long have I been out?"

"Nearly a week."

Caitlyn gasped, accidentally allowing some of the fire to seep back in. "How?"

"You slept through most of it while I held you."

"What do you mean *it*?"

Grigore's chest expanded as he took a deep breath. "Your change."

"My recovery?"

"No, Sunshine, there was no way you were going to recover. You would have died—" Grigore growled, obvious pain cutting short his words. "Can we talk about this later?"

"What aren't you telling me?"

"Tell me you don't feel different." He snuggled his hold. "Your senses are heightened. Let it in."

Caitlyn drew her lower lip between her teeth, noting her surroundings, hearing the muted conversation from somewhere in the clubhouse now clear as day. Her name was being tossed about synonymously with the word vampire. Her nostrils flared, scenting the heavenly bouquet of… What? His blood?

"What the fuck is going on, Grigore? You need to tell me."

He leaned in, aligning their cheeks. Never had she felt so cherished, more in tune with him. "Relax, Sunshine, unless you want this fire nipping back at your veins. You need to work with me, not fight me on this."

"Why can I hear the conversation in the living room as if they're standing right here beside us? And worse, why does the smell of your blood cause my stomach to rumble in hunger?"

Caitlyn worked her jaw, feeling the bones pop and move. What the hell? Fire heated her gaze, though not in the same painful way, but more like a pleasant warmth. Her gums ached, her canines lengthened... She sucked in a breath as fangs scraped her lower lip. Dear, Lord!

"Grigore?"

He blew out a breath. "You're a vampire, Sunshine."

The extreme heat that had been plaguing her left, leaving her feeling different, somehow stronger. Her vision brightened. Grigore dropped his hold and she turned on him so fast, he flinched.

"A what?"

"I must say this new look on you is quite becoming. You're rocking it."

"Not funny, Grigore."

Cait jumped from the bed and ran to the mirror hanging over the dresser. Her face had contorted much like Grigore's when they made love. Her eyes looked as though someone had replaced them with shiny, black marbles. And her teeth? She pulled back her upper lip, producing two razor-sharp fangs.

"A vampire," she whispered.

Grigore stood, strode over to her and wrapped her in his embrace again. "A vampire. More specifically, *my* vampire."

She caught his gaze in the mirror. "Yours?"

"We're mated, Sunshine. I hate to be the bearer of bad news, but that's for eternity."

"Like Tamera, Kimber, and Tena?"

"Yes."

She took trembling fingers to her lips. "The fire, will it come back?"

He shook his head. "You've completed the change."

"How?"

"I gave you my blood before you died. Had I not, I'd be standing over your casket instead of holding you. Trust me?"

Her brow creased.

"Trust that I will love you through eternity." His smile was warm, the love he spoke of shining in his black gaze. "I'll never fail you again, Sunshine."

CHAPTER TWENTY-TWO

H IS GREAT-GRANDSONS' FRIENDS AND THEIR MATES MILLED about the living area of the clubhouse. Stefan ran about the room, weaving between the legs of the adults, while the women took turns cuddling baby Lucian. The legacy lived on. Today they celebrated Grigore Lupei and Caitlyn Summers newly mated status.

Vlad sat in a chair to the far corner of the room, observing the festivities. Lefty, and his new found friend Chad, had ashed Vlad's disobedient servant Nina nearly a week ago, sending her to Hell where she could damn well pay her penance.

One down, one to go.

He needed to intercept his brother before the imbecile went and did something foolhardy like create another mate, or worse yet a little army. Vlad growled beneath his breath. This intolerable situation was entirely his fault. Mircea should've died at Kane's hands long ago. But foolishly, Vlad had allowed family and sentimentality to rule his actions.

Mircea simply couldn't be redeemed.

He knew that now. Mircea had damn near made good on his promise to take out both of his grandsons in one fell swoop. Just looking at Kane and his now nearly healed scrapes and bruises were enough to incite violence.

His brother wouldn't get a second chance.

Vlad's gaze moved from Kane to Grigore and his new mate Caitlyn. The woman was stunning, to say the least. Grigore had chosen well. Normally, Vlad preferred blondes, but today it was a brunette who came to mind, captivating him.

Janelle Ferrari.

No good would come of seeing her again. Vlad had needed to alter the DEA's theory of what had gone down the day of Mircea and Nina's violence against the four dead cartel members. Job accomplished. They now believed it to be the work of rival cartels, fighting over territory. Let the barbarians go to war over his brother's misdeed and destroy each other. What did he care? The world was a better place without the drugs they peddled.

Meeting with the sexy-as-hell DEA again? Shouldn't happen. No good would come of another one-on-one. But damn, Vlad couldn't stop thinking about her. Even now he felt a tightening in his groin. He couldn't remember the last time a woman had completely captivated him.

He bet she'd be a handful and then some.

Vlad chuckled. He never was one to step down from a challenge.

"Vlad."

His spoken name caused him to startle, caught unaware someone had approached. Christ, he never let down his guard, proving the DEA special agent was making him lose focus.

"Caitlyn?"

"Yes." Her smile was pure sunshine. "Why are you sitting over here all alone? Would you like to join us?"

"I'm not one to mingle." He smiled, appreciating her concern. "As a matter of fact, I've overstayed my welcome. I have some family business that needs taken care of."

Grigore walked over, draping an arm across her shoulders. "I see you met my mate."

Vlad smiled, liking the couple. They seemed well-suited, proving opposites attract. He and Special Agent Ferrari couldn't be more opposite, but he'd certainly like the chance to show her what he was capable of between the sheets. Right now, though, his focus was better suited for his brother. He didn't have time to get sidetracked. Mircea needed to be found.

"She has a beautiful soul. I can see why you fought for her." Vlad stood, adjusting the sleeves of his pale blue cashmere, V-neck sweater. He had heard about Caitlyn's career, knew what exposure would cost them. "I'm sure the two of you will figure this out, keeping our secret intact."

"I assure you it's a priority," Grigore said.

Caitlyn's smile warmed her blue gaze. "We haven't had time to talk it over, but once we deal with this mess my dead manager caused, I am planning to leave the business for a more quiet life."

"Caitlyn—"

"As you can see, I have yet to convince Grigore," Caitlyn cut Grigore's argument short. "But he'll come around to my way of thinking."

Vlad laughed. "I like your spirit. Now, if you'll both excuse me, I must say my goodbyes."

A knock sounded, drawing their attention. Kane strode over to the entrance and opened the door. His brow creased, telling Vlad that Kane didn't know the caller. A familiar scent had Vlad excusing himself and approaching the door. He stepped around his grandson.

Special Agent Ferrari stood in the doorway, hands clasped in front of her. Her gaze quickly flitted to his. "Mr. Tepes."

Kane nodded to his grandfather, then left them to their privacy and headed back to the celebration.

Vlad cleared his throat. "This is certainly a surprise."

"I'm sure it is."

"Is there something I can do for you, Miss…?"

"It's Special Agent Ferrari, but then you already know that too."

Vlad was dumbfounded as to how she remembered their initial meeting, not to mention found him. He played dumb. "Do I know you?"

Humor twinkled in her eyes. He felt her smile like a punch to the gut. Janelle Ferrari wasn't merely stunning, she was a fucking goddess.

"You were in my office the other day. I intend to find out why."

How the hell she remembered his presence was beyond him. "Surely, you're mistaken."

"I'm rarely wrong, Mr. Tepes. Nor are my visions." She reached into her pocket and pulled out a card. "I suggest you call this number when you're less busy. You owe me that much."

He took the offered card, his gaze never leaving hers. This woman was trouble with a capital T. Even knowing this, he knew he'd be calling the number on the card.

"How did you find me? One of your *visions*?"

"I'm used to non-believers, Mr. Tepes. But I think the proof lies in me standing here talking to you. I saw the Sons of Sangue rockers in my vision. Since there is only one Sons of Sangue clubhouse in Oregon, you were easy enough to find."

He wet his lips and cocked a crooked grin. "Did your visions show us fucking?"

She sucked in a breath, before quickly composing herself. "I have visions of truth, Mr. Tepes, not far-fetched dreams."

Vlad leaned forward, his lips just shy of touching her ear. He didn't miss the shiver that his nearness caused to pass through her. "I'll be calling you, Special Agent Ferrari. Not because I intend to answer your questions, but because I plan to find out if you're nearly as good as my fantasies."

Color rose up her neck and reddened her cheeks.

"Good day, Special Agent Ferrari."

Janelle's jaw hardened and her shoulders stiffened before she turned and stormed off to the shiny black Chevrolet Tahoe sitting to the rear of the lot. She turned and glared at him, just before climbing behind the driver's seat. If she had managed to find him due to these visions, then how long before she exposed him and his secrets? This was one meeting he wasn't intending to miss.

"WE NEED TO TALK."

Grigore shut the door on the last of their guests, leaving Caitlyn and him alone for the first time in hours. Not that he didn't appreciate the welcome and outpouring of love his friends had given Caitlyn in accepting her into the family, but they had things to discuss.

"How are you feeling?"

She shrugged, taking a seat on one of the leather sofas, tucking one of her long lean legs beneath her. It was one of his favorite assets of hers. Her legs seemed to go on for miles. Tonight, they'd look even better wrapped around his waist.

He nearly groaned. They still hadn't made love since their return, which now seemed like ages. Grigore planned to end that dry spell tonight, right after he taught Caitlyn to feed. But first, they needed to address the elephant in the room.

She adjusted the skirt of her flowery white sundress over her knees. "Not bad, though I've been better."

"Once you feed, Sunshine, you'll feel greater than you ever have. You need sustenance."

Her face paled and she wetted her lips. "I'm not sure I can do this, Grigore."

He sat beside her, the sofa cushion dipping beneath his weight, and pulled her against his side. "We've all been there. Trust me, it isn't so bad. In fact, I promise you'll even grow to like it."

"Can't I just feed from you? Why do we need to follow the others to the Blood 'n' Rave?"

Using the pad of his thumb, he tilted her chin up and locked gazes with her. "Your blood no longer possesses the properties I need to nourish my body, nor does mine to feed you. You know this. That's why we have donors. We'll be following the others soon and I'll be right there beside you to teach you. We can still enjoy each other's blood. In fact, you'll definitely like the benefits of doing so."

"Why, if there is no advantage?"

Grigore chuckled. "Oh, there are perks. Even better than those you received when I fed from you. Surely, you remember."

Her pale complexion reddened, telling him she hadn't forgotten. He could scent her desire elevating.

"Now multiply that feeling ... from what I understand." His grin widened. "I've never been mated, but I've heard what the others have said. It's something we'll explore and soon, once we get you fed."

"Then why are we here and not following the others?"

His nostrils flared, telling him they were yearning for the same thing. If she tapped into her senses, she'd know just how eager he was.

"Because there's something else we need to discuss without the others present."

She placed her palm against his whiskered cheek. "What could possibly be more important?"

Damn, she was making it hard on him to do the right thing. Grigore had wanted her to feed first, to end her slightly weakened state from the lack of nourishment she must be experiencing.

"Your career."

"Not negotiable, Wolf. I'm not going back."

He tightened his hold and kissed the top of her head, inhaling the bouquet of her blood, fueling his need. "You have a tour to finish, fans who are counting on you, employees who need their paychecks, not to mention time to find new jobs. You can't just walk away, Caitlyn. It would be irresponsible of you. You have people who depend on you, not to mention fans who adore you."

She shifted in her seat, putting space between them, her warm gaze now shadowed with trepidation. "And how am I to do that without a manager?"

Grigore gripped her hand and entwined their fingers. "Let me help. I'll act as your manager. We'll finish this tour, reschedule the canceled dates, then put out a farewell album for your fans. Once that's done, you can disappear from the limelight and retire. At best, its a two-year plan. We may have to spend time at your home in Crescent City where we'd be closer to the recording studios in L.A."

"Speaking of my home, what did you do with Ryan's body? The authorities—"

"Will never find out. Some of the Sons and prospects went and took care of cleaning up the mess. The car was scrubbed and left in an empty lot. You'll never see a single reminder of Ryan's betrayal in your home. It's good as new."

She crossed her arms beneath her breasts, her creamy flesh spilling above the low neckline of her sundress. His gaze dropped to the soft globes, causing his mouth to water. It took very little action on her part to make his fangs emerge. She had a great set of tits. Grigore had a hard time concentrating on their conversation when she was within reach, knowing she was all his.

His.

Damn, he liked the sound of that.

"You'd be with me?" she asked.

She really had no idea how this mated thing worked.

"Sunshine, you couldn't get rid of me if you tried. We're mated; that's for life. Vampires don't get divorced, so you're stuck with me."

Her gaze did a sweep the clubhouse. "What about your MC?"

"What about it? I'm not walking away from the Sons of Sangue. We're brothers until the end. You're just part of a bigger family."

"What if someone finds out that we're vampires? The media follows me everywhere. There are days I can't even go to a restaurant to eat a meal without being hounded."

"We'll keep a low public profile, go through the backdoor of the Blood 'n' Rave when we need to feed. Draven will provide us the privacy. If we need to feed while on tour, I'll make sure our secret stays safe. We're in this together, Caitlyn."

Grigore ran a knuckle down her cheek. In all the years they'd been separated, never had his heart felt as full as it did now. She completed him, the other half to his whole. No one had ever come close to taking her place.

"You mean the world to me, Sunshine. I'm not thrilled you almost died because of my fuck up."

"It wasn't your fault. Ryan was crazy."

"As a loon. I won't argue that, but I should've known. I should've somehow sensed he wasn't on the up-and-up. I failed you. That won't happen again."

She scooted across the couch, palmed his cheeks and lightly kissed his lips, eliciting a growl from him. Caitlyn had no idea that she played with fire. Much more of this and they'd be waiting for that lesson in feeding while he took care of an entirely different need.

"I love you, Grigore. I never stopped. That's what matters."

"Every day we spent apart, for fifteen years I tried to deny my love but never could. You are my heart. Trust me?"

"With everything that I am. I won't ever have to worry about losing you again."

"That's for damn sure. No one could take your place as my mate." He gripped her hand and placed it over his sternum. "This beats for you. This is yours for all of eternity. I promise I'll never let you down again, Sunshine. I'll make it my life's work to keep that smile permanently on your face."

"You silly vampire. You're disappointing me now."

Grigore's heart dropped to his stomach. "What did I do?"

"Everything right..." Humor filled her gaze. "Well, almost everything."

"Christ, tell me what's wrong and I'll fix it. I'll go to the ends of the earth to make sure you never have to worry ever again. Surely, you know that."

Her smile lit her pretty hazel gaze right before they transformed to black. Her razor-sharp fangs peeked just beneath her luscious upper lip. Never had she been more beautiful. Grigore was having a hell of a time keeping control.

"What I want is for you to stop worrying about my career. I'll concede to your two-year plan, but only after we seal the deal."

Her pink tongue darted out, wetting her lips. His gaze heated and his dick strained against the rough material of his jeans.

"What exactly did you have in mind, Sunshine?"

Caitlyn stood, reached beneath her skirt, then shimmied out of her white lace thong and tossed them aside. Lifting a leg, she straddled his lap, rubbing her center along his hardness. Jesus, he hadn't felt like a schoolboy in years. Much more and he'd be embarrassing himself like one.

"Before I need to feed, I think there is one little issue that needs your attention."

Grigore smiled so large his cheeks hurt. God, he loved this woman. "Oh, yeah? Am I going to like this?"

"No. I think you're going to love this."

Lifting off of him enough to reach down and undo the front of his jeans, she reached inside and encircled his erection, releasing him. She slid down his length and settled fully onto him. His eyes damn near rolled back in his head.

"So about that deal," she said, right before she lowered her head to his neck and sank her fangs into the flesh, nearly making him come.

He gritted his teeth against the pressure building in his groin as she started to rock slowly on his cock. Fuck, she was going to be the true death of him. Caitlyn certainly knew how to get their union started, making him look forward to the next thousand years.

"What about that deal?" he hissed.

Withdrawing her fangs, licking the twin holes, she sat back and grinned. "Consider it sealed."

Grigore smiled. She was now his for forever and a day.

ABOUT THE AUTHOR

A daydreamer at heart, Patricia A. Rasey, resides in her native town in Northwest Ohio with her husband, Mark, and her two lovable Cavalier King Charles Spaniels, Todd and Buckeye. A graduate of Long Ridge Writer's School, Patricia has seen publication of some her short stories in magazines as well as several of her novels.

When not behind her computer, you can find Patricia working, reading, watching movies or MMA. She also enjoys spending her free time at the river camping and boating with her husband and two sons. Ms. Rasey is a retired third degree Black Belt in American Freestyle Karate.

CPSIA information can be obtained
at www.ICGtesting.com
Printed in the USA
LVHW040507240622
722041LV00012B/57